Seams
Deadly

Seams
Deadly

A MEASURE TWICE
SEWING MYSTERY

Maggie Bailey

CROOKED
LANE

NEW YORK

Published in the United States by Crooked Lane Books, an imprint of The Quick Brown Fox & Company LLC.

Crooked Lane Books and its logo are trademarks of The Quick Brown Fox & Company LLC.

Library of Congress Catalog-in-Publication data available upon request.

ISBN (hardcover): 978-1-63910-469-7
ISBN (paperback): 978-1-63910-676-9
ISBN (ebook): 978-1-63910-470-3

Cover illustration by Joe Burleson

Printed in the United States.

www.crookedlanebooks.com

Crooked Lane Books
34 West 27th St., 10th Floor
New York, NY 10001

First Edition: July 2024

10 9 8 7 6 5 4 3 2 1

To Missy: As far as Lydia and I are concerned, you are the mayor of Peridot. You are the reason this book exists. And you deserve all the root beer floats.

Chapter One

"Did you at least put your hair up with a nice clip?"

"Fran!"

"Well, Lydia dear, messy buns are fine for the store, but I think you should look your best tonight. A nice clip might be a nice touch."

Fran was being nice, Lydia reminded herself. And she had to admit she did have a habit of throwing her long, dark hair up in very messy buns. But a nice clip? Like one of those big claw clips from the eighties?

"Fran, I promise I'll do something nice with my hair, okay?"

"What was that now?"

Lydia sighed and picked up her phone from her bed. She had tried to have it on speaker phone while getting ready for her date, but Fran's house in the mountains had spotty reception, and she kept having to yell about her outfit choices. Looking in the mirror, Lydia repeated to Fran, "I will do something nice with my hair. I promise."

"And what are you wearing?"

"A new make, a green linen Bardon dress by Peppermint Patterns."

Her friend sighed. Even though it was Fran who had introduced Lydia to sewing, Fran stuck to quilts. Lydia, though, had fallen in love with garment sewing and constantly regaled her friend with new dress patterns and special fabrics, like the dress she was wearing tonight.

Turning in the mirror, she admired the sundress, tiered with a ruffled bottom. It was casual, but the lovely European emerald-green linen she'd ordered elevated it for an evening look. She hoped.

"Sounds lovely. I'll see you at the shop tomorrow morning. I can't want to hear all about it. Brandon is lucky you said yes." And before Lydia could respond, Fran hung up.

Lydia placed her phone in her purse and headed to the front door of her apartment. Fran would never know she'd decided to leave her hair in a messy bun. She wanted to look nice, but she didn't want to deceive the poor guy. What was the saying? Start as you mean to go on? She didn't do fancy hair or fancy makeup, she made her own dresses, and too often she forgot to use the lint roller to remove the dog hair.

At least tonight she'd remembered to do that, though her rescue dog, Charlie, had watched her with a slightly offended look, as though his hair all over her clothes was a good look and she was just being absurd.

Now she looked at Charlie, asleep on her couch, happily twitching his feet in pursuit of the elusive dream squirrels. In real life, Charlie was more than a little lazy, but in his dreams, he really gave those squirrels a fair chase. She could join him on the couch, text Brandon, claim she was getting a cold or something equally lame.

When Fran had told her about the dinner, Lydia had tried to get out of it right then and there. They had been at work in Measure Twice, the fabric shop Fran owned. They had been happily chatting about how Lydia was adjusting to life in Peridot, having moved to the North Georgia mountain town earlier that summer.

Lydia loved Peridot. The old-fashioned town square. The huge magnolia tree. The apartment above the shop she rented from Fran. The whole time they were talking, Fran smiled a little too much. Fran was wildly kind but usually not the kind to grin like that. Then Fran spilled the beans and the grin's reason became all too clear.

"It's just dinner."

That had been Fran's refrain as Lydia tried to worm out of it. Brandon worked at the bookstore on the square, a few shops over from Measure Twice. Sure, he was in his thirties and Lydia had just turned forty, but that was fine, wasn't it?

Leaving Charlie asleep on the couch, Lydia walked out into the heavy, early September evening air. Awkwardly, Brandon was her neighbor on the left side of her apartment, but he must have stayed late at the bookstore, Turn the Page, and headed to Rosetti's straight from work. She had worried about having to walk to dinner together, a strange prelude to dinner, and was relieved to head down the stairs to the square by herself. Plus, she had made it past the apartment of her other neighbor, Jeff, without having to chat with him. Jeff was nice but between the brightly colored, silk, button-down shirts he always wore and his obsession with model trains, conversations with Jeff always had a way of being a little strange and a lot longer than she ever intended.

The night was off to a good start. And as she walked the wide brick sidewalk of the square, lit with streetlights and busy with people out enjoying Labor Day Weekend, she realized it was just dinner. Right?

True, it was her first "dinner" since she'd left her husband. Her ex-husband. And Brandon was really cute: bookish and well dressed. Thankfully, by the time she reached Rosetti's, the town's nice Italian restaurant, she'd run out of time to psych herself out any worse.

How bad could one dinner be? It wasn't a date—not really. It was just dinner with someone close to her age in her new hometown. She breathed in slowly, then exhaled and walked into the restaurant.

Brandon was already sitting at a table and stood up, smiling at her. Yeah. He was really cute. Lydia walked over, and they both said hello and sat down at the table. Lydia unrolled her silverware from the napkin, to buy her some time. Surely, Brandon would start the conversation? Nope. Lydia tried to tuck her stray hair into her bun and wondered if she *should* have found a clip to wear. The silence grew. Brandon stared at the menu. Lydia smoothed the napkin in her lap.

"Read anything good lately?" Well, Lydia would never win any awards for scintillating conversation, just like she would never be known for her pristine hairstyles. At least it worked.

Brandon looked up from the menu, beaming. "Oh, thanks for asking. I absolutely have. I read a book of poetry that really blew me away."

Lydia opened her mouth to say that she also enjoyed poetry, but Brandon kept right on talking.

"And I read a great nonfiction piece that really explores the vital role of the hellbender in the region. Just fascinating."

Lydia almost spat out her water. "The *what?*"

"Sorry—I keep forgetting you're new to the area. The hellbender is a kind of salamander. They're hard to find, but you can spot them around here if you look hard enough. I go with a group some weekends when I'm not needed in the shop. We meet up in the Walmart parking lot. It's pretty great. You know, the hellbender is the largest salamander in North America. Fascinating creatures, really. Some locals have the best names for them. One guy who comes with the group, this older guy named Hank, told us his grandmother called them snot otters! So then, on the next outing, Darrel—have you met Darrel? From the bakery? Darrel brought this hilarious word game that generates your own hellbender nickname! It was a riot."

Lydia tried to force a small laugh.

"Wait—hold on." And Brandon stood, fishing something from the back pocket of his jeans. It was a piece of paper with columns of words. "Okay, perfect, I still have it. Lydia, what is your birth month?"

"June." Lydia was filled with a sense of mild dread.

"And your favorite color?"

"Green."

"That makes you a . . . hold on . . . slime puppy!" Brandon let out a laugh. "I got . . . wait—let me see . . . yeah, I got . . . muck dragon!" He kept laughing.

Lydia looked at the table, the gently flickering candle, the empty breadbasket. Then she looked around the room, at the women with nice jewelry and the stylized photos of Italian vistas on the walls. There was soft classical music playing in the background, and the lighting was dim and golden. Brandon was still looking over the nickname generator and laughing, quietly saying different combinations like "swamp gator" and "mud beast."

Suddenly, Lydia realized Brandon had brought that list on purpose. He had planned to find and share their lizard nicknames. He had wanted the evening to go well, and this was his solution. Because?

This was a date. A real date. Fran had said Brandon could show her around Peridot. A new friend would be great. But now, as they looked at their menus at Rosetti's, Lydia finally admitted to herself that this wasn't a friendly get-together; it was a date. Of course it was.

"Sounds like that group is a lot of fun," Lydia offered, trying to be nice in light of her realization.

"We have a blast."

Lydia looked at the menu. "What do you recommend?"

The lizard topic had run its course.

"I really like the linguini Alfredo." Brandon didn't quite make eye contact, as if uncertain of what to talk about next.

Lydia nodded, hoping she wasn't blushing, although the burning in her cheeks left little doubt that she was.

"Or, um, if you like burgers, the Town Square Burger is pretty good too. It has local onions on it." Brandon seemed to still be looking somewhere between the menu and Lydia's face.

Onions? At least maybe he wasn't hoping for a goodnight kiss. How did that even work these days? Lydia had only really dated her ex-husband, Graham. She had no idea what was normal now. She was getting ahead of herself. Again.

Although looking at Brandon, who was reading the menu as if it held the answers to all the questions of the universe, she thought maybe he didn't either.

"The burger looks great! So, how long have you been working at Turn the Page?" Lydia grimaced slightly. Not the most inventive question, but it was better than silence. And a lot better than lizards.

"I started right when they opened, about five years ago. I'm from Jasper?" His voice rose, turning the statement into a question.

"Jasper? Is that near here? I'm afraid I'm terrible with North Georgia geography. I'm a transplant from the north." Lydia smiled.

Brandon didn't return the smile but continued explaining how he came to work at the bookstore. "I studied English in college and have always, um, . . . I want to be—well, um, I'm a writer?"

Again, his voice rose at the end. Lydia was starting to suspect this was just how he talked. Or did he want her to confirm he was an author?

"Really? Brandon, that's so interesting. I taught junior high English for almost twenty—"

"I'm writing a novel. The next Great American Novel."

Lydia stifled a sigh and pretended to rearrange her silverware. Not the NGAN, which was how she thought of the next

Great American Novel. Whenever she told people she taught English and had a degree in literature, she risked being informed of the listener's plan to write the NGAN. Half the time, the person in question had yet to write even a word. Still, Fran had gone out of her way to set up this date, and Lydia needed friends in her new town, so she tried to look as interested as possible, raising her eyebrows as if to say, *"No way—tell me more!"*

It worked.

"It's a story of betrayal. Of lies. Of a small town and how people think they know each other, but of course they never really do," Brandon expounded.

Lydia stifled a sigh. This was hardly uncharted territory, but she didn't have it in her to be a downer.

"Wow, Brandon, that sounds gripping!"

"Thanks, Lydia. Would you want to read a few chapters?" Hope rang out in his words.

Oh goodness. The only thing worse than hearing about an NGAN was being asked to be a beta reader. Well, in for a penny, in for a pound, as the "M's" would say.

Lydia smiled thinking about the two older women she had become friends with, Mary and Martha. Classic Southern ladies, well-coiffed and perfectly turned out, they might say, *"In for a penny, in for a pound,"* but they also might insist Lydia have a chaperone on her date.

Brandon must have assumed her smile was for him and not her prim and proper elderly friends. He smiled back. "Great! I'll get the manuscript to you!"

The waitress came and they ordered their meals, both opting for the Town Square Burger. The waitress seemed irritated by their choices, but Lydia tried to ignore the woman's sharpness. Then the waitress started to read out the side options. "Would y'all like green beans, a mixed salad, or French fries?" Looking directly at Brandon she added, "Let me guess, French fries with extra ketchup?"

Was that an insult of some sort? Was there a ketchup shortage in town? Maybe it was just a busy night at Peridot's nicest restaurant. Maybe the waitress thought it was tacky ordering burgers at an Italian place.

Brandon, however, clearly noticed the sharpness and seemed unnecessarily put out by it. He kept glancing at the waitress as she made her way around the dining room, taking other orders. Was he the sort of guy who would be rude to a waiter? Lydia hoped not. That was a deal breaker in her book, far worse than having an NGAN.

Brandon ate the last piece of bread in the breadbasket, and they sat at the table in awkward silence. The waitress had somehow ruined the mood.

Maybe he was sensitive. A lot of novelists were, in Lydia's experience.

"So, what brought you to Peridot?" Brandon got the conversation started again.

What *had* brought Lydia to Peridot? Where to start her answer? For a moment, she was back in her palatial house in Buckhead, walking into her bedroom, dropping her take-out diet lemonade on the floor.

Her husband, Graham, was in her bed, their bed. Next to him was her teaching assistant, Emma Grace. Lydia was home early from a boring meeting at the Junior League of Atlanta. A meeting Graham had suggested she attend. He had wanted her to do those things: tennis round-robins, dinner parties, charity fundraisers. In retrospect, maybe he had just wanted her out of the house.

Brandon looked at her expectantly.

She wasn't about to explain that she had fled her disaster of a marriage in Atlanta for this small mountain town in order to have a chance to start over. Too cliché. Too depressing.

"Well, I started sewing a few months ago and really fell in love with it. And I . . . needed to make a change . . . and after I found Measure Twice, I was spending so much time in Peridot, it just made sense to move here."

Brandon, thankfully, didn't ask for any details about why she had left Atlanta. Lydia sipped her water, trying to shake off the memory of that diet lemonade pooling all over the floor. Not the memory of another woman naked in her bed with her husband. Diet lemonade.

"So, are you working at Measure Twice now that you live in town? Or . . ."

The waitress came by and refilled their water glasses. Slowly.

Brandon wasn't looking in the direction of the waitress, but he was looking so firmly away from her, it gave the same impression. Why did she bother him so much?

"Yep! Fran has been a complete angel and hired me to work part-time, in addition to letting me rent her apartment above the shop. As you know." Lydia smiled since Brandon lived right next door and knew exactly how she had come to be his neighbor.

"Do you like working there?" Brandon finally seemed to be warming to the pattern of conversation.

"I love it! Have you ever been in?"

Brandon shook his head but at least had the decency to look chagrined.

"Well, you have to let me show you around one of these days." Was that awkward? She decided to keep going. "I actually have some big ideas for Measure Twice, if I can get Fran onboard. Right now, Measure Twice is really a quilt shop, not a fabric shop . . ."

Brandon looked at her blankly.

". . . so it carries all the cotton fabric you need to make a quilt, but not the other sort of fabrics you need for, say, making clothes." Lydia raised an eyebrow and asked, "Does that make more sense?"

He shook his head.

"Right, so this dress I'm wearing? I made it. It's the Bardon dress pattern, and I made it out of European linen. Lots of people make their own clothes these days, so I'm trying to convince Fran to carry the stuff to make dresses like this. In the shop."

Brandon smiled. "That's really cool you made your dress."

"Thanks. I really think I can help the store move in a new direction. I'm just really excited about being here and starting a new chapter, so to speak." They both chuckled at her lame book pun.

Their burgers arrived. The waitress didn't put the plates in front of them so much as she dropped them, letting them clang on the table. Lydia's burger was deconstructed, all the ingredients spread out across her plate. She quickly glanced around the room and confirmed her suspicion: the burger wasn't normally served this way. Even stranger, while Lydia had a heaping portion of fries on her plate, Brandon had three. Three French fries. Each fry had its own spot on his plate, followed by a few empty inches and then another fry. After the third fry was an absolute lake of ketchup. Was Brandon going to address his fry shortage?

"What does Fran think about your ideas for the shop?" Brandon seemed to be ignoring their bizarre plates.

What did Fran think of her plans? Brandon meant it as light conversation, but the truth was, Lydia wasn't completely sure of the answer. Meeting Fran was the best thing that had ever happened to Lydia. Thanks to Fran, she had a place to live and a dream job. But was Lydia the best thing that had ever happened to Fran? Was she anywhere close?

Brandon ate his burger, and Lydia tried to follow suit, but it was awkward as she piled the ingredients back on her bun. She wanted to be at least a little ladylike and wasn't having any success. Next time, if there was a next time, she'd order something easier to eat.

After a few bites, Lydia answered, "I think Fran likes the new ideas. I haven't totally convinced her yet, though. She's run Measure Twice the same way for twenty years. Change can be hard."

Brandon looked up from his dinner, his eyes lit with a sudden intensity. "Change can be really hard."

For a heartbeat, Lydia felt like Brandon was about to confide in her. But the moment passed.

"What do you do for fun? When you aren't at the shop or sewing?" Brandon asked.

"Oh." Lydia adjusted to the change in topic. "I like to bake. Brownies, cookies, that sort of thing. I love thrifting too. I'm always on the lookout for vintage Pyrex mixing bowls. Mary and Martha at Blessed Again tease me about it, but they do keep an eye out for them, which is awesome."

Brandon had finished his meal and looked about as impressed by Lydia's love of mixing bowls as she had probably seemed about North America's largest amphibian. Dating was harder than she'd remembered.

The waitress was back, taking their plates. Lydia still had uneaten French fries on hers. She wanted to snatch them off and shove them in her mouth. Who on earth wasted a perfectly good French fry? But the fact that she was on a date was enough to stop her.

"Can I get y'all anything else? Maybe a nice dessert? Something romantic?" The waitress only looked at Brandon. Not just looked, stared. The very attractive waitress was *staring* at Brandon while asking if he wanted a romantic dessert.

Brandon, for his part, was staring at the table like it held the first review of his beloved manuscript.

The waitress stared at Brandon. Brandon stared at the table. Was the waitress hitting on Lydia's date? But then why had he only gotten three French fries? Or maybe this was a sales tactic discussed by the waitstaff before opening. Lydia could almost imagine the manager explaining, "If you say the dessert is romantic, I think we can raise sales by at least ten percent, especially if you make eye contact while listing the options."

Lydia looked at the woman's name tag.

"Um, Sarah Jane, we're good. Thanks." Lydia willed her to stop looking at Brandon.

But then the waitress did just that and turned her full attention to Lydia. "How about a coffee? Maybe a sundae?" Sarah

Jane flashed a wide smile at Lydia. "The fudge sauce is local, you know, from Garrison's, around the square. Nothing beats real hot fudge sauce made from scratch, don't you think?"

Had she met this woman before? Why was she acting like Lydia's new best friend?

"Um." Lydia tried to figure out how to get out of this bizarre exchange. She looked over at Brandon, who shook his head no while still refusing to look at either Sarah Jane or Lydia.

"I think we're going to skip dessert tonight, but thanks for letting me know about the fudge. That sounds really delicious. I will, um, have to keep that in mind." Lydia smiled back awkwardly.

"Okay, then. I'll bring the check by, but don't y'all feel rushed. Take your time, all right?"

And with that, the blond-haired, blue-eyed waitress turned sharply and walked away.

Lydia waited for Brandon to joke about the weird interaction, but he acted as though it had never happened.

"Well, I should probably head on home. I do most of my writing in the evenings. That is, when I really feel the muse."

"Oh, I'm a total night owl too. I love sewing new outfits at night."

He seemed distracted. Was it something she'd said? Was he already thinking of the next chapter he wanted to write? Authors could be distracted like that. Well, at least she could tell Fran she'd tried.

When the check came, Brandon quickly filled the little folder with cash and stood to leave. Lydia followed. Maybe she was mistaken, but it looked like he had left quite a sizable tip.

Fair enough. Sarah Jane hadn't been the nicest waitress, but Peridot was a small town, and locals probably made a habit of tipping well. It was nice of him to buy her dinner, which she said as they left the restaurant.

"My pleasure, Lydia. I had a really nice time." Brandon smiled shyly.

Lydia took a moment to look at her date under the streetlights of Peridot's town square as they walked back to their neighboring apartments.

Whenever Lydia met someone new, she liked to think of a pattern they would wear. Some people swore by the Meyers-Brigg type indicator or enneagrams, but Lydia thought in terms of sewing. What pattern would the person be? Would she ever want to make it for them? It was a fun game to play. Looking at Brandon, she struggled to decide on a pattern.

He wasn't tall. Lydia was five feet five, and she guessed Brandon was only a few inches taller. But he had such good posture he seemed even taller. His hair and eyes were both dark brown, with his hair cut short and styled up a little at the front. He had chosen dark, well-fitting jeans and a worn-in polo shirt for their dinner. The combination made him seem hip rather than shoddily dressed. Worryingly, his shoes were nicer than hers. Lydia lived in a rotating cast of clogs and Birkenstocks, but Brandon had on polished loafers, even in the early September heat.

Lydia thought of "Goldilocks and the Three Bears" as she looked at her date. He wasn't skinny, but he wasn't broad either. And the minute he smiled, his face went from average American guy next door to handsome, charming actual next-door neighbor.

She scolded herself silently. He was really cute; that was all it was. And that was when she realized what pattern he was: the Archer button-up shirt pattern by Grainline Studio. A classic. Maybe a little advanced for her to make, but well worth the effort.

In the time it had taken her to decide on the pattern, they had reached their building.

Technically, Brandon had walked her home, but since Lydia's new apartment was next to his, she couldn't tell if he'd wanted to or simply couldn't avoid it.

For a moment, they stood facing each other under the light that lit up the door to her little apartment. Lydia stuck her hands in her pockets, unsure what would happen next. Stray pieces of her shoulder-length brown hair, still pulled back in its messy bun, the only way she knew to battle the summer heat, had fallen down, framing her face.

Brandon reached out and gently tucked one strand behind her ear, his fingertips brushing her jawline as he dropped his hand.

Lydia's stomach flipped.

She looked at the ground for a moment, and when she looked back up . . .

Not a kiss.

Instead, Brandon had stepped back and held out his hand in a fist. Lydia stared at the fist. Then it clicked. She raised her fist and gave him a bump. In return, he opened his hand as he pulled it away, waving his fingers. Lydia had thought she might be getting a goodnight kiss. What she got was a goodnight fist-bump and faux explosion.

Lydia realized Brandon was waiting, so she followed suit. He smiled.

"See you later, slime puppy," Brandon said, truly adding insult to injury, and then he turned and walked to his apartment next to hers, unlocked his door, and disappeared.

Lydia called out, "See you later, muck dragon," and then turned to her own door and did the same.

Leaning against her closed door, she looked at her new apartment. It was small, but it was cozy. Plus, it smelled fantastic. Lydia looked at her kitchen counter. Brownies? Check. Banana bread? Check. Sprinkle cookies? Check. Since moving into her new apartment, Lydia had really taken stress baking (and comfort eating) to the next level. They hadn't had dessert at the restaurant. Maybe she could offer Brandon some brownies? It was only eight, after all.

She checked her appearance in the living room mirror. Her bun was a mess, so she retied it. She still had a bit of a summer tan, so it was less noticeable that she wasn't wearing any makeup besides a little mascara. Smiling, she watched her crow's-feet crinkle at her eyes. Well, she was forty. No hiding that. Should she just call it a night?

As if he could read her mind, her rescue dog, Charlie, shuffled over to his leash hanging by the front door and spun around a couple times. Right.

"Sorry, Charlie! Of course, you need a walk."

Lydia clicked the leash onto his collar, left her apartment, and locked the door behind her.

It was technically September, but her New England heart refused to accept that fact. September meant sweaters and pink cheeks and hot apple cider and brown leather boots for the new school year.

Here in Peridot, in the Blue Ridge Mountains of North Georgia, school had started weeks ago, the apple cider was served like a slushy on ice, and the idea of a sweater made her practically break out in hives.

She told herself to think of the Labor Day Weekend as part of summer instead of the gateway to fall, but she still cherished the slight breeze in the evenings.

Lydia had gotten in the habit of taking Charlie to the park each morning and then ending the day with an evening stroll around the square. It made her new life feel that much more real now that she had routines, a structure and pattern to her day.

When she had taught middle school, there had been a clear rhythm to her days. She could still remember the anxious caffeinated energy of first period on Monday, and just as clearly, she felt the raw, ungovernable spirit of last period on Fridays.

Working at Measure Twice wasn't quite that much of a roller coaster, but the shop had its own heartbeat. Lydia paused for a moment outside the front window display. Charlie, used to Lydia's habit of admiring shop windows, waited patiently for the walk to continue.

The Peridot streetlights illuminated the front of Measure Twice, allowing Lydia to both see into the shop and see her own reflection. In the shop, there were piles of colorful fat quarters, which were quarter-yard pieces of fabric beloved by quilters, as well as the fall quilting kits Fran had already organized and displayed, and even the sale corner of Fourth of July–themed fabric and notions, with the holiday in the rearview. She smiled, which made her reflection smile, and her green eyes sparkled and echoed the green of her dress. She was shorter and chubbier and messier than her ex-husband had ever seemed okay with, but now that it was up to her, she was pleased with what she saw, even if her date had ended with a fist bump rather than a first kiss.

Lydia paused, remembering how she had shown up at the shop after discovering Graham and Emma Grace in her bed. Thankfully, Fran had still been at the shop, doing inventory, when Lydia pulled up, having driven straight to Peridot, almost in a fugue state. Before she could even knock on the shop door, Fran had spotted her pale face and opened the door, ushering her inside.

Fran had led Lydia straight to the break room at the back of the store. The cozy room had a few well-loved chairs and a couch no doubt from Blessed Again, the town's church-run thrift store; a few tables; and a little mini-kitchen well stocked with mugs and assorted teas, as well as an electric kettle.

Flicking the kettle on, Fran had guided Lydia to the couch and simply waited. That was one of the many magical things about Fran. She knew when to be quiet.

Minutes passed. Fran got up and made them each a cup of peppermint tea with a healthy glob of honey and sat back down.

Warming her hands on the mug, which read "A Real Lady Never Discusses the Size of Her Fabric Stash," Lydia began. "I dropped my lemonade. My diet lemonade."

Fran, true to form, stayed quiet and waited.

"They were in my bed. Our bed. Graham and Emma Grace," and with that unpoetic beginning, Lydia spilled out the whole tawdry tale to the woman she had met only a few weeks before when she'd first discovered Measure Twice, but who was quickly becoming one of her closest friends.

Then Lydia admitted the real reason she was at the shop. "Fran, I don't know where to go."

Lydia's cheeks had felt hot with the shame of it. She knew she had every right to drive back to Atlanta and kick them both out. That house was as much hers as it was Graham's. But she just couldn't. There was no rational explanation, but Lydia felt in her bones that she simply couldn't go back to that house. Not yet. Not any time soon.

How could she explain to Fran that everything in Atlanta felt tainted? Her social circle was Graham's social circle. Her work friends were Emma Grace's friends. The only thing she had for herself was the drive up to Peridot for a shopping trip at Measure Twice. And Fran.

Finally, Fran spoke. "Screw him." Her mouth had settled into a flat, angry line.

Technically, it was a mild exclamation, but Lydia had never heard Fran say anything like it.

"Screw him," Lydia repeated, a little feebly.

"You need a chance to regroup. You need a chance to heal. I think you should stay in Peridot for a bit." Fran's face softened into a smile.

Lydia exhaled loudly and took a large sip of her honey-sweetened peppermint tea. She was still too shaken to be embarrassed. "Oh, Fran, I was hoping you'd say that. Can I stay in the break room for the night?"

Fran and Lydia both turned to look at Charlie, asleep at Lydia's feet. "I mean, can *we* stay?"

"In the break room?" Fran replied, incredulous.

It was too much to ask. What was wrong with her? She had her wallet. There was bound to be a hotel that allowed dogs somewhere around here, she hoped.

"Don't be silly, Lydia. You both"—Fran gestured to Charlie—"can stay in my apartment above the shop. For as long as you need."

She could still see Fran's face when she'd said "as long as you need." Fran seemed to know then that Lydia wasn't hiding out in Peridot; she was coming home.

Home, Lydia thought, as she climbed the stairs back up to her apartment now, Charlie slowly following. Fran was her fairy godmother; it was as simple as that. Her small, spry, wiry godmother who dressed in head-to-toe L.L. Bean. It had been all Fran's doing that Lydia had gone to dinner with Brandon.

Without realizing it, Lydia made the exploding fist motion with her hand. So embarrassing. Then she thought of the counter covered in baked goods, waiting in her apartment. She'd keep Charlie with her to make it clear she wasn't inviting herself in or anything.

Lydia kept Charlie on his leash as she dashed inside to grab the brownies. Plus, Brandon had said he liked to write at night, so he would probably still be awake. And maybe in need of a sugar high.

Outside his door, she took a deep breath, told herself to buck up, and knocked.

But, as she knocked on the door, it swung open.

"Well, that's weird," she said quietly to Charlie, as she stepped into Brandon's apartment. "Brandon? Hey, Brandon, sorry to bug you, but I have these brownies, and I thought you might want something while you write." No one answered.

She stepped farther into the room and turned to the place where, in her mirror-image apartment, she had placed her sewing desk. She figured that must be where he put his writing desk.

Then she heard the plate of brownies shatter on the floor.

Then she was outside, sitting on the floor of the walkway, shaking, with her head in her arms, pressed against her knees.

When she closed her eyes, she saw Brandon, slumped over the writing desk. She saw a pair of dress shears plunged deep into his neck. The blood was spreading down his neck to his arm, pooling on the carpet beneath his rolling desk chair. His skin was almost blue-white. She opened her eyes.

Lydia looked at her hands and saw blood. That was right. She had walked past the shattered plate of brownies on the floor, dropping Charlie's leash, and reached to feel for Brandon's pulse.

The blood on his wrist was now on her hands. From when she had reached out. Put her fingers on his wrist, telling them to feel a pulse. Telling herself he was still alive. When he wasn't. Brandon was cold and gone: no pulse, no sign of life.

She had dropped his hand and walked outside, sat down, and was still sitting there. Charlie leaned against her legs, whimpering quietly, but she refused to comfort him, too afraid the blood would get on her dog. The blood. Brandon's blood. She needed to call the police.

Chapter Two

"Nine-one-one, what's your emergency?"

"He's dead."

"Who is, ma'am? Can you tell me your address? Is the person still breathing?"

"I am trying to tell you. Brandon is dead. No one is breathing."

"Ma'am, are you hurt?"

"No, no. I'm fine. He is dead. You need to get here."

"Can you tell me your name?"

"Lydia Barnes."

"And what is your location, Lydia?"

"77 Main Street, apartment 2B."

"Okay, Lydia, I am going to need you to stay put, okay? Help is on the way. Can you stay on the line with me, Lydia?"

Lydia hung up. There was nothing that woman could do. And she couldn't bear to hear the helpful, kind voice ask any more questions.

She held onto her phone, even though the call was over.

There must be sirens, Lydia thought. But she couldn't hear a thing. She just stared at her hands. Charlie kept pressing against her legs. And she waited. Lydia sat outside Brandon's door, on the rough walkway that connected the apartments above the storefronts. The September evening wasn't cold, but Lydia was shivering. Or was she shaking? Did it matter? What about the brownies? Were they evidence? Or trash? Would the officers want to eat the brownies? Or maybe she should offer them other cookies, from her apartment? Should she go and sit in her apartment? She wanted to stop shaking, but she couldn't. Instead, she simply sat and listened to the night. A mournful sound echoed across the square. Was that an owl? Did Peridot have owls?

She looked at her hands again. Her right hand was bloody from touching Brandon. Someone had killed Brandon. Who? Where had they gone? Suddenly, Lydia went from feeling numb to feeling skittish. What if the killer was still in Brandon's apartment? She hadn't looked. Why hadn't she checked?

Standing up, Lydia pulled Charlie's leash and rushed into her own apartment. She hadn't even locked her own door when she had left. But she did now and turned to slump against her couch.

A knock at the door sent her flying back to her feet before she could think that a killer would hardly knock. She looked out the peephole and saw an older, tall officer in uniform.

Lydia cracked open the door but kept the chain on.

"Miss, are you Lydia Barnes?"

The voice was deep, but not unkind.

"Yep," Lydia answered, still too afraid to fully open the door. Thankfully, the man didn't ask her to, simply talking to her through the crack in the door.

"I'm Sergeant Simpson," he explained. Lydia noticed he smelled like aftershave. Her grandfather had used aftershave. Was that still something people used? Her ex-husband never had; he'd used a fancy cologne instead. This man wasn't old enough to be her grandfather, but he had to be at least late sixties, surely, with the salt-and-pepper hair and creased face.

"Miss?"

"What? I'm sorry. Did you . . .?" Lydia realized the man had been trying to talk to her while she ruminated on aftershave.

"That's okay. I asked you if you had called us."

Lydia nodded.

"Okay, great. You just hold tight for one minute." He turned to the other officers she could glimpse milling around Brandon's apartment, quietly giving instructions. Then he turned back to Lydia. "I am Sergeant Simpson. I am in charge of this case, miss. And I would like to talk to you at the station. Can you do that?"

"What?" she responded slowly.

"How about we go to the station?" He was talking to Lydia like she was a child, but Lydia wasn't offended. It was comforting. The idea of making any decisions was repugnant to her; it felt like a relief to have this tall, old-fashioned police officer guiding her.

Unlocking the safety chain, Lydia opened the door fully and looked at the man in front of her. Tall. Very tall. With a distinguished mustache that matched his short hair.

"All right now. No need to lock up. My officers will take care of everything."

He placed his hand on her elbow to guide her to the staircase that led down to street level.

"My car is right over here, miss," he told her.

Lydia noticed he didn't touch her hands. Evidence. He didn't touch her hands because they were evidence.

Lydia looked at her watch. It was only ten o'clock. On a Friday. On Labor Day Weekend. Thankfully, her corner of the square was quiet, since it was only shops. Across the way, she could see people coming and going from Shenanigans, the only live music venue in Peridot. Normal people having a normal night. She felt like she was going to throw up.

Sergeant Simpson noticed Lydia slowing down and placed his hand on her elbow one more time, guiding her to his parked car before anyone could see, under the quaint street-lights of the Peridot Town Square, that one of her hands was bloody.

Leaning her head against the cool glass of the car window, Lydia looked out at the night. Moonlight filtered through the large magnolia tree that had pride of place next to the court-house in the center of the square. It was beautiful, but given what she had just seen, felt obscene to Lydia. She wanted the whole world to stop, which meant no moonlight on glossy green leaves and showy white petals.

Sergeant Simpson glanced back from the front of the car and noticed her looking at the tree.

"That tree there is over a hundred years old. Magnolias are incredible. I bet you didn't know that magnolias are older than bees. That's a fact. How amazing is that?" he asked as they drove past the tree and out to the edge of the square.

"Bees?" Lydia replied lamely.

"Bees pollinate most trees, but not the magnolia. They are so old—over one hundred million years old. Bees didn't even exist way back then, so beetles pollinate magnolias, not bees. Isn't the natural world amazing?"

Lydia worried she was starting to disassociate, and all this talk of bees wasn't helping. Surreptitiously, she pinched the flesh on the back of her left hand with the fingers of her right. Nope. Not a dream. Not a nightmare. Just blood on her right hand. Just a nighttime drive with a policeman, talking about beetles and avoiding talking about murder.

"I didn't do anything to Brandon," Lydia blurted out.

"That may well be, miss, but let's talk about that at the station, okay?"

Miss? Lydia might be a transplant to the South, but she had been there long enough to know she qualified as a ma'am and not a miss. At forty, she was firmly in ma'am territory.

"Right, right, I am sure there must be a procedure for this. I'll make a statement, of course. Whatever you guys need. I just wanted . . . I just think you should know . . . I would never have hurt him. It was a bad date, but it wasn't that bad!"

"Let's talk about it at the station, miss," he responded.

Lydia stopped talking.

*　*　*

In a matter of minutes, they had parked, and Sergeant Simpson was walking with her, almost herding her like a sheepdog, into the police station. Once inside, he walked her straight to a small, windowless room, flicked on the light and the ceiling fan, and gestured for her to sit down.

The room felt stale, unwelcoming. Lydia sat in a plastic chair with metal legs on one side of a table, and Sergeant Simpson sat down on the other.

Looking around, she noticed a video camera in the top corner of the room, but nothing else. What had she expected? A mirror? Some sort of recording device?

"Now Miss Barnes, as I said before, my name is Sergeant Simpson. I want to be clear with you: you are free to leave this room if you choose to do so. You are not under arrest. I would simply like to ask you some questions. Do you understand?"

She nodded.

"Good. When did you last see Brandon alive?"

Lydia had expected the question. She loved murder mysteries on TV and read enough thrillers. There were certain things you could expect. Like the detective asking when someone last saw the victim alive. The victim. Brandon. Brandon wasn't alive.

"Miss Barnes? When did you last see Brandon Ivey alive?"

"Tonight. We went to dinner at Rosetti's and then walked back to our apartments. We live next door to each other."

"What time was that?"

"We had dinner at six, and we said goodnight around eight."

"And then what?"

Lydia looked at her hands. She bit her nails, sometimes even her cuticles. It showed.

"I walked my Charlie. My dog. I walk him every night around the square."

"When did you finish your walk? What time was that?"

"Oh. I'm not sure. It normally takes us about twenty minutes, maybe half an hour, to walk around the square. Charlie is pretty lazy." Lydia felt weirdly ashamed of describing her dog that way, but before she could clarify, the questions continued.

"And then what happened?"

"And then. I like to bake?" Lydia said, but it came out sounding like a question.

Sergeant Simpson looked at her, baffled.

"Um, what I mean is, I like to bake, so when I got home from the walk, I thought it might be nice to bring over something I had made. I had some cookies and brownies in my kitchen. Baking relaxes me."

The officer made no effort to put her at ease.

"I thought maybe Brandon would like some brownies. So I put some on a plate and I went to his door, with Charlie, just to offer him some brownies—not to try to come in or anything, and I knocked, and when I knocked the door moved because it hadn't been shut, and it just sort of opened, and I called out to him because I thought he might want a brownie, even though we had just had these huge burgers at Rosetti's, and I wasn't hungry, but Brandon said that he did some of his best writing at night and I thought some sugar might be good, and I was just holding the plate when the door swung open, so I called out because, you know, our apartments are set up in the same way, and his writing desk was right where my sewing desk is, which is what I had guessed when I stepped in the apartment, and then I saw him and he was . . ."

Lydia stopped talking, like an overwound toy winding down, and wiped at the tears starting to form in her eyes.

"Okay, so what you're saying is that you took some brownies to the deceased's apartment and found the door open. Is that correct?"

"Yes, sir," Lydia said through her tears.

"And what time was that?"

"Right after the walk. So maybe like eight thirty? I didn't check."

"And when you found the door open, you decided to enter his residence. Is that also correct?"

"Yes, sir."

"Can you tell me, in as much detail as possible, what exactly you saw when you entered Brandon Ivey's apartment at approximately eight thirty this evening?" he asked.

She couldn't put this off forever. She sighed and began: "I walked into Brandon's apartment. I think I must have dropped the plate of brownies. I know I walked over to the desk, and I saw Brandon. I saw the dress shears in his throat."

Sergeant Simpson interrupted, "Dress shears? Tell me about that, miss."

Explaining sewing notions was much preferable to talking about a murder scene. She tried to focus only on sewing, explaining, "When you sew, you cut patterns out of fabric," Lydia waited.

Sergeant Simpson nodded.

"But you don't want to use normal scissors . . ." Lydia stopped.

"Because?"

"Shears and scissors are not the same. Shears are generally longer and sharper, and they have a larger bottom loop, so you can use more fingers, which means you can apply more pressure and have more control. Like if you were making a quilt, you could use shears to cut a lot of layers of fabric at once, and the cut line would also be a lot cleaner. Dress shears are larger than regular shears and are really good for larger pieces of fabric. Every sewist . . ."

"Every what now?" Sergeant Simpson asked.

"Sewist. Sorry. People who sew like to be called sewists. It's a thing. Seamstress is outdated, and no one wants to be mistaken for a sewer."

"Right."

"As I was saying, every sewist wants at least one if not two pairs of high-quality shears in their sewing kit. There are a lot of jokes in the sewing world about how if someone uses your fabric shears for something other than fabric, the punishment should be death." Lydia gulped. "I didn't mean—I wasn't trying to say—it's just a saying . . . a nice pair of shears is important, which is why . . ." She stopped.

"Why what?" he pressed.

Well, there was no hiding it anyway; she may as well tell him now. "That's why we have them branded with the store name and stock them by the register."

"Miss, are you telling me that Brandon Ivey was stabbed with a pair of scissors from the store where you work?"

"Dress shears. And yes."

Lydia and the police officer sat in silence.

"After you went on a date with him? In his apartment that is directly next to yours? And you found the body?"

"That's what I was trying to say. I realized he had been stabbed in the neck with the shears. I thought there was a chance he was still alive, so I went over and felt his wrist for a pulse, and there was no pulse." Lydia looked down at her still-bloody hand. They hadn't let her wash her hands yet. "Then I called the police."

"Now, when we arrived, you were in your own apartment?"

"Yes. I, um, I called from the walkway, but then I thought, what if someone was still in there? The killer? So, I went into my own apartment and locked the door and waited for the police—for you—to come."

"That was a good decision, Miss Barnes. I can see why you did that. Thank you for walking me through your evening. That will be of great help. I'm also going to need to know about you."

"Me?"

"You are new to town, are you not, Miss Barnes?"

"Yes."

"Tell me about that."

Lydia was starting to feel like a broken record. Was a police interrogation just a nightmare version of a bad first date? Did he want to know her hellbender nickname? She needed to concentrate.

"I moved here a few weeks ago from Atlanta. Do you know Fran Whiteside?"

"I know Fran," Sergeant Simpson replied, with something at least a little close to a smile.

"Fran offered me a job at Measure Twice, the fabric shop on the square. And since she wanted to move to her mountain house full time, she said I could rent her apartment above the shop."

"That's convenient."

Lydia could not read the policeman's tone.

"Yeah, I'm really lucky. I needed a change, and Fran has really offered me a whole new start."

"Why?"

"I guess Fran is just a really good person."

"No, I mean why did you want a new start?"

"Oh." How much was she supposed to say? This wasn't about Graham. But also, she didn't want to seem secretive. "I just got divorced."

"You left your husband?"

"What? No. He . . . he was seeing someone else. I found out. We called it quits. And I moved to Peridot."

"And when did you start seeing Mr. Ivey? Was that before you moved here?"

"Mister . . .? You mean Brandon? No! Listen, please, Fran wanted me to get out of the apartment, make some friends. She knows I taught middle school English, that I love to read, so she set up a dinner for me with Brandon. Since he works at Turn the Page, the bookstore. I had seen him before but never really talked to him. Honestly. It was just a first date. That . . . that ended like this."

"How exactly did this first date end?"

"I told you." Lydia wanted to be polite—heck, she even wanted Sergeant Simpson to like her—but now her exhaustion was starting to win out over her innate desire to please others. She wanted to go home.

"Did he kiss you, Miss Barnes?"

"Excuse me!"

"Did Mr. Ivey, Brandon, did he kiss you goodnight?"

"What? No! I mean, he did not kiss me, but why do you even need to know that?" she sputtered, indignant and embarrassed, though more the latter than the former.

"Thank you for answering. Let me explain, Miss Barnes—"

"Lydia."

"Pardon?"

"Why don't you just call me Lydia?"

"Thank you, but no. As I was saying, let me explain: you are new to town, as you yourself explained; you are just out of a bad relationship, as you said; and your date has been murdered. With scissors from your store."

"It is not *my* store. I just work there."

"So, the date ended badly. You had wanted a kiss, maybe more. You went back to your apartment. Seethed. Thought about the rejection. Got angrier and angrier."

Lydia just stared at the man in disbelief.

"Maybe you just meant to scare him. Is that it? Maybe you just wanted to tell him how hurt you were? What happened? Did he insult you further? Mock you? You must have been very angry. Just tell us what happened, Miss Barnes. We'll find out anyway. It will be better coming from you. Are you ready to tell us what happened? What really happened?"

"I told you exactly what happened. I mean. When we said goodnight, he didn't kiss me; he gave me a fist bump. I should have said that earlier. So, there, that really is everything. That is what happened. You don't think that . . ." Lydia let the words drop, waiting for him to assure her he did not suspect her of murder.

"A fist bump?"

"Yeah. Like this," and Lydia mimed the fist bump with her own two hands. It felt ridiculous. Again. "That was why I thought I would bring the brownies by. It had been awkward. I wanted to end the night on a better note. I wanted . . . I didn't . . . I swear . . ."

Sergeant Simpson just watched her.

They both waited for the other to say something more.

Lydia knew she was innocent, but she didn't know if she sounded innocent.

"Am I being arrested?" she asked, her voice suddenly much quieter.

"No. No, you're not, Miss Barnes. As I said, you are free to go at any time. I simply have some questions."

"Oh. Okay. The may I please go home now?"

"Yes, you can. We will need to take your fingerprints. And are you willing to let us search your phone, or do I need to get a warrant?"

"What? Sure, you can have my phone."

"Thank you. I will make sure it gets back to you in a timely fashion. After we take your prints, I will have an officer take you home."

"Why . . .?"

Sergeant Simpson spoke over her, continuing his thought. "But I want to make something very clear to you."

"Okay."

"We are not arresting you. We are not keeping you here. But as far as I can see, Miss Barnes, you are our main suspect. Right at the top of the list."

Lydia felt like she was going to throw up, again.

"If I were you, Miss Barnes, I would give some thought to who else wanted to hurt Mr. Ivey. If anything comes to mind, please call me"—he slid a card across the table as he continued—"and tell me what you come up with. Otherwise, the next time we talk, it might be a very different conversation."

With those menacing words, he stood up, opened the door to the interview room, and gestured her out.

Standing in the general hustle and bustle of the police station, Lydia wanted to be home so badly she could almost scream. Instead, she hurried to follow Sergeant Simpson as he walked away, still talking to her.

"Officer McGrath will take your fingerprints just over here, have you done in a jiffy."

True to his prediction, Officer McGrath walked her through the process, cleaning her hands, pressing each finger into the ink and then onto a waiting paper card, with curt efficiency. *That woman looks like she irons her uniform every morning,* Lydia thought, glancing down at her own rumpled linen outfit. Lydia washed her hands as thoroughly as she could, but some ink remained. Proof of this nightmare being real. She needed to be home.

Walking back over to Sergeant Simpson, Lydia suggested, "Why don't I just walk home?" desperate to get out of there.

"Miss Barnes, it is almost midnight, and you are in considerable shock, understandably. I realize you want to get home"—his stern mustachioed face softened with the last word—"and Officer Eisen is just about to clock off for the night. He would be happy to drive you home, isn't that right, Luke?"

The man who must be Luke nodded.

What a study in contrasts. Sergeant Simpson looked exactly how Lydia wanted an officer to look, rugged, wise, and a little tough. Officer Eisen, on the other hand, looked like a kid she could have taught, an old student who might reach out to say, "Thanks for being nice to me in middle school, Miss Barnes!"

Lydia thought about when she had adopted Charlie, how the lady helping her at the shelter had said paws could show you how big a puppy would grow to be. That was what Officer Eisen reminded her of—a puppy with big paws, gangly and a little energetic. Worse still, while Sergeant Simpson had a dignified, if old-fashioned, mustache, this lanky young man had an ill-advised goatee. It looked less like a choice and more like he had tried to grow a full beard and failed.

"I sure can, Miss Barnes. I'll drive you home right now if that works for you?" he asked, almost shyly. Was he blushing?

Was *she*? Well, he was handsome, she had to admit, but he couldn't be more than twenty-five years old. She must still be in shock—that was all.

Thankfully, Officer Eisen was driving home in his own car, a beat-up Jeep Wrangler with no doors. She didn't have to sit in the back of a police car behind a plastic partition like the perp in a cop show. She didn't even have to open a door.

She buckled up and they sped off into the dark night. The warm breeze moving through her hair made her feel weirdly awake. It was probably shock, but suddenly it seemed okay that the night was beautiful. Lydia felt, selfishly, so very happy to be alive. She held her hand out the window, moving it up and down in the wind as they drove.

Had Sergeant Simpson told this poor young man not to talk to her? Suddenly, she couldn't stand to be quiet.

"I hope this isn't taking you too far out of your way. I know it's late." She smiled at her driver, hoping he'd take the bait. He did.

"No, ma'am." Ah, yes, back to "ma'am" territory. Well, she was used to it. "I live on the other side of the square, so this is no problem for me. Besides, Sergeant is right: you shouldn't be walking home all by yourself. You're new to Peridot, aren't you?"

"I moved here at the start of the summer, up from Atlanta—needed to start a new chapter, you could say." Lydia let herself enjoy the mundane conversation.

"What made you pick Peridot?" the young man asked, echoing a question Lydia had answered so many times in the last few weeks.

"I had been up to shop at Measure Twice a few times, you know? Like, I would drive up from Atlanta and sort of make a day of it. Classic day-tripper, really. I even bought one of those sweatshirts," Lydia admitted, watching Luke's face for his reaction.

Luke grimaced. He knew what she meant, and she knew he felt secondary embarrassment. All the stores in Peridot sold those T-shirts, sweatshirts, and hats with John Muir's famous quotation, "The Mountains Are Calling, and I Must Go," written across them in stylized bohemian script.

No one, absolutely no one, who lived in town would be caught dead in a sweatshirt like that. Caught dead.

Luke started to talk about his least favorite tourist wear, clearly trying to make her laugh, but Lydia could not concentrate on his words. She pulled her hand back into the car. Suddenly, all she wanted was to fall asleep.

Luke was still talking, and Lydia forced herself to pay attention.

". . . and that is what city people don't see—you know what I mean?" he asked, earnestly, clearly building on a larger, just-presented argument. Lydia had no idea what he was talking about, so she nodded.

"Right?" Luke was pleased with her response. "You know, we meet up on Wednesdays. There's a room above Frank's. We're always looking for new people. People who get it."

The Jeep jerked to a stop. They were in front of Measure Twice, with her apartment waiting just above. Looking up and to the left, she could see the crime scene tape, the police hard at work. Brandon wouldn't still be there. She knew that. She did. By now, he would be somewhere safe, with a doctor there to uncover the details of what had happened. Luke looked up as well, watching his coworkers swarm around the apartment next door to her own.

As Lydia started to clamber out, Luke put the Jeep in park and came around and helped her down to street level.

"Listen, Sergeant Simpson will figure this out, no doubt. If you get worried, though, you can always call me too." As he said this, he reached into his worn leather wallet and pulled out a card, offering it to her. "And I meant what I said. I hope to see you on a Wednesday night."

"What's happening on Wednesday?" Lydia asked, baffled, as she tucked the card into her tote bag.

"The *Dungeons and Dragons* game? Above Frank's?" Luke slowed down his speech.

"What? Oh, right, yep, for sure. Thanks for this," Lydia added, meaning the card and the ride, and turned to walk up the stairs to her apartment. *Dungeons and Dragons?* Was that a board game? The last few steps to her place felt impossible. She noticed an officer writing down her movements. She nodded at him, adding, "I can go in, right?" and pointed at her door.

"Yes, ma'am, you can. And don't be scared; officers will be here all night. Just put your dress in this and give it to one of the officers, okay?" Luke added, handing her a plastic evidence bag.

"Yes. Of course. Thank you," Lydia replied, taking the bag. As she shut the door, she realized with a heart-sinking lurch that she hadn't even thought to ask if she would be safe.

*   *   *

Back in her apartment, she wondered what time it was now. Somewhere on the other side of midnight. Beyond that, Lydia had no idea, and she didn't want to figure it out. She wanted to fall asleep and wake up yesterday.

Looking down, she looked at her handmade sundress. She had been so proud of it when she'd first completed it, marveling at how her finishes had improved, the smooth bias binding at the neckline, the clever inseam pockets at the waist.

Even the fabric had been an upgrade, ordered from a small company in Canada. The linen had a lovely drape while remaining breathable. Emerald green, to bring out the green in her eyes. Now the police needed it.

Lydia went into her bathroom and placed the dress in the bag, she knotted it and dropped it to the floor.

Then she finished getting undressed and stepped into a scalding hot shower.

In her coziest pajamas and slippers, Lydia scooped up the bag and brought it over to a slightly alarmed officer next door. She told him Sergeant Simpson would want it and promptly went back to her apartment, kicked off her slippers, and locked the door.

Lydia curled up in her bed, with her quilt high up around her shoulders, the air-conditioning on full blast. Charlie normally slept at the foot of her bed, but tonight, instead, he lay down next to her in the full-size bed, pressed back to back.

Thank goodness for dogs, she thought.

With the bedside light on, Lydia looked at her quilt. She'd made it in classes at Measure Twice as she got to know the shop regulars. The quilt, a simple carpenter star pattern, wasn't fancy or complicated, but to Lydia it charted her new friendships in her new home.

What was it that Heather, the young store assistant, had said about quilting? It was the most narrative of the fiber arts. At the time, Lydia had nodded. The young, apple-red-haired woman intimidated Lydia, so she pretended she understood what that meant.

But now she thought she did. Quilts were put together, square by square, fabric by fabric, the way chapters or stanzas built a story or a poem.

Lydia turned off the bedside lamp and clutched the quilt in both hands. As she fell asleep, she told herself the story of her new life in Peridot, trying desperately to pretend the story ended in a floral patch of quilting cotton, not with a desk—and a man covered in blood.

Chapter Three

Lydia woke up to Charlie's nose against her cheek, cold and wet. His favorite way to request his morning walk. For one moment, she hugged the dog close to her and burrowed under the quilt, her first finished quilt, listening to only the birdsong outside her window.

But the moment couldn't last. She heard the movement next door in Brandon's apartment. That would be the police. Because Brandon was dead. Murdered. And what had Sergeant Simpson said?

"The next time we talk, it might be a very different conversation."

Those words echoed over and over in her mind as she quickly got dressed and took Charlie out for his morning walk.

When Fran had first shown her the apartment above the shop, she had imagined this part of her day as a quaint ritual. Now she had to take a different staircase down to the street level since the police tape cordoned off the whole area surrounding Brandon's apartment. Even though she knew she had no reason to feel guilty, Lydia felt herself hunching as she hurried down the stairs, past the store, and toward the small park that was off center from the main square.

Charlie sensed her discomfort and picked up his speed from his usual waddle to a slightly more strenuous shuffle. Looking at his short legs working harder, Lydia wondered about getting his DNA tested. He looked like a low-rider car, his body the sleek black of a Labrador, but his legs the stout appendages of a basset hound. She dismissed the idea as quickly as she had it, happy to let Charlie be a noble mutt and her perfect dog.

At the park, Lydia slowed down and let Charlie smell and wander at his own pace.

Peridot was starting to feel like home, and Lydia liked the morning temperatures the best. The afternoon heat always weighed her down, but in the morning, she felt full of new things: new ideas and hopes and projects.

The park filled up in the afternoon with families, but the mornings were quiet, just other dog walkers and the fitness people running quickly past her.

Even though it was the Saturday of Labor Day Weekend, the park still had the morning stillness she loved so much. But it didn't bring the usual optimism.

Brandon was dead. Sergeant Simpson thought she had something to do with it.

Lydia sat down on an empty bench and tried to think through the man's questions the night before.

"Lydia?"

Lydia looked up.

"Oh. Hi, Clark."

It was Clark. At the park. The dog park. With no dog.

Truthfully, she didn't know much about the man sitting on the next bench over. He owned one of the nicest shops in the square, The Pampered Pantry, but he always made a point of coming in Measure Twice to chat with Fran and talk sewing projects. In fact, Lydia had him in mind when planning the new garment classes she wanted to add to the store's repertoire. He struck her as a bit uptight, but Fran swore he was a great friend, and Fran's endorsement was enough, especially if he could be convinced to sew some trendy jackets or slacks.

Lydia realized she was just staring at him, so she offered lamely, "I didn't know you liked to come to the park in the morning."

"Well. There were police sirens last night that were far too loud. Who knows what that was about? Did you know they want to open a brewery in the square? Outrageous. It's bad enough with that clap-trap T-shirt shop selling tacky souvenirs. Really, the community needs to band together . . ." Clark looked at Lydia and noticed she was staring off into space.

"That is a topic for another time, I'm sure. We'll need to get you on some committees this fall. But clearly there was some sort of scuffle last night, hence the sirens. Ruined any chance I had of a good, restorative rest. Since I couldn't get back to sleep, I figured I would come back to the park," he added, slumping his shoulders.

"Back to the park?" Lydia prodded, not ready to admit she knew exactly what the sirens were about.

"I used to walk here every morning with Rutty."

Rutty? The name sounded like a pet, but Lydia had been wrong before and hurt people's feelings when it came to unconventional names. She wanted to be sure, so she prodded again, "Rutty?"

"Rutherford B. Hayes," Clark clarified, gazing off into the middle distance.

Well, that didn't help at all.

Charlie came up and bumped Clark's hand for a rub, which startled him into continuing, though he declined to pat the dog.

"I had a vizsla named after the nineteenth president of the United States. Absolutely majestic breed, vizslas."

Did Lydia imagine it or was that statement punctuated with a look of distaste in Charlie's distinctly mutt-ish direction? Maybe Charlie was part vizsla for all he knew!

Clark continued his lecture. "They're Hungarian—just terrific animals, very intelligent, hunters—of course, extremely active. I would take Rutty here every morning for his exercises."

"Has he gotten too old for that?" Lydia offered, wondering for the millionth time why Clark had to say things like *exercises* instead of just *fetch*.

"Rutty was in the prime of health. Really the epitome of the breed. His breeder in Dawsonville said exactly that. But he's gone. Dead. Taken." Clark pursed his lips together. In anyone else, it might have looked like annoyance, but Lydia had quickly grown fond of this peculiar man and knew the grimace masked a much deeper emotion.

"I am so sorry," Lydia offered, imaging poor Rutherford hit by a car or some other commonplace tragedy.

"I'm not sorry. I'm angry. Fran will probably tell you the whole sordid tale, so you may as well hear it from me. Rutty was an excellent dog, very attuned to me as his owner. He could be . . . some claimed he was . . . somewhat aggressive, but really, dogs are meant to be that way, not like the dopey, mindless retrievers you see these days, all the instinct bred right out of them."

Clark looked down at his hands that had clenched into fists while he was talking. Lydia looked out at Charlie, who she imagined must be below even retrievers on Clark's hierarchy of canines. Charlie was on his back, rolling around in clover, tongue hanging out in the sunshine.

Clearing his throat, Clark unclenched his fists, smoothed his pristine khaki shorts, and continued, "One day, I was walking Rutty around the square and noticed that Turn the Page was setting up a discount book cart on the sidewalk. Now, Peridot has very strict parameters when it comes to outdoor vendors, and I made a point of letting the shop know they were in clear breach of said regulations. That man April and Wade hired, Brandon, well, he had a differing of opinion regarding the sales cart. I did not appreciate the tone Brandon took. Neither did Rutty. I am not accusing Brandon of violence, but he did step toward me, which was certainly beyond the bounds of appropriate behavior . . ." Clark trailed off.

Lydia could see that his hands were again clenched in his lap.

She had to tell him. Clark clearly didn't know that Brandon was dead. How on earth was she going to tell him?

"Simply put, Rutty protected me. He bit Brandon. On the arm. Drew blood. Brandon was fine—no stitches were required. As if that mattered. Brandon took the matter straight to the police, simply would not drop it, threatened to sue. I still do not understand why they were swayed by his absurd overreaction. They ordered. It was decided. I had to put Rutty down. You see, Lydia, he did not just die, he was taken from me. That man Brandon Ivey killed the best dog I have ever known. That man is a bastard, plain and simple. Someone should put *him* down. Now that would be justice."

Clark stared off into the middle distance, and Lydia tried to think of a segue.

"Was. Brandon *was* a bastard. He died last night," Lydia said, cringing. Would she ever learn how to have tact? It wasn't looking likely.

"What now?" Clark asked, baffled.

"Last night, someone murdered Brandon. The police are at the apartment. Right now. Investigating." Lydia didn't add that she had already been interviewed and was clearly the prime suspect. Even though she was new to Peridot, she had no illusions that she could keep that a secret. Still, she didn't have to tell anyone just yet, did she? Clark was clearly waiting for her to continue.

"I had dinner with Brandon last night. It was Fran's idea. And after dinner, well, after the date—the dinner date . . ." Lydia took a deep breath and tried again. "Last night I had dinner with Brandon. Afterward, I wanted to bring him some brownies"—it sounded as bad out loud as she'd thought it would—"and when I went to his apartment, he was dead."

"Lydia. How did Brandon die?" Clark sounded exasperated.

"Um. Well, I'm not sure exactly. But, um—he was . . . there was—someone stabbed Brandon in the neck with dress shears?" There, she had done it: said everything. Why didn't she feel any better?

"Dress shears?" Clark rummaged through his smart leather satchel and found his sewing kit. "I packed this for tonight's class. I always prefer to use my own tools." Unzipping the pouch, he pulled out a Measure Twice–branded pair of gleaming silver scissors and asked, "You mean like these?"

Lydia flinched. "Yes, Clark, just like those."

"I can prove it wasn't me!" Clark joked loudly. When Lydia failed to respond, he went on, "You know, like in Clue, it couldn't have been Clark in the apartment with the dress shears. I have my scissors here. Exonerated, your honor."

Charlie tugged at his leash, tired of being in the hot sun and ready to head home for some cool water and a morning nap. Lydia stood up, unsure how to leave the conversation.

"Sorry if that was uncouth. I can't say I have ever been told about a murder before. I would say I am quite shocked. Can we forget I said that, about justice and whatnot? I had no idea, of course."

"Sure, Clark. I'll see you tonight for the sewing class at the shop. If Fran doesn't cancel . . ."

"See you then, Lydia," Clark replied, not moving from the bench as Lydia followed Charlie home.

What was he thinking about now? Lydia wondered, as she walked home from the park. Was Clark a little pleased that Brandon was dead, or was that unfair of her to think? Sergeant Simpson had told her to think of who else would have hurt Brandon.

Looking down as Charlie made his slow way back to their new apartment, Lydia tried to imagine how she would feel if someone had him put down. Lydia really felt like Charlie was her family. With her marriage in the rearview, Charlie meant more to her than ever. On the mornings when it was hard to get up and try all over again, Charlie was there, nudging her with his wet nose, demanding to be walked, rewarding her later with snuggles on the couch.

Lydia no longer had a car to put a bumper sticker on, but sometimes she still felt the desire to buy one of the ones that said, "Who rescued who?" with a paw print or something equally cringy. Graham had wanted a dog from a breeder, a goldendoodle, perfectly hypoallergenic. Lydia had demanded they adopt. Graham surprisingly acquiesced and set up Google alerts for doodles at the local shelters. They were supposed to adopt one the day she found Charlie. The doodle was the hit of the shelter, with families lined up to meet him. Charlie, in comparison, sat silently in his kennel, curled right against the far corner. A dog of uncertain age, no clear lineage, and only a white stripe down his snout and a white patch on his black chest to make him stand out in any way. Lydia had put her foot down. When Graham left, at least there had been no risk he would take Charlie with him.

Back in the apartment, she gave Charlie his water and breakfast and changed from her exercise clothes into a checkered gingham linen dress.

It was nine in the morning already. And Measure Twice opened at ten on Saturdays. She had to get to the store to help get it ready for the day. Fran and Heather were expecting her. And they had no idea what had happened the night before.

* * *

The bell above the door rang out as Lydia walked into Measure Twice, her favorite place in the world.

Fran and Heather were checking inventory, the two wildly different women both lost in the task at hand. Fran looked, as always, like a model from an L.L.Bean catalog, a little older than Lydia, but far thinner, with her graying hair cut close to her head. She looked ready to go on a hike or lead a committee meeting. Heather, meanwhile, was in her twenties, pale with bright, dyed-red hair and a penchant for short skirts and big boots. Still, Heather was trim and slim, built like Fran, and for a moment, they seemed oddly well paired, even though Lydia knew for a fact that each found the other's sartorial choices baffling.

Lydia cleared her throat to break their concentration.

Looking up, Heather informed her, "Lydia, your order of Ruby Star Society fabric is here."

"Thanks, Heather!" Lydia said, hoping her enthusiasm would warm the young woman toward her. They were friendly, but Lydia had a feeling Heather still didn't really consider Lydia a friend.

"Yeah. No problem. What's going on upstairs? Did someone steal something from Brandon's apartment? Let me guess, a priceless first-edition novel of some sort? Something British?" Heather smirked.

It was so hard to tell when Heather was joking. Sure, her face was smirking, but wasn't it always?

Heather looked up from the counter, clearly waiting for Lydia's response, just as Fran came out from the back break room, arms full of rickrack and binding.

Lydia looked at her watch: nine forty-five AM, so they had fifteen minutes until they opened. The hand-lettered sign in the shop window still read "Closed." Good.

"Heather, it wasn't a robbery. I think we should all take a quick breather, maybe have a cup of coffee," Lydia suggested, walking to the break room without making eye contact with either woman.

Thankfully, she could hear Heather's Doc Martens clomping behind her and Fran's murmurs of confusion as she followed.

But before Lydia could reach the break room and explain the nightmare she had endured, there was a knock on the door.

The M's: Mary and Martha.

The first time Lydia had seen them, she had assumed they were twins. Then she looked more closely at their faces. They didn't look alike, not the way sisters would. It was a false impression based on their clothes, their hairstyles, even their posture. The M's weren't sisters, but they were inseparable. And almost identical from a distance in their pristine, proper look.

Lydia knew "proper." Her own New England grandmother, Oma, had cared about things like handwritten thank-you cards and which fork to use with which course. But this—this was something different, and all Lydia could think was, *This is Southern.*

Today, they both wore button-down shirts topped with cardigans. They both wrapped floral scarves around their necks, tied in neat, subdued knots. They both even wore the same style skirt, a soft sort of pencil skirt that came down well below the knees. Peach-colored stockings and surprisingly white Keds sneakers finished off both ensembles.

Although they were clearly older than Fran, Lydia hesitated to classify them as elderly, even to herself. She thought she would be quick to offer them a seat or a hand down a steep staircase, but she also suspected that, if need be, both women could be far faster and more tenacious than anticipated. Woe to whoever thought they could overcharge the women or lead them down the primrose path.

What on earth were these matriarchs, and possible members of the Daughters of the American Revolution, doing in Measure Twice on a Saturday morning before the shop was even open?

"Mary! Martha! How wonderful to see you both," Fran exclaimed, moving back to the front of the shop. Lydia and Heather followed.

"Quite," was Martha's terse answer.

"What can I help you with this morning?" Fran persevered.

"That remains to be seen. As you know, Mary and I have volunteered to donate a quilt to our church's annual silent auction. The auction is only one week away, and while we have already placed our order for quilt batting . . . frankly speaking, Fran, it has yet to arrive." Martha's icy tone seemed better suited to a long-standing family feud than an issue with an order, but Lydia wondered what was going to happen next.

"Oh my goodness," Fran replied, sounding suitably chastened. "I am mortified. You are both such valued customers. And I know how Peridot Baptist relies on your quilts to be the stars of their fundraisers."

Lydia thought Fran was pouring it on a little thick, but looking at Martha, she realized her friend knew just the right tack to take.

Fran continued, "I think we just got some new batting in the store. Why don't you take what you need for the quilt with you today? And then when the package arrives—and believe me, I will be on the phone with our supplier immediately—when the package arrives, you can keep that as a thank-you from the store for your wonderful support."

Mary spoke up now, her voice similar to Martha's elegant Southern tone, but softer, quieter. "Well, now, Fran, you didn't have to do that. How kind of you."

Heather bagged up the batting and gave it to Martha, and the two women turned to leave the store.

Just as they reached the door, Sergeant Simpson appeared to hold it open for them.

Lydia watched as the two women faced an impossible choice.

Why was Sergeant Simpson, in full uniform, heading into Measure Twice on a Saturday, before opening time, no less? They would desperately want to know. But as he held the door open for them, if they chose to stay, they would be revealing themselves to be, at the least, curious, and at the worst, nosey.

"Have a wonderful morning, ladies," Sergeant Simpson said, closing the door behind them.

Lydia watched the two women walk away, sneaking glances over their perfectly poised shoulders.

"Sergeant Simpson, to what do we owe the pleasure?" Fran asked, blithely unaware of why the man was in her store.

The policeman looked at Lydia and raised one eyebrow, as if to say, *You haven't told them?*

"Well, now, Fran. We need to talk about what happened last night in your building."

"I saw that. Was there a break-in?" Heather asked.

"Miss, I don't believe we've met. I am Sergeant Simpson with the Peridot Police."

"I'm Heather Moulton. I work here," Heather replied. At least she was equally unfriendly, Lydia supposed.

"Thank you, Miss. Fran, is there somewhere we could have a chat?" Sergeant Simpson asked, still smiling, keeping the conversation pleasant. When would he tell them?

"Sure thing." Fran led them back to the break room and offered the man coffee.

"No, Fran, but thank you," Sergeant Simpson answered, remaining standing while the three women sat down. "I am sorry to be the one to tell you this, but last night, Brandon Ivey was murdered in his apartment."

Fran let out a sort of shout, and Heather went even paler than usual.

"I have already talked with Miss Barnes, here."

Heather and Fran turned to her in shock. She stared at the floor.

"But I need both of you to tell me what you were doing last night from around seven to nine, and then I will need both of you to come by the station this weekend to sign your statements. Can you do that?"

The two women nodded.

"Last night, I went home from the store at around five, like I normally do. I drove to The Laurels, my house on Cherry Log Mountain, which took almost an hour. When I got home, I had some dinner, and then I sewed for a bit and went to bed around nine."

"Thank you, Fran. Can anyone vouch for you?"

"What? No. There's a caretaker on the mountain that looks after a number of houses; he might have seen me pull into my driveway, I guess, if that helps."

"That does help. Can you write down his number for me?"

While Fran hurried to comply, Sergeant Simpson turned to Heather, prompting, "And you, Miss Moulton?"

"I was at the hospital," Heather answered flatly.

"What?" Fran gasped, her concern for Brandon superseded by her new concern for the young shop assistant.

"Knitting," Heather elaborated.

"What?" Fran repeated, this time more confused than worried.

"You were knitting at Peridot General?" Sergeant Simpson asked, with a little bit of confusion creeping into his official tone.

Heather sighed as if their confusion were absurd. "I'm in a Friday night knitting group. We meet at the hospital and knit hats for the NICU babies."

"What babies was that?" Sergeant Simpson asked, trying to keep up with Heather's increasingly confusing alibi.

"NICU," Heather annunciated slowly. "Neonatal Intensive Care Unit. For babies that are born early or have problems. They need little hats to stay warm. I meet with a group that knits the little hats. For the babies." Now Heather looked uncomfortable.

Everyone was quiet for a moment. Heather, with her black clothes and dyed candy apple–red hair, seemed . . . well, Lydia had never thought . . .

"I had no idea you did that, Heather," Fran said, saving Lydia from thinking about her own shameful assumptions.

"Yeah. Whatever. I like to knit for kids. It is not the kids' fault that things are tough for them," Heather said.

"Can anyone verify that?" Sergeant Simpson asked.

"There are, like, ten of us. Just go ask at the hospital," Heather answered.

"Thank you, Miss Moulton. I will do just that. Now, I need you both to come by the station in the next few days to give official statements and sign them. But for now, what I am going to ask you is this: if you can think of anyone who wanted to hurt Mr. Ivey or had a reason to not like Mr. Ivey, I would like you to give me a call." With that, he gave each woman a card like the one he had given Lydia the night before. "Can you do that?"

Both women nodded, Fran enthusiastically, Heather less so.

"Miss Barnes, why don't you walk me out?" Sergeant Simpson suggested in a way that sounded like a command rather than a request.

Fran and Heather stayed behind in the break room, talking quietly about what they had just learned.

When they were near the door, Sergeant Simpson handed Lydia a zipper-closed plastic bag, saying, "Here is your phone, miss. Thank you for letting us look at it. Have you given any thought to our conversation?"

Had she? In a way, Lydia had thought about nothing else. And Clark had admitted he hated Brandon. Isn't that exactly what Sergeant Simpson wanted to know? Lydia knew the conversation was strange, maybe even important, but she also knew she wasn't ready to tell Sergeant Simpson that one of her only friends in her new town had a reason for hating the man who had just been murdered. It could wait. Couldn't it?

"Miss?"

"Oh, sorry, Sergeant. I'm tired. And, um, no, nothing has come to mind. But I will keep thinking."

"You do that. Then you tell me what you come up with. All right?"

Lydia nodded and looked back to the workroom. Fran and Heather were watching the conversation.

"I will be expecting your call." And with that, Sergeant Simpson walked out into the summer sunshine, and Lydia turned to face her friends, their questions, and the truth of what had happened the night before.

* * *

"Lydia, dear," Fran began as Lydia joined them in the break room. But then she fell silent. Heather stared at her.

"Last night, after we had dinner, I went to Brandon's apartment, to see if he wanted some brownies, and when I got there, I found him. Dead. Murdered. I'm the one who called the police. They interviewed me last night. I wanted to tell you both, but then the M's got here and I just, I wanted to wait until—and then . . . I'm sorry. You should have heard it from me."

Fran stood up and started pacing around the break room. Whatever composure she had maintained for the sergeant had disappeared.

"We can't. We can't open the store today. Brandon is . . . he was our friend." Fran paused, forcing herself to take a steadying breath, "Heather, I will still pay you for today. I know you were counting on longer hours for the holiday weekend."

Heather tried to interrupt Fran, but Fran just waved her off and continued, "Don't argue with me, Heather. I am going to do what I think is right. This is still my store."

Shrugging, Heather grabbed her bag and walked toward the door, but before she left, she turned to Fran and quietly added, "Just call if you need me."

Still? Lydia wanted to ask what Fran meant by "still my store," but Fran was speaking to her now, and the moment was lost.

"Lydia, can you stay and help me lock up? I had started setting up displays for weekend shoppers and want to put a lot of that away. Then, I'm going to head back to The Laurels. I'm very tired. This is very . . . I think I will take a rest this afternoon." And with that, Fran stood up and walked back into the main shop to lock the door, her back bent forward as if she had aged ten years in one conversation. She looked, Lydia realized, suddenly incredibly frail. Sergeant Simpson wanted her to think about who was guilty. But what about who might still be in danger?

Chapter Four

"Why don't we have one more cup of coffee before we head out?" Fran suggested, turning back toward Lydia in the break room. Lydia felt relieved. She could tell Fran had more to say, and she knew she wanted to say more to Fran. As always, Fran would know what to do.

Sitting in her favorite spot on the long couch that dominated the back wall, Lydia admitted something to Fran she hadn't wanted to say in front of Heather.

"Fran, before Clark knew that Brandon was dead, he told me that he hated Brandon. Like, really hated him," Lydia confided in her friend. "Last night, Sergeant Simpson told me that if I could think of anyone who wanted Brandon dead, I should tell him. Immediately. But I didn't say anything just now. Should I have said something? I mean, do you think? . . . You don't think . . ."

"That Clark killed Brandon?" Fran scoffed. "No, Lydia, dear, I don't think that."

Lydia let out her breath. "Right, I'm sorry. I haven't really slept. And it was just . . . he sounded so angry. What Sergeant

Simpson didn't say is how Brandon died. Fran, someone stabbed him in the neck with a pair of dress shears. One of our pairs."

Fran looked shell-shocked. "What? What are you saying?"

"When I found Brandon last night, someone had stabbed him. In the neck. With dress shears from Measure Twice. And listen, Sergeant Simpson said it looks like the killer knew Brandon. Do you think that means we know the killer? Why else would it be a pair of our scissors, Fran?" It felt good to finally speak her fears out loud.

"I didn't know. How terrible," Fran replied. "But Lydia, those scissors are right by the register; they would be easy to steal. And we have stocked them for as long as the shop has been open. Lord knows how many pairs I've ordered over the years. It is horrible, but it does not mean we know who did this . . . this terrible thing."

"But Clark said—"

"It doesn't matter what Clark said," Fran interrupted her, adding, "Lydia, you are new to Peridot. Small-town life is different." Fran paused, looking around the walls of the break room, the corkboards filled with notes about reorders of fabric and store maintenance. "People know each other's business. People get involved in each other's lives. Sometimes, people have grudges. And sometimes, grudges . . ." Fran gestured vaguely with her hand.

Lydia waited for her friend to finish the sentence. When she didn't continue, Lydia prompted her, saying, "Grudges sometimes do what, Fran?"

"Well, when you see someone every day, you can lose perspective a bit. And Brandon. Well, Brandon was a strong personality."

Brandon? The guy who couldn't seem to decide what to order for dinner? The guy who took forever to say goodnight and then decided on a fist bump?

"Clark had good reason to be upset with Brandon, but he wasn't the only one. Brandon had a great mind for business. I really think Wade and April have him—had him," Fran corrected herself, "to thank for the success of Turn the Page. Still, you don't become successful without ruffling a few feathers, as the M's would say." Fran offered a weak smile.

Lydia nodded.

"Clark is not the only person that has struggled with Brandon. Turn the Page wasn't the first business in that spot—you know that, right?" Fran asked Lydia, her smile tightening.

"What do you mean?"

"Well, Turn the Page bought the storefront from a business that was failing. It wasn't exactly predatory, but . . ."

Lydia wasn't sure why this mattered, but she knew better than to rush Fran, so she played along, asking, "What was the store before? I can't imagine anything there except a bookstore." And she meant it; the store seemed perfectly shaped to the rows of shelves, with the cozy nooks for reading.

"For good reason. It was a bookstore." Lydia must have looked as confused as she felt, since Fran rushed on to explain. "It was a bookstore, just not Turn the Page. It was called The Rising Phoenix, and it was more, you know, *woo-woo*."

Lydia had no idea what *woo-woo* meant, so she just stared at Fran blankly, hoping her friend would explain further.

"Well, it had crystals and dream catchers and that sort of thing. Cynde was just sure . . ."

"Cynde?" Lydia's mouth hung open in surprise. Cynde, a shop regular, was quickly becoming a good friend, but Lydia couldn't imagine the cheerful, but very practical, court stenographer interested in dream catchers, much less running a store that sold them.

"Yes, that is what I was getting to. Cynde owned the shop that used to be in that spot, a bookstore called The Rising Phoenix, and it was really her dream. She just poured herself into the bookstore. Used all her savings. It only lasted six months before trouble hit.

"The store wasn't failing, exactly. But *you* know, Lydia, dear—you see it with Measure Twice: it looks a lot easier to run a business than it is. The Rising Phoenix was wonderful, but it wasn't making money. It was Brandon who suggested Cynde sell. Before your time, of course, Lydia."

Fran looked out through the shop window into the square, but she gazed as if staring right into the past.

"Brandon had been offering a continuing education course at the college, creative writing something or other. April took the class—that's how they met. I'm not sure who dreamed up Turn the Page first, Brandon or April. April had just married Wade, and I think they were trying to figure out what their next move was going to be, with Wade moving to Peridot and all.

"Brandon, and I guess April, saw an opportunity in Cynde's failure. It wasn't Brandon's fault that her dream failed, of course. And Cynde never claimed to hold a grudge. But I think about how I would have felt if Measure Twice had failed and I had sold out and given up on my dream, only to watch someone else move in and make it work for them. I'll tell you what, Lydia, and this is the truth: I would have been awfully mad. Measure Twice is my dream and no one else's."

They sat together in silence, considering the implications of Fran's admission. How angry had Cynde been? And why did Fran seem angry too?

"Okay, Fran, I understand . . . well, I understand that maybe I don't really understand what it's like to live in a small town. And I get what you're saying about watching someone else live out your dreams." For a second, Lydia saw her diet lemonade spreading across the floor of her bedroom. "But Turn the Page isn't new or anything, so why would it suddenly matter now?"

Fran moved her head back quickly, surprised, "Well, the party. I think that's what has really been hard for Cynde."

Lydia stared at Fran.

"You don't know about the party?"

"Party?"

"This is Turn the Page's fifth year in business, so April decided to have a party to celebrate. I'm surprised she hasn't mentioned it."

Had she? Had Lydia been too selfishly absorbed in her own troubles? She would be sure to ask her that night. For now, Lydia just said, "I don't remember hearing about it."

"Oh, it has been the talk of the town. Everybody is involved in one way or another. She wants to do it in a few weeks and has already asked Clark to cater. He was thrilled, of course. I think they're going to have some guest authors come, maybe do a reading? April is so excited. Excited and a bit stressed. You know how she is. I don't know what will happen now. I can't imagine they'll want to go through with it without Brandon."

The terrible reality of Brandon's murder crashed back in on their conversation that, for a moment, had been lightened by talk of book parties and rival storefronts.

A man was dead. Murdered.

Lydia shivered.

Fran noticed and stood up to add a little more coffee to Lydia's cup. Once she was seated again, she took a deep breath.

"That is enough about that, Lydia, dear. Small towns can breed frustration. Clark is not special in that. And he is not a murderer. The police will do their job and find the madman who did this. Sergeant Simpson is very good at his job, not that Peridot ever has any murders."

The silence returned.

Lydia felt relieved. This time, she tried to change the subject, "Thanks, Fran. Do you want me to stay and do some inventory? Since you're closing for the day?"

Taking inventory was Lydia's least favorite task at the store, but right now the methodical nature of counting spools of threads sounded heavenly.

"No need, Lydia. I think it's best for you to let the store be for today. Did you have any plans? What will you do for the rest of the day?" Fran asked, clearly worried Lydia would go home and either bake all day or spend the whole day eating what she had already baked.

"Actually, I'm having lunch with Cynde. We set it up before . . . before everything. She invited me to eat with her outside the courthouse; you know how she does that?"

Fran nodded, looking wistful, though Lydia couldn't imagine why.

"I'm going to join her today. She doesn't know. I mean, I don't think she . . ."

"You might be surprised just how fast news makes its way around Peridot," Fran countered.

"Oh. Okay." Maybe she wouldn't have to break the news again. She could hope.

"That said, Lydia, I wouldn't mention The Rising Phoenix. Maybe you could keep this conversation between us?"

"Sure," Lydia replied. She had no problem keeping the conversation to herself, but it wasn't something Fran had ever asked her to do before. It felt unsettling, as if something familiar had become secretive.

Trying to avoid Fran's gaze, Lydia looked at one of the many corkboards that covered the walls of the break room. This one had a flier advertising that night's class, Lydia's first-ever garment-making class at Measure Twice.

Oh no.

Pointing at the flier, Lydia asked meekly, "Do you want to cancel class? April and Wade Lanier asked me over for dinner tonight beforehand—before all of this happened—but I don't know . . . Maybe I should just cancel everything—dinner, the class, all of it."

Fran had agreed about a week ago to let Lydia teach a garment sewing class that night. All the shop regulars were coming. She had been counting down the days until her first chance to really prove to Fran that the shop should consider stocking garment fabrics, patterns, and notions. Now what would happen?

"No. No, I do not, Lydia. You don't need to be home alone with your worries. April and Wade will be glad of the company.

And as for Measure Twice? I think it is the right thing to do to close the shop for the day. But the class? That's for our friends. We all need to be together, now more than ever. So, I will see you tonight at eight on the dot." Fran smiled. "Clark, Cynde, Mary, and Martha are all coming. Heather too. Maybe by then, someone will have a better idea of what happened to Brandon," Fran added darkly. Then she turned to Lydia abruptly.

"Lydia, dear. Do you think you're happy here? Do you think you can live here, considering what happened? Here you left the big city only to have this happen in our small town. Will you stay? I understand if you need to go home. No one would think badly of you, you know. Will you go home to Atlanta?" Fran asked.

Where was this coming from? Wasn't Fran the one who had told her she had finally found the place to plant her roots? Hadn't they just agreed that class would go on? Fran was just overwhelmed. They all were.

"Fran, Peridot is my home. Like you said, Sergeant Simpson will figure it out. It's terrible what happened, but I know I'm right where I'm meant to be." Lydia hoped she sounded like she meant it, and giving her friend a quick hug, she headed out of the store.

* * *

As she rushed back to her apartment to grab the lunch she had packed earlier, she ruminated over Fran's words. Why would Fran be worried Lydia would leave Peridot? True, what had happened was terrible. But this was her home, wasn't it? Fran was right about Lydia needing to stay busy. Already, the images from the night before were threatening to overwhelm her. Instead, she thought about Cynde.

The court stenographer, and apparently former bookstore owner, was a regular at Measure Twice, a plumper, softer counterpoint to Fran's trim efficiency.

Lydia nodded to the policemen at Brandon's apartment, ran into her place, and grabbed her lunch, stopping only to give Charlie a dog treat. It felt better to keep moving. And the courthouse was only a short walk away.

As she approached the brick building that anchored the center of the Peridot town square, Lydia paused to look at her friend. Cynde hadn't seen her yet and was resting on a bench outside the courthouse, soaking up the late summer sun. Lydia always felt like she was melting in the full Georgia heat of August, but Cynde was like a lizard on a rock, happy and still in the strong sunshine.

Fran had a uniform, but Cynde was a little more adventurous in her clothing choices. Lydia always thought of L.L.Bean when she looked at Fran, but Cynde struck her more as a boutique shopper. Maybe she bought all her clothes at the shop in the square that seemed to have new, bias-cut pant-and-shirt combinations every week. Cynde loved a good coordinating set and an accent scarf.

August was too hot for a scarf, but Cynde's top had bright flowers appliquéd diagonally across it, and the flowers suited the mood of her friend, who was pleased to be on her lunch break.

Cynde wasn't a pattern as much as she was a type of fabric. She made Lydia think of novelty quilting fabric, the cotton material with bright animals or unexpected flamingos. Cynde was like that: bright, a little silly, and always good for a laugh. And even though quilting cotton could be a little brash, it lasted for years and years, growing softer with every wash. It was gentle, just like her bright and exuberant new friend.

How was Lydia going to tell her about Brandon? First Clark, then Fran and Heather. Now Cynde. How had Lydia become the bearer of such bad news? Then she thought of what Fran had said, that Cynde wouldn't "be mourning much." Brandon hadn't been a bad guy—Fran was adamant about that—and the date might have been awkward, but it wasn't terrible. Still, though Brandon was a "not bad guy," a lot of people seemed to be less than devastated by his death.

When Cynde had suggested, at the last craft-and-chat night, that they meet for lunch, she had made it clear that it was BYOL: bring your own lunch. Graham had made his frustration regarding Lydia's cooking abilities, or lack thereof, more than clear in their brief marriage. Now that she wasn't bothered about cooking, she was finding her way to a few recipes that she enjoyed. It was far, far too hot for the lasagna recipe she had been tweaking, so she had packed herself a turkey-and-Swiss sandwich and two bags of barbecue chips instead. Graham might have cared about portion size, but Lydia was more than happy to throw caution to the wind when it came to delicious potato chips.

Cynde cared even less about cooking than Lydia. Lydia sat down, uncertain what to say, but Cynde beat her to it.

Smiling widely at her friend, Cynde asked, "Do you mind if I start? I am starving!" She pulled out a plastic container of takeout Chinese.

"No, no, go ahead. Listen, Cynde, about last night . . ."

"That's right! Last night was the big night! So"—Cynde twirled lo mein around her fork—"tell me all about the date! No offense, but you look exhausted, which I am going to take as a good sign. Spill!"

Lydia didn't know what to say.

"And what on earth is going on over by your place? Is there something wrong with the roof?" she added, gesturing toward that corner of the square.

Roof? Lydia bought herself some time opening the first bag of potato chips, slowly eating a few before responding, "There's nothing wrong with the roof, Cynde. That's police tape."

Cynde was so bright, and she had to be quick, since her job as a court transcriptionist demanded speed and attention to detail. It was just that Lydia never seemed to see that side of her friend.

"Police! Did someone have a break-in? I'm telling you, these holiday weekends—"

"No one broke into the building, Cynde. Listen to me," Lydia's change in tone was enough for her friend to set down the takeout and pay attention. "Last night, after our date, I found Brandon in his apartment. Dead. Someone killed Brandon. He was murdered."

Nope. Still couldn't say it in a normal way. Maybe it would go better the next time she had to explain it? Somehow, Lydia doubted it.

Giving Cynde a moment to absorb the horrible news, Lydia focused on her potato chips.

Finally, Cynde responded, "Brandon is dead? Someone killed Brandon? Do they know who killed him? Why would anyone do such a thing? I mean, he wasn't the easiest guy to get along with." Lydia tried to hide her wince with the sound of crunching chips. Sugar might help shock, but salt really helped grief.

"You guys were friends, right?" Lydia asked, hoping to hear something different from what Fran had told her that morning. Fran might be magical, but she wasn't infallible. Maybe Brandon and Cynde got along better than she realized.

"What? No. Brandon and I are not . . . *were* not . . . friends." Cynde attacked her lo mein, and the two women sat without talking, watching the life of the square move past them. Thankfully, none of the tourists seemed to realize that Lydia was connected to the crime scene tape only a few buildings away. How long would it take for the rumors to start?

"Have they caught the guy?"

"Who?"

"Whoever killed Brandon—have they caught him? I mean, statistically speaking, it's bound to be a guy, right?"

"Um, Sergeant Simpson is on the case and working to solve it."

"I have never known anyone who . . . this has never happened to me . . . poor Brandon. No one deserves that. Not even Brandon."

The two women looked at the apartment. Lydia felt the panic of the night before starting to creep back.

Shaking her head to clear her thoughts, she asked Cynde, "You have work today, huh? I'm surprised that there are cases on a Saturday. Especially a holiday weekend. Is that even allowed?"

"What?" Cynde looked miles away. "Well, no cases are being tried today or anything. But sometimes I like to come in and catch up on filing and whatnot. That way I don't end up in the weeds. Technically, I'm the court stenographer, but really I fill in wherever I'm needed for office tasks. There's always something that needs doing. It's fine, even if not exactly inspiring." With that, Cynde's normally happy face settled into a frown.

Lydia felt validated in her choice to pack two bags of chips. Cynde clearly had more to say, and it was starting to look like Fran was right.

"Don't get me wrong—it pays the bills, and everyone at the courthouse is really lovely." Both women paused to look at the stout brick building that anchored the center of Peridot. "When I first moved here, I had other plans, you know?"

"We've never actually had a chance to talk about it. You've always been so great about listening to me complain about Graham. I should have asked you more questions!" And Lydia meant it. Everyone in Peridot had welcomed her, but it was Fran and Cynde who had listened to all her sob stories. Literal sob stories, embarrassingly.

"No need, Lydia. Nothing much to say. But when I first moved here, I had plans that had nothing to do with the courthouse, to be honest. Turn the Page wasn't the first bookstore in the square, you know."

Lydia did know because Fran had told her as much that morning, but she just nodded and looked busy eating her turkey sandwich.

"I had a bookstore—The Rising Phoenix." Cynde gazed in the direction of Turn the Page. "I wish you could have seen it, Lydia. I stocked crystals. Candles. Beautiful local artwork. It was more than a store, really." She smiled to herself, lost in the memory. "The M's were scandalized! Claimed it was New Age witchcraft." Cynde's smile turned into a snorting laugh. "In a way, I guess it was. I stocked self-help books and books about spiritualism and even had some tarot card decks in the back. The store was ahead of its time. But I wish I had held out a little longer, believed in my dream . . . not listened to . . ."

Cynde and Lydia sat in silence, staring across the square at what was now Turn the Page.

Cynde broke the quiet first, trying to shake the gloom, "Well, it is terrible, just terrible that this happened. Peridot really is a safe town, Lydia. Brandon must have been into things we didn't know about. You know. Drugs. You never do know someone's secrets. I trust our police department, so I have no doubt they will find this deranged individual in no time. We can't get lost in our sorrows, Lydia. Besides, isn't today the big day?"

Chapter Five

"What?" Lydia asked, baffled.

"Oh." Cynde looked embarrassed. "Did you decide not to go through with it?"

"With what?"

"Baby Lobster?" Cynde asked, now looking worried about Lydia.

Lydia smacked her palm against her forehead and then felt like a cartoon character. Baby Lobster! She had completely forgotten.

"No! No, I didn't decide not to go through with it. I . . . well, I'm embarrassed to say it, but I completely forgot. Last night was so—I just haven't been . . ."

Cynde smiled kindly. "I'm sure you can call the shelter and tell them things have changed."

Lydia thought back to the listing for Baby Lobster on the shelter website. Lydia had clicked, just based on the extraordinary name, and then learned that the calico cat had been in the shelter for over a year, no takers. The cat looked sad and angry. Lydia knew that feeling, so she had called and asked to adopt the cat. Which was supposed to happen today. The day after she

73

found a dead body. She could call and cancel. No one would blame her. But she thought about those eyes, so full of disappointment already. Baby Lobster would blame her.

"No. No. It's not the cat's fault, what happened. I have everything ready. I can't believe I even forgot. Cynde, thank goodness you reminded me! I need to go! But, um, Fran, well, she closed the store for the day but is still doing my class tonight. So will I see you then?"

"Absolutely. I can't wait to hear all about the newest member of your family."

And with that, Lydia left Cynde to bask in the sun for the rest of her lunch break, and hurried home to prepare for her new arrival.

Back in her apartment, Lydia stood near her window air-conditioning unit, shaking her linen dress to move the cool air through. She thought for the millionth time, *I am not made for this heat.*

Hopefully, her new cat would like air-conditioning. Lydia had wanted a cat for years. Unsurprisingly, Graham had been completely against it. He wasn't allergic; he just thought cats were not "the look." Lydia never really understood what that meant, but she had a feeling that cats just weren't cool enough for the catalog-perfect life Graham wanted to build.

Well. Lydia wasn't that cool either. Now that she had her own place, it was time to get a cat. The first night after she had left her marriage, Lydia had scrolled the pet adoption websites into the early hours.

It was a day after she had moved into Fran's apartment in Peridot that she found Baby Lobster, surrounded by cats with

Seams Deadly

names like Mittens and Snowflake. Now, facing the prospect of living next door to a murder scene, Lydia felt even more strongly that a cat *and* a dog combination was the way to go.

Lydia had never had a cat, but she was pretty sure wearing a handmade linen dress to a pet shelter was asking for trouble, so she quickly changed into shorts and a T-shirt that read, "Yes, I Sew. No, I Won't Hem Your Pants." She thought it was funny, and at least she didn't care if it got ruined.

Charlie looked up from his usual spot on the couch and then, with a snuffle-like noise, simply fell right back asleep. Thank goodness for her lazy dog. She didn't have time to walk him before she went to get his new . . . sibling? Cousin? Roommate?

She shook her head at her own nonsense, gathered up the cat carrier and the supplies she needed, and braced herself for Jeff, her neighbor on the other side of her apartment.

Jeff Johnson was a nice guy. Nice and perfectly normal. Lydia hoped if she repeated that refrain enough, she wouldn't find him so . . . off-putting. That was the only word for it: Jeff was off-putting. Still, Lydia didn't have a car, and the shelter was farther than walking distance.

Which meant she needed a ride. Which brought her back to Jeff. Lydia had thought Fran would be busy at the store, and the local taxi service was both spotty and expensive. Uber, which she completely took for granted in Atlanta, had yet to crack the coveted Peridot market. When she had mentioned her predicament to Jeff, he'd been quick to offer a ride, claiming he was always glad to rescue a damsel in distress. Lydia was grateful enough for the ride not to scold him for calling her a damsel, much less one in distress.

75

Again, she opened the door to her apartment and nodded at the police still milling about. Then she quietly knocked on Jeff's door. Jeff answered the door so quickly, Lydia wondered if he had been standing behind it, just waiting for her to arrive. Lydia considered, looking at her neighbor, what pattern he would match. He was a hard one to peg. Peridot was a laid-back town—lots of jeans, lots of fundraising T-shirts. On any given day, Lydia would see a shirt supporting the high school band or another advertising for a fun run sponsored by the local tire shop. Jeff, however, was the exception. Today he sported one of his trademark garishly bright silk shirts. This one had horses galloping across the front and the top button undone. Lydia couldn't help trying to place the fabric, but realized it had to be Italian, and, um, not easily purchased. Maybe he had a hookup in Europe? Some sort of horse shirt dealer? Lydia forced herself to stop thinking about the logistics of such a . . . bold . . . shirt, and she worked equally as hard to keep her eyes from the hairy chest exposed by the undone button. Who was she, in her sewing-themed T-shirts, to judge someone else's sartorial expression?

Maybe Jeff could be a duffle bag pattern.

Rather than step out onto the walkway, Jeff gestured for Lydia to come into his apartment, a smaller version of hers, that functioned as his home as well as his business.

Jeff picked up one of the countless model trains that ranged about the living room, filling bookcases and tabletops. He held the train gently and methodically cleaned it with a wet wipe. He stared at her. Silently.

"How's business, Jeff? I can't tell you how much I appreciate you giving me a ride today."

"Business is brisk, Lydia—thanks for asking. I just had an online auction for this beauty. I'm sending it off to its new home tomorrow." He gestured at the train he lovingly cradled in his hands. "Here, why not take some business cards for the shop? Maybe one of your sewing people will have a train to sell." Jeff passed her the business card, on heavy card stock, that read *Jeff's Trains*, his business buying and reselling model trains from his home.

She took the cards and tucked them into her bag. He continued to stare.

"So, have you been to the shelter before?" Lydia asked, unsure how else to goad him into action.

"Trains and pets don't really mix, Lydia," Jeff said, guffawing as he adjusted one of his many large gold rings.

Hmm. That hadn't worked.

"The shelter gave me a pretty strict pickup time, so if you don't mind . . ."

"Gotcha. Let's head downstairs. You can wait for me while I jog over and grab Maria." With that enigmatic remark, Jeff ushered her out of his apartment, following very closely behind her; locked the door; and headed downstairs. Lydia wondered why he hadn't mentioned the police swarming about the building.

Waiting for Jeff, and possibly Maria, Lydia looked at the window display for Measure Twice. The flier advertising the garment-making class was placed in the corner, visible but not boldly highlighted.

She tried not to feel disheartened. Fran was letting her teach the class. She would impress her with the Shirt No. 1, and then maybe the next class advertisement would have a bigger flier.

The sound of Jeff's horn honking broke Lydia from her reverie.

Turning around from the shop window, Lydia took full stock of Jeff's car, which she had never before had reason to pay careful attention to.

An old red Saab, the car had only two doors and a boxy frame that spoke to designs from ages past. Jeff honked again.

She opened the passenger side door and climbed in, stowing the new cat carrier she had bought at her feet. Inside, the sound of opera filled the small car.

"Lydia, meet Maria. Maria, this is my neighbor and close friend, Lydia."

Close friend? Lydia wanted to dispute that claim, but she was too distracted trying to find Maria. The car only had two seats, so where was the woman.

Did Jeff have a woman in the trunk? Lydia felt lightheaded, the blood draining from her face.

"Maria Callas," Jeff added as if that helped.

Seeing her shocked expression, Jeff continued his clarification. "Maria Callas, one of the greatest stars of opera ever to have lived? I named my car after her: Maria," he repeated, patting the dashboard.

Phew. Jeff did not have a woman in his trunk. He had simply named his old Saab after a dead opera singer. What a relief.

Even though the temperature was already climbing into the nineties, Jeff didn't have the air-conditioning on. On second glance, Lydia realized the car didn't have a working air conditioner. Feeling the sweat starting to bead at the back of her neck,

Lydia rolled her window down and looked out at Peridot as they passed through the square and out into the sprawling edges of town, dotted with strip malls.

After a few minutes, Jeff reached over and turned down the opera.

"So do the cops think you did it?"

Jeff turned to Lydia, smiling. *Smiling!*

"I saw you walking down to the cop car last night. Did you find the body? Do they think you did it?"

For a moment, Lydia's mind was completely blank. It was true that Fran had asked similar questions, and she knew that more questions were bound to come. But this was so much blunter than she had expected.

Jeff was still smiling, waiting for her reply.

Who started a conversation that way? She wanted to scream that this wasn't a TV show, but she was in his car, so she tried to be pleasant.

"I found him. I found Brandon." She squeezed her eyes shut tight, as if to banish the memory, and rushed forward with the information Jeff wanted. "And Sergeant Simpson had some questions for me at the station."

Surely that would be enough to satisfy his curiosity.

Nope.

"Did they grill you? 'Good cop, bad cop' sort of thing?" Jeff looked right into her eyes as he asked.

She wanted to tell him to pay attention to the road. But they were only five minutes away from the shelter. Looking down at the carrier at her feet, she thought about the new collar she had sewn up with a cute lobster-printed quilting cotton.

Sighing, she answered him, "There was no grilling. He just wanted to know why I was there. And. Well. They had a few questions about the dress shears."

"The what?"

Lydia could see the profile for Baby Lobster in her mind. Why on earth had she mentioned the dress shears?

"Dress shears. Scissors for fabric."

Jeff looked baffled.

Why had she mentioned it? Maybe she could fill the time with sewing information? She tried to explain dress shears, in a weird echo of the night before.

"Okay, so, when you're working with fabric, you want something better than normal kitchen scissors. Which is why you use dress shears. They're stronger and longer and cut better. It really makes a difference."

"Longer?" Jeff smiled.

Lydia grimaced, "Yeah, they have longer blades so that the cut is cleaner and more controlled."

"Sounds pretty deadly." Jeff smiled. Again.

"I mean, not when you use them correctly," Lydia replied, feeling a strange need to defend her sewing tools. "You would be more likely to hurt yourself with a rotary cutter or even the needle on the sewing machine than with dress shears."

"I didn't realize sewing could be so dangerous," Jeff replied.

Thankfully, before he could say anything else, they arrived at the shelter, and Lydia practically jumped out of the car as soon as he parked.

Without waiting, she walked into the shelter, carrying the cat supplies she had brought. The building was chaotic, far less organized than she had expected.

Lydia took a deep breath and then regretted it. The shelter smelled like . . . well, it smelled like urine. And it was a lot louder than she had anticipated. She checked in, Jeff standing right behind her, just a little too close, at the front desk and was quickly shown through the rows of cages in the back. Lydia thought back to the day she had adopted Charlie from a shelter in Atlanta, that time trailed by her apathetic ex-husband, Graham, rather than the overly invested Jeff.

Today, though, she was led past the barking dogs to a quieter room with both individual cages and a larger area of the room filled with carpeted stands that were in turn covered in cats. Those cats, scattered about the open area, looked plump and calm, purring or curled in tight balls asleep. But their guide did not stop there, instead leading them to a cage with a mangy calico cat sitting in its own litter box, howling like some sort of ancient demon.

"Here she is—Baby Lobster."

Lydia could hear Jeff snicker behind her. Baby Lobster, who had looked sad but not terribly unfriendly in her online profile, was clearly the pariah of the shelter.

Her suspicion was confirmed when the shelter woman helping them reached for a pair of oven mitts before trying to open Baby Lobster's cage.

What had she gotten herself into?

Who adopts a cat based only on a photo and an awesome name?

When the cage opened, the cat jumped straight out, bypassing the volunteer completely, and attached herself to Lydia.

The tired woman glanced down at her clipboard and back at Baby Lobster, fully Velcroed to Lydia's shoulder. She sighed and looked at the empty carrier in Lydia's hands.

Lydia moved her free hand to try to pry the cat loose, only to set off another series of ungodly wails. She dropped her hand and the noise immediately stopped.

The woman's name tag said "Julie."

"Julie, listen, I know I'm supposed to take her out in the carrier. And you can see I have a carrier." Lydia gestured with her free hand and felt Baby Lobster's claws tighten. "And I have the adoption fee," she added, holding the check out toward Julie. "Why don't we just call it a day, and I'll take her home?"

Julie looked at the check. Then she looked back at the rows of cages of animals that needed her attention. Looking at the ridiculous combination of cat and woman in front of her, she just said, "Happy adoption day, Baby Lobster." Then she clipped the check to her clipboard and walked back toward the main office.

Lydia placed one hand on the cat to try to calm her, and the three of them walked out of the shelter, all a little too close for comfort. At least she could focus on the cat and not the murder. Hopefully, Jeff would do the same.

"Were they Brandon's sewing scissors, or whatever you called them?" Jeff asked as they climbed back into his car. "Did he sew?" Well, there went the hope he had forgotten about their conversation. Lydia looked up from Baby Lobster, who was now curled tightly in her lap, and noticed Jeff's smirk. Of course, Jeff probably thought it was unmanly to sew. Toy trains were apparently completely different.

Barely containing the desire to roll her eyes, Lydia answered him. "Brandon didn't sew. It was a pair from the shop. They have 'Measure Twice' on the side, so I could tell it was one of ours."

"Ooooohhhh," Jeff cooed. "That doesn't look good for you, does it?"

Lydia stiffened. Feeling the change, Baby Lobster raised her head and hissed at Jeff.

Lydia tried to hide her smile.

"You're going to have your hands full with that cat. Want me to turn around? I'm sure they'll take her back and give you a refund. That Julie lady seemed a little too eager to see the back of us. Just sayin'."

Baby Lobster dug her claws even more deeply into Lydia's lap, as if she understood Jeff's proposal.

Lydia stroked the cat's back in what she hoped was a calming fashion and explained to Jeff, "No. She's coming with me."

"I guess she can be your guard cat," Jeff said and let out a grating bark of a laugh. "I mean, really, Lydia, do you feel safe in your apartment? Maybe you should consider coming to stay with me."

"Excuse me?" Lydia yelped before she could stop herself.

"Well, it's hardly safe for you to stay in your apartment, is it? Right next to a murder scene? The police interviewed me this morning. It doesn't sound like they're anywhere near finding whoever did this. You'd be safer with me."

Lydia swallowed hard. Jeff had a point. Her apartment—well, really, Fran's apartment—didn't feel like the safest place in the world at that moment. She looked over at Jeff. Had he unbuttoned another button on his shirt? She hadn't noticed the second button being undone before. No, staying with Jeff was not an option.

"Wow. Thanks, Jeff. That is so kind of you."

Jeff smiled, pleased with himself.

"But I'm going to stay put for now. After all, I need to get Baby Lobster settled in. And the police don't seem to think I'm in any danger," Lydia said, not adding that they thought she *was* the danger.

"You know where to find me when you change your mind," Jeff replied.

When. Not if.

"Keep me in the loop, won't you?" he continued. "I wonder if the Laniers will keep Turn the Page open after this. Are you seeing them anytime soon?" Jeff asked. Did he know she was having dinner with them that night? How could he? But how did he know any of the things he seemed to know?

Jeff continued before Lydia could respond. "Because I would be interested if they decide to sell. Town square real estate doesn't become available very often, and I've been thinking about expanding."

Lydia raised an eyebrow.

"Taking my business to the next level. Keeping the online transactions, of course, but I want to pivot into the brick-and-mortar space and really generate some foot traffic."

Lydia's second eyebrow went up to the meet the first.

"Trains, Lydia. Trains. The model train market is hot," Jeff elaborated, looking at Lydia as if she were a few French fries short of a Happy Meal.

Lydia's stomach rumbled at the thought of French fries, and Jeff grimaced in disgust.

"Offer stands, Lydia. Good luck with Demon Crab," he smirked.

"Baby Lobster," Lydia said under her breath, opening her door and struggling to get inside with the carrier and the cat who refused to be carried in it, wondering just how many people in Peridot wanted Turn the Page out of business.

Chapter Six

Lydia heard the door click shut behind her and leaned against it, exhaling. The cat sprang out of her arms and ran to the couch, perching on the back edge.

"Welcome home, Baby Lobster," Lydia said, trying to sound enthusiastic. The cat looked unconvinced.

Lydia read over the handout from the shelter. Among the tips and suggestions were ones to make sure to give your new cat time to acclimate to its new home and to consider starting your cat out in a smaller room, like a bathroom, for the first few days.

Lydia slowly walked toward the cat, trying to make the "pssp pssp pssp" noise she had heard the lady at the shelter make. The cat just hissed. Lydia held out her arms, hoping she could somehow catch the cat and put her in the bathroom while she went to dinner at April and Wade's house.

Baby Lobster streaked into the kitchen and sat, pleased with herself, right under the kitchen table.

Lydia looked at Charlie, who had remained in his place on the couch during the failed cat capture attempt. He didn't seem to mind his new roommate.

Letting out a loud sigh, Lydia told the cat, "Okay, Baby Lobster. The litter box is in the bathroom, just so you know. I am going to dinner, but then I will be back to feed you and"—the cat glared at her—"maybe have cuddles?" Probably not.

* * *

Lydia didn't want to put back on the linen dress she'd been wearing earlier, since she had left it in a pile on her floor, and it was looking more than a little sad and rumpled. Her T-shirt was covered in cat hair and puncture holes from Baby Lobster's aggressive "cuddling" in the car. She didn't have time for a shower, but she looked in her closet and grabbed one of her newer makes, a rayon dress with a bright floral pattern. Hadn't Fran said that April loved to garden? Floral dress it was!

"Okay, you two, have fun!" Lydia called to the sullen-looking cat and the sleeping dog as she left her apartment, heading down to the square and ignoring the police tape that draped the building.

* * *

At least it was a short walk to dinner. The Laniers lived just past the center of town, on one of Peridot's many quiet residential side streets. Lydia looked at her phone as she walked to Wade and April's house. She could call and say she wasn't coming. They would understand. Who had dinner with friends after finding a dead body? No one. No one did.

Then Lydia thought about eating dinner in her apartment. Alone. With her demon crab of a cat. Jeff would probably stop by to check on her. If she managed to get rid of Jeff, she would have all the time in the world to think about Brandon and wonder if the killer would come back.

She put her phone back in her bag. True, they had invited her before everything had happened, but April had also texted that day, telling her to still come.

Which was so like April. Lydia thought about her new friend. Lydia had met her before she had any idea Peridot would become her new home. She had simply come up to the mountain town for the day, like so many Atlantans, wanting a bit of fresh air and a little shopping.

Turn the Page had been her first stop, after the bakery on the square, PeriDough. Donut from PeriDough in hand, she had wandered into the bookstore, only to have April immediately introduce herself.

"Hello! Welcome to Turn to the Page. Can I help you find a book today? Is that the Gold Miner? One of my favorites! We have some new releases right over here, and then in the back is our secondhand section, if you're looking for something a little less current but also a bit easier on the wallet."

Lydia had just stared. Then she realized the Gold Miner was the donut she was eating. Looking at April, she realized this talkative woman was just as sweet as the donut, earnestly pointing out various books to Lydia, even though Lydia had yet to respond.

Lydia had stayed for over an hour on that first trip and had learned April's name and how she ran the store with her husband, Wade. When she left to walk around the square, she'd left with April's card, a stack of slightly worse-for-the-wear mysteries, and the giddy excitement of a new friendship.

* * *

The door opened before Lydia had even finished knocking, April hurrying her in and fussing over her. Wade waved and headed toward the back of the house. April followed Wade, and Lydia followed April.

Lydia wasn't sure what she had been expecting at Wade and April's house, but whatever it was, this wasn't it. As she stepped farther into the modest ranch, what struck her first was the lack of books. She had just assumed that bookstore owners would have a million books in their home. Instead, the house was remarkably spare: no clutter, no knickknacks, very few books.

She trailed Wade and April through the living room to the kitchen that clearly also served as a dining room. The back of the kitchen had glass French doors, and Lydia could see in the summer twilight proof that April truly had a green thumb, the backyard a riot of flowers and leafy green bushes.

Further proof sat on the table. A huge vase of peonies dominated the center of the table, rich, pale pink petals practically spilling out toward the dinner plates.

"Wade has dinner on the grill," April said quickly, gesturing to the table. "Why don't you have a seat, and I'll get you a drink. What would you like?" Wade, as if on cue, walked past Lydia and out the French doors to the backyard, clearly headed for some grill tucked away out of sight.

"Do you have any ginger ale?" Lydia asked sheepishly. What she really wanted was a Shirley Temple, but she doubted that was the sort of drink April was offering.

"Sure, I do," April responded, anxiously looking in the back of a cabinet for the unexpected request.

Lydia took the moment to look at her new friend. What pattern matched April?

The trouble with playing that game when it came to April was that Lydia always dressed to be seen. She loved bright colors and fun styles. Ruffles? Great! Flouncy sleeves? Sign her up! April, on the other hand, seemed to want to blend into her surroundings. Now that she thought about it, Lydia couldn't even think of what April liked to wear. When she cast back into her memories, she could see her friend's anxious, smiling face, but no outfits.

April, always moving, always apologizing, always a little frazzled. Rushing around the bookstore in a mild panic. Welcoming newcomers with a stream of information as she moved from one display to the next.

Maybe April would be a Dress No. 1? The pattern was one of the most straightforward Lydia had encountered, the dress equivalent of the shirt she was going to be teaching that night. A simple shift dress with an A-line swing to it. Just two pieces cut from the same single pattern piece and sewn together—no darts, no sleeves, no collar. Just a dress. Maybe she would make one for April in a comfy floral pattern? Add some large pockets for garden tools?

April interrupted her daydreams, asking, "Would seltzer be okay, Lydia? I am so sorry. Wade isn't much for soda, and I just never get around to buying any. I could ask the neighbors if you want . . ."

"Seltzer would be great." Lydia hurried to assuage her host's worries.

April hurried about, fixing the drink and pouring herself a glass of white wine. April placed the just opened wine bottle on the table.

The women drank in silence.

"So, did you make the dress you're wearing?" April finally asked.

Lydia smiled. Leave it to April to see the effort she had made. Lydia stood up and did a little twirl, saying, "Yep. This is the first time I'm wearing it out. It's the Ashton Top by Helen's Closet, but I hacked it to add a skirt and tulip sleeves."

April stared at her, her smile wavering. She had no idea what Lydia was talking about.

"Helen's Closet is the name of a pattern designer. And she made the pattern for the top of this dress. Then she released sleeve patterns you could add. And I made a skirt to attach to turn it into a dress." Lydia twirled one more time.

"That is really neat, Lydia."

Lydia wanted to tell her more. Tell her all about her plans for Measure Twice. Maybe talk to her about the Dress No. 1 pattern, offer to teach April to make one for herself. Making her own clothes had brought Lydia so much unexpected joy. Maybe she could even convince April to start sewing. Lydia had brought it up once before, when they first became friends, and had gotten no traction whatsoever.

Lydia drank her seltzer water as the silence grew.

Wade still had not returned from the backyard, so Lydia cast about for another subject. She didn't want to make April talk about Brandon until she was ready, so she went for a soft pitch and asked, "So, April, how did you and Wade meet? I realized I never asked."

April's smile brightened.

Lydia congratulated herself silently for picking a good topic.

"I had been going through a hard time."

April paused and Lydia waited. Was April going to elaborate?

"So, I started taking a writing class at the university," April continued, and Lydia knew she mean the University of North Georgia, whose campus nudged up against Peridot's town square.

"After class, I would walk home, past one of the athletic fields, and that was where I first noticed Wade, drilling the ROTC cadets. He always seemed so . . ."

Lydia waited, curious to see how her new friend would finish the sentence. In her opinion, Wade was very military-ish. Was that a word? Lydia thought it should be. If April was always rushing, Wade simply stood and glowered. Not only was Wade over six feet tall, but he also had thick eyebrows that always seemed furrowed in concentration—or maybe frustration. Lydia would not want to be one of his cadets who stepped out of line.

". . . dashing," April said, finishing her thought. "And then one day I dropped some papers, and he asked if he could help me gather them up—very clichéd, but so sweet of him, really. He had all his cadets running around picking up my papers in the wind, giving them orders like it was a planned drill." April's smile widened further as her cheeks turned pink.

"He walked over to me with this neat pile of dirty pages and asked me to dinner that very night, and here we are."

Lydia thought about her ex-husband in Atlanta. She had met Graham at a college party and followed the expected steps until they were married and in a nice house, arguing over Lydia's mismatched Pyrex collection that he claimed didn't suit their aesthetic. Really, it was Lydia that didn't suit Graham's aesthetic.

Lydia realized April was waiting for her to respond to the anecdote, so she shook off the thought of Graham and Emma Grace and said, "Wow, April, that's like something out of a Hallmark movie!"

"It really was," April replied more quietly and poured herself another glass of white wine. "Let's see if dinner's ready," she added, standing up and opening the French doors, ushering Lydia into the backyard and toward the grill.

When they reached the plume of smoke reaching into the evening sky, they found Wade opening and closing the lid to the smoker.

"Just burping the egg," Wade explained, smiling.

April smiled back, as though this were a completely expected remark, and then added, "I'm just going to zip back inside and make sure dessert will be ready in time. Wade, why don't you tell Lydia about what you're making for dinner?" April was true to her word and darted away, leaving Wade and Lydia together in the backyard.

Lydia stood next to the meat smoker. She had lived in Georgia long enough to know that a Green Egg was high end, but she still didn't really understand the large egg-shaped contraption standing next to them.

"Nice egg," Lydia offered.

Wade chuckled. It was a pleasant laugh, low and gentle. Had she ever heard Wade laugh before?

"I take it you don't do much grilling?" Wade asked, smiling.

Lydia thought about the cookies and brownies she churned out on a regular basis. "Nope, can't say that I do. How does this thing work?" Lydia inquired, reaching toward the handle.

"Whoa, now—that stays closed. You can't open the egg while the meat is cooking, Lydia. Unless you're doing it to bring in some fresh air, and then you do it in short little raises like I was doing before. That's what they call 'burping the egg.' You see, great brisket is about three things: heat retention, air circulation, and temperature control. Leaving the dome closed most of the time lets the heat circulate the meat like a convection oven. It can be tricky to master, but it really is the only way to cook meat."

Lydia looked at Wade, who was looking at the Big Green Egg. Was this what she sounded like when she talked about the latest pattern release? Yep.

Wade looked up to see Lydia watching him and shook his head, adding, "Not that you need to know all of that. Ha. Anyway . . ."

For a moment, Wade looked lost. First the laugh, now this? Lydia saw Wade as almost a caricature of a person, the former Marine whose pants always had a crease. It shocked her to see him look so uncertain.

"April has been so excited about you coming over for dinner, Lydia. She insisted on making her famous banana pudding," Wade continued, not seeming to realize it was a non sequitur.

Lydia tried to hide her immediate reaction, pretending to adjust her hair. She hated bananas. The only thing worse than bananas? Banana pudding. Wade clearly wanted to talk about something. She tried to forget about the dessert. Maybe Wade finally wanted to talk about what had happened the night before. They still hadn't really talked about Brandon.

"Sounds great. I wasn't sure you would still want to have me over . . ." Lydia let the sentence hang in the air.

"No, we're so glad you're here. I've been wanting to talk to you. To tell you the truth, I've been worried about April for a while. I'm not talking about what happened last night. Of course, that's upsetting for all of us. But this is something different. And I was hoping to get your advice."

Wade wanted her advice? Wade? They were friendly, of course, but Lydia was friends with April. Wade was April's husband. That was the extent of it, as far as she knew. What did this hulk of a man want to discuss with her? She didn't have to wait to find out, as Wade started to explain immediately.

"The five-year anniversary party for Turn the Page is coming up. April may have mentioned it to you. She got it in her head to throw a big party to celebrate. At first, I thought it was a good idea. But the strain of the party seems to have really gotten to her, Lydia. Something is wrong with April."

"Really?" That surprised Lydia. With Brandon's death, she had worried for her anxious, busy friend. But in general, April seemed happy in her life at the bookstore, in Peridot, with Wade. And Wade, with his military bearing and clipped approach to conversation, didn't seem like a man to worry too much over his wife. He seemed like a man to spend hours worrying over his perfect brisket, maybe, but not April's moods.

"Yes. Listen, Lydia, I love Turn the Page. We have put our hearts and souls into that place. But it's just a store. Do you understand what I mean? I love April more than anything in the world."

Now Lydia truly felt like the world had tipped upside-down. Wade wasn't just talking about April's feelings; he was talking about his own. But Lydia still had no idea what he wanted from her. She was overwhelmed with the tragedy of what had happened to Brandon, what she had seen when she walked into his apartment only the night before. How could she help? Seeing Wade look so lost, so vulnerable, made her want to help, certainly. She just had no clue how. Of course, Wade did.

"I would like to ask a favor of you, Lydia. Could you take April to coffee? Talk to her. Listen to her. Then you could suggest—just suggest—that she cancel the book party. When I tell her we can cancel, she won't hear of it. She wants to make me happy, Lydia. She thinks I really want this party. She won't listen to me. I think she'll listen to you."

"Sure, I can do that, Wade."

He exhaled loudly. "That is great to hear, Lydia, great to hear. I've been worried. Don't tell her I said any of this, will you? I've noticed her drinking more, sleeping less. She seems distracted, sad even. It has to stop." He said the last line firmly, and Lydia could imagine him in his Marine days. He was a man who gave orders, and others hurried to follow them, but in this case, it was almost sweet how worried he seemed.

"Wade, do you think it could be—"

"Now what are you two talking about over here?" April asked loudly, coming toward their corner of the yard and unknowingly ending their conversation.

"I was just telling Lydia here about what makes the Green Egg the superior way to cook brisket." Wade looked at his watch and then checked the various thermometers that seemed to grow on the surface of the green contraption. "As always, April, your timing is perfect."

As Wade opened the Green Egg, Lydia noticed that April had a platter and tools waiting. The two were like a well-oiled machine: April oohed and aahed as if on cue from an unseen director and held out the platter while Wade filled it with brisket.

Lydia watched them, reminded for a moment of her own parents, even though they were at least a decade older than Wade and April. She had been so embarrassed when she had told her mom about the collapse of her own marriage because her parents, almost fifty years married, were clearly still so in love.

Were April and Wade the same?

Wade obviously adored his wife. He had made that clear tonight. And April always fussed over Wade, her knight in shining armor all the way back to the day they'd first met. Lydia couldn't shake the feeling that Wade was right. Something was off with April. Was it really about the book party?

Before she could follow her worry any further, the couple led the way back into the kitchen, and Wade proudly placed the platter on the table. April refreshed Lydia's glass and gestured for them all to sit down.

Lydia considered raising her seltzer water to toast Brandon. April saved her the trouble and bowed her head, reaching out to hold Lydia's and Wade's hands. Lydia grasped April's small, dry hand and reached to close the circle, opening her hand to Wade's. Whereas April felt almost unnaturally cool to the touch, Wade's large hand was hot and slightly sticky. Lydia repressed an immediate urge to yank her hand back. Of course his hand was hot; he had reached into the Green Egg for the brisket. What had he said about it being hot like a convection oven?

With her head still bowed, April spoke quietly, interrupting Lydia's musings on barbecue. "Our Father, Father in Heaven, we just—Father, we lift to you—Father God, we lift to you our dear friend Brandon, and we know, God, Father God, we know he is with you even now. We know that in Your love, there is no goodbye, only a 'see you soon.' In Your Son's holy, holy name we pray, Amen."

Lydia looked at April, who still had her eyes closed. She looked more at peace than she had the whole evening. Wade, though, had also opened his eyes and looked at his wife with what, for a fleeting moment, looked to Lydia like contempt. When Wade caught her eye, though, he smiled broadly enough for his ears to rise slightly, softening the look of his tight, military haircut. It must have been worry. Wade was worried about April, and now Lydia was starting to feel worried too.

April opened her eyes and let go of their hands.

"Guests first. Help yourself, Lydia," April said, encouraging her and gesturing to the plate of brisket Wade had brought in.

Lydia glanced around the table, looking for vegetables or rolls. Nope.

Wade noticed her gaze.

"Hope you don't mind, Lydia. I'm a meat man, myself. Can't stand vegetables—not a one. And April here lets me be. But don't worry: this brisket is top quality. We'll have you buying a Green Egg in no time," he finished, beaming with pride.

Lydia didn't mind meat, but she wasn't used to having a meal with no sides.

Still, it was clear her hosts were waiting on her to serve herself before they would, so she dug in and piled some brisket on her plate.

April took barely a forkful and then Wade quickly loaded his plate to the edges. He hadn't been joking when he'd said he was a meat man.

"That was a lovely grace you said, April."

"Thank you, Lydia," April replied, the vague look of worry back in her eyes. Lydia noticed April pour herself another glass of wine, her third. Wade must have been right. Why hadn't she noticed sooner? At least Wade had confided in her, so she knew how to help. Even if she didn't know what to say right now.

They ate the brisket in silence, Wade chewing loudly as he plowed through his heaping serving.

The silence stretched out. Lydia fidgeted in her seat. She could talk to April later about the book party. But what about last night? Were they going to talk about what had happened to Brandon?

"Do you want me to talk about what happened?" Lydia finally offered.

April gasped and Wade shook his head.

"Oh no, Lydia, you have been through so much. We don't want you to relive any of that . . . unpleasantness," April said. *Unpleasantness* was one word for it, Lydia supposed. April continued, "Some officers were here earlier. They told us what happened. So tragic."

Wade and April focused on their brisket as if the subject were closed.

Lydia knew she should let it go, but she couldn't.

"I was at the police station for hours last night," Lydia admitted, though no one had asked her. "Sergeant Simpson had so many questions. Did the police ask either of you for an alibi?" Lydia was hoping Sergeant Simpson had given other people in town the same piercing glare he had given her. Maybe it was just procedure, she kept telling herself.

Wade frowned. This was clearly the opposite of what he had in mind when asking Lydia to help talk to April. April, however, answered quickly, "They had someone come in and take a statement, even though, of course, we didn't have much to say. We were together all night." And with that she reached across the table and grabbed Wade's hand again, squeezing it.

"We're planning a big event for Turn the Page, to celebrate five years since our opening, so we checked out some of the authors from the area. You know, to do a reading? Wade had the great idea that a local author would be a bigger draw. Have you heard of the poet Joe Stanton? He's a veteran and a poet from Georgia." April kept talking as she stood and walked into what Lydia assumed was their living room. She reappeared, still talking, but now with a slim volume in hand.

As she gave Lydia the book, she continued, "Now this Joe Stanton wasn't a Marine like my Wade, but he still served his country, and we want to support him. Not to mention he can actually write a good poem!"

Wade was right; April was way too invested in the bookstore party. Was that it? She wasn't going to say anything else about Brandon? True, Lydia had been offended by Jeff's vulgar curiosity, but this felt too far in the opposite direction.

April gestured back to the book, "So we had a quiet night in last night, reading poetry. Please take a copy of the book, Lydia. We have plenty."

Wade looked like he wanted to take the book back from Lydia, which made sense given his earlier confession. But Lydia held on to it. She could read it and use that as an opener to get April to reconsider the party. That could wait, however. She still wanted to know more about what the Laniers had talked to the police about.

"The police kept asking me who would want Brandon dead, and I don't think they really believed me when I said I barely knew him." That was an understatement, Lydia thought to herself, not wanting to admit they considered her the prime suspect. "Do you have any idea what might have happened?" she asked Wade and April.

April turned to Wade and then answered for them both, saying, "I can't think of anyone who would want to hurt Brandon. I mean. I guess that's what people always say. But I mean it. I mean. He could be a little . . ." April paused, looking at Wade as if he had the word she wanted. Wade said nothing. ". . . Pushy," she continued. "But that was a good thing most of the time, you know? Especially when it came to Turn the Page. You need to have a little bit of an edge in business. Brandon got things done. You know? Turn the Page was just a dream until he made it a reality and I can't imagine how . . ."

And just like that, her I cracked. It was a small crack, just quiet tears running down April's face, but, in a way, Lydia was relieved. Lydia had experienced death in her life. Who made it to forty without attending a few funerals? Still, she had never lost anyone to violence. Accidents, illness, old age. Death was never easy to handle. Grief always felt heavy and unwieldy.

But murder? Murder made the whole world feel upsidedown, and sitting at their table, eating a huge pile of beef, and talking about poetry didn't feel right, no matter how stressful the anniversary event was.

April stood up, wiping her tears and apologizing for making a scene, although none had been made. Lydia watched her pour her fourth glass of wine, as she said, "I am so sorry, Lydia, really, it's just that . . ."

Wade interrupted his wife. "At least we know his death had nothing to do with Turn the Page. Brandon helped run the store and organize the programming, but April and I control the books. There was nothing suspicious there." Wade glared at Lydia, clearly blaming her for his wife's tears. Lydia admitted defeat and changed the topic.

"What is that?" Lydia asked, pointing at a shadow box that clearly had pride of place in the room. She could tell it was some sort of military ribbon, but she couldn't infer any more than that.

April straightened in her chair, looked with pride at the shadow box, and explained, "That, Lydia, is a Purple Heart. Awarded by the president to soldiers injured or killed in action. Wade here was awarded the Purple Heart when he served as a Marine. It is the highest honor."

"Wade, I hadn't realized. I don't have any servicemen in my family, so I didn't recognize . . . How impressive. . . . Thank you for your service."

Wade didn't say anything, and Lydia worried she had offered the wrong type of congratulations. April just sat at the table, beaming at Wade, her tears forgotten. Then April stood and began to clear the table.

"Lydia, I hope you left a little room for dessert. This is my momma's secret recipe. Banana pudding!" April exclaimed, bringing the dish to the table.

All Wade wanted was for Lydia to cheer up his wife. First, she had brought April to tears. Now she had to deal with April's pride and joy, a dessert Lydia loathed.

She pushed the dessert around her plate, eating the Nilla wafers and complimenting April's cooking. Wade ate three helpings with military precision, but Lydia noticed that April only drank her wine. She wanted to say something, something helpful or kind or useful. But it was also getting late, and hadn't Wade said she should talk to April one on one, anyway?

Lydia tried to look at her watch without being obvious. She had already mentioned she had a class at Measure Twice when they had first invited her, but she didn't want to be rude, especially given what happened.

Wade caught her looking and stood up, saying, "Well, Lydia, thank you for a lovely evening."

"Thank you for having me, especially since . . ."

Wade just nodded and walked her to the door while April stayed behind, clearing the table.

But as Lydia turned to leave the well-tended yard, April slipped out of the house and walked her to the sidewalk.

Once out of earshot of the house, April leaned in close and whispered, "Lydia, we should talk."

Lydia realized April had never been that close to her before. Normally, she hovered at a distance, but now she whispered close to Lydia's ear, and she could smell the white wine and some sort of old-fashioned perfume. Shalimar? Lydia needed to get to Measure Twice. Fran was really making an effort, offering to keep the class running in light of what had happened. However, she could hear Wade's request to talk to his wife echoing in her head. Maybe she could kill two birds with one stone? She flinched, but April didn't notice. *There had to be a better expression,* Lydia thought. Maybe she could bake two cakes in one oven?

"Lydia," April repeated, snapping her back into the moment.

"April, I really need to head over to start this class, would you like to come with me? Then we could chat on the way over?" Lydia offered.

"No. No, Wade and I have our reading time together tonight." Lydia craned her neck to hear better, as April was still whispering. "But I want to talk to you. Something has been bothering me. About Brandon. I just need to talk it through with someone."

Lydia stopped walking and turned to look at April. The older woman looked exhausted and somehow defeated.

"April, of course. I really can't imagine how hard this must be for you. You have so much on your plate. And now . . . Why don't you come over to the shop tomorrow morning? Maybe a little past noon? I can show you the new long-arm quilting machines that just came in and we can talk through all of this. How does that sound?"

April looked visibly relieved, her shoulders dropping as she replied, "Yes. Yes, that sounds great, Lydia, thank you. I'll let myself in and meet you in the classroom. Yes, thank you, this is just what I wanted."

Surprisingly, April gave her a quick hug and then scurried back to her house. That was what she looked like, a small woodland creature, scurrying back to its home.

Chapter Seven

Lydia let the bell on the front door of the shop ring out as she entered. She stopped for a moment to look around before she headed downstairs to the classroom. Having moved around a lot in her childhood, Lydia wasn't one to get sentimental about places. She was good, maybe too good, at packing up and moving on. But now she tried to imagine leaving Peridot, packing up her fabric and her pets, and starting again somewhere else. Her throat tightened. For what might be the first time in her life, Lydia finally felt like she didn't want to be anywhere but here.

She took a deep breath and headed to the back staircase to the classroom. Technically, everyone had gathered at Measure Twice to learn how to sew garments. Technically. But as she walked down the stairs, she could hear the quiet discussion around her trip to the police station, which fell silent the minute she was visible to the group. Lydia looked at the people settled at the machines in the classroom: Clark, Mary, Martha, Cynde, Heather, and of course Fran.

What they really wanted was to hear about Lydia's interview at the police station. No, it was more than that. They wanted to hear about Lydia's discovery of Brandon. *Then* they wanted to hear about the interview. And *then* they wanted to discuss who might have killed Brandon, assuming none of them suspected Lydia.

But it was clear they would let her at least talk about the sewing first. No one was going to ask straight out the way that Jeff had. And hopefully, no one would try to brush it under the rug the way April and Wade had.

Trying to bring herself back to the moment, Lydia thought about the pattern she had chosen for the evening. She couldn't be happier that she had a chance to share the Shirt No. 1 love with her little group. Fran was laying out the patterns and lining up the scissors. Lydia got out the rings of bobbins and set up the rack of thread.

The pattern was blessedly simple. The front and back were made with the same piece, so the sewist had to line up the pattern, which looked like half of a T-shirt, on the fold of the fabric and cut it out, twice. Boom. Front and back of the shirt, cut and ready for sewing.

Of course, once the pieces were sewn together, you could choose the bias binding for the neckline that made the garment look professional, as well as any trim desired for the bottom. Trim was where Lydia's appreciation of minimalism ended. A good shirt was only made better when you put some hot-pink pom-poms all along the bottom, right?

With that in mind, in addition to all the needed supplies, Lydia had also brought down to the classroom her own personal stash of trim a few days ago, a riotous mass of pink and orange and even yellow. The brighter, the better was her theory when it came to pom-poms.

The actual directions for the shirt encouraged the sewist to trace the wanted size onto a piece of tracing paper and keep the pattern whole as a reference; that way you could make other sizes down the line. That said, tracing paper could be fiddly and easy to rip, and it definitely required patience. She wanted to convince this group that garment sewing was fun! Which it was. To keep it as easy as possible, she had precut their sizes out of the stiff pattern paper and ditched the whole idea of tracing. Besides, this group was pretty committed to their current sizes. The M's seemed like they had only ever been whip-thin women of a certain age, more likely to take up gymnastics at that point than gain even five pounds.

"Okay, everyone. I have cut out your patterns, so the first thing I need you to do is take out your fabric and press it using the irons Fran has already set up around the classroom."

Lydia watched as each member shook out their fabric choice, as unique as each sewist. The pattern worked with basically any fabric, which was one of the reasons Lydia had chosen it. Cynde had decided to use some leftover quilting cotton for her "toile," which was just a wearable first attempt at a pattern. True to her vibrant personality, Cynde's cotton had cats chasing unraveling balls of yarn in a riot of colors—pink cats chasing blue yarn, purple chasing yellow, and so on.

The M's had also stayed true to type. While the women did make an effort to contribute to the success of Measure Twice, Lydia had long suspected they had some other source for most of their fabric. They never seemed to run out of yards and yards of crisp cotton covered in small tight flowers. The fabric always made Lydia think of old houses that had wallpaper and glass carafes for water by each bedside. Houses that would have only linen napkins. This time, Mary had a soft yellow flower set against a muted cornflower blue background, and Martha had blue flowers on a cream background. They had to be some sort of historical prints brought back to life as fabric, but Lydia knew better than to ask where they had bought them.

Clark was more comfortable with garment sewing, so he, unsurprisingly, pulled out a dapper chambray that he intended to make into a modified Shirt No. 1 with buttons, collar, and cuffs. He might be frustrating, but he had a great eye.

Heather had brought in a sliver of modern sewing with her gorgeous Lady McElroy rayon, a black background covered in the white outlines of a woman's face. It was bold and clean and effortlessly cool, just like Heather herself.

Lydia took a deep breath.

"Okay, everyone. I am going to give really basic directions, and if you feel like you can move ahead at any point, feel free— sound good?" Before anyone could respond, Lydia continued, "Once your fabric is pressed, fold it, right sides facing, so that the selvage edges are touching."

Lydia paused and held up her own fabric she had prepared earlier, a soft double gauze covered in zodiac constellations. She folded it so that the brighter side was on the inside, lengthwise. Like a hot dog, as Fran would say, not a hamburger.

The room felt sharp with the focus of each sewist, bent to their tables, folding fabric, placing patterns and pattern weights, and cutting or tracing with tailor chalk as they were comfortable. Lydia moved to the bookshelf and turned on the old radio. Fran had never really "updated" the shop, but Lydia wasn't looking for top-forty hits, anyway. With soft AM classical music playing in the background, Lydia took a deep breath and let herself think, for the first time, that this might work.

The directions required them to cut out the pattern only twice, each time on the fold. The end result was two matching boxy T-shirt shapes, ready to be sewn together to make the top.

Pinking shears, those strange, heavy scissors that cut notches into the seam allowances, meant that they didn't even need to finish the seams with a serger. Just cut the two pieces, sew them together, finish the seams with the pinking shears, and then add bias tape to the neckline. A quick, small hem on the sleeves and the bottom of the shirt and you were done!

In reality, sewing clothes wasn't any harder than sewing quilts. Still, it meant stepping out of a comfort zone. Mary and Martha, for instance, were used to the wide, single-folded binding used to bind all the layers of a quilt together. The bias-cut, double-folded binding used to make a neckline look polished was a version of what they were used to, but a distant version that required slightly different skills.

Lydia had seen it before in the craft world: small differences that led to lifelong schisms of interests. One friend was an ardent knitter, the other a crocheter, each claiming to find the other's hobby baffling. One person would wax lyrical about needlepoint while another would calmly explain to Lydia that needlepoint was just dumbed-down cross-stitch.

Walking around the room, Lydia let herself feel a tiny bit of pride. A little surge of optimism. Everyone was hard at work on their shirts. If this worked, that meant regular classes, and regular classes meant she could argue for stocking the patterns, fabric, and supplies suited for garments rather than just quilts. Mary and Martha were already pressing open the seams they had finished with the pinking shears. Clark was absorbed in his pattern hack, adding a working placket of buttons down the center of the shirt. Heather had produced her own bias binding and was quietly pinning her neckline into shape.

Some people hated bias binding. Lydia loved it, even though she sometimes got turned around and almost got started in the wrong direction. Bias binding was more or less just a folded strip of fabric, cut on the diagonal so that it could stretch. You sewed it first on the outside of the neckline, and then folded it over and sewed it into the inside of the shirt. It captured the raw hem and left the neckline of the shirt looking smooth and polished. That moment of folding it over and enclosing the hem felt like magic to Lydia. It reminded her of a photography class she had taken in high school. You put what seemed to be a blank piece of paper into what seemed to be a tub of water, and then you watched as a photograph materialized.

Lydia strained to listen for any sound of an animal fight in her apartment above the store, even though she knew it was hopeless down in the basement. Maybe she should have brought Baby Lobster downstairs to the shop? She hadn't even told the group about her newest family member. Maybe . . .

A cough interrupted Lydia from her cat reverie. It was Clark. Of course.

Lydia knew Clark wanted to say something. He looked like a little kid trying to keep a secret, squirming with frustration.

"I, for one, cannot just sit here stitching away, pretending a man was not killed in this building. Right above us!"

Well, Lydia thought, *that's one way to break the ice.* Thank goodness Clark never felt the need to be circumspect when it came to other people's business.

"Lydia, we have been sewing for ages. When are you going to tell us what happened?"

It was a fair request. Everyone had finished the majority of the pattern. She may as well tell her tale.

"Okay, Clark. I had dinner with Brandon last night"—Mary and Martha turned to each other, slightly scandalized—"and after dinner, I walked Charlie, and then I went by Brandon's apartment to see if he would like some of the brownies I had made." Everyone knew that Lydia baked when she was stressed. She continued, "When I went to his door, it was open, so I stepped inside." At this point, Lydia didn't even bother to check if the M's were shocked. It was a given. "And I found him, at his desk, dead. He had been stabbed in the neck with dress shears. A pair from the shop."

At this last revelation, everyone's eyes went to the scissors at each sewing station, bright silver, with the words "Measure Twice" clearly etched on the side.

"Then what happened?" Heather asked calmly.

"Then I called the police. And they came. And Sergeant Simpson drove me to the station and, um, talked with me for a long time." Hopefully that sounded better than what had really taken place: an interrogation.

"Who do they think did it?" Clark asked, having regained his composure.

"Um." Lydia realized it would be better to be honest. "They think I did it."

If the M's had been scandalized before, now they were affronted.

"Our Lydia? Never. Oh my. Well, it just goes to show you that police these days are nothing like the men in uniform we grew up with, isn't that right, Martha?" Mary asked, her voice rife with indignation.

"That's the truth, Mary, just the truth," Martha agreed.

"Sergeant Simpson did say that I should tell him if I could think of anyone else who would hurt Brandon. But I don't . . . I didn't really know him." Lydia looked at Fran, who nodded. "I was hoping, do you think you could tell me if you know . . .?" Lydia left the sentence unfinished.

Looking around the group, she realized Cynde was holding her phone and scrolling through, looking for a photo.

"So. Look at this," Cynde commanded. She turned the phone screen to the group, slowly moving it so each person could see, like a kindergarten teacher reading a story to the class.

The only problem was that Lydia had no idea what was on the screen, and she knew that if she couldn't figure it out, the M's didn't stand a chance.

"Oh!" Lydia exclaimed, uncertain if she had even seen the intended picture or just a receipt from a store or something. She figured this was the best way to get Cynde to say more. She was right.

"Exactly! I am so glad you see why it is so important, Lydia. Brandon was married!"

Married? Lydia looked down at her left hand, expecting to see her own wedding ring, even though she had left it behind on her dresser in her old life in Atlanta. She had told Brandon that she was separated. He hadn't said anything at the time. Why hadn't he said anything? Lydia felt hurt. Which was absurd. Which made her feel hurt and embarrassed. The poor man was dead; why did it matter if he was also married? But somehow, to Lydia, it did.

"I was not, *technically*—Cynde drew the word out— "supposed to be looking at his files, but I was just a few letters away in the filing cabinet, and this practically fell out when I was doing other work. And after I had lunch with Lydia, and she told me what had happened, I just thought it wouldn't hurt to . . . see what I could learn."

Not a single person in the sewing group bought that excuse, but they all nodded, nonetheless, urging Cynde to continue reporting on her find.

"Brandon was married to someone named Sarah Jane. Now, I 've never heard of her, but there is no record of a divorce filing, so technically they might still be married."

Cynde continued, musing about Brandon's mystery wife, but Lydia was stuck on the name, Sarah Jane.

"Sarah Jane?" Lydia asked, wondering if she had misheard Cynde. She had to admit she was guilty of confusing some of the Southern double names she had come across since her move to Georgia. Case in point: Emma Grace, her husband's new . . . his new . . .

"Yes, Sarah Jane. Now, as I was saying—"

"I know her."

"What?" Cynde coughed, her moment as the center of attention ruined by Lydia's outburst.

"At least I think I know her," Lydia clarified. "When we went out to dinner"—had it really only been the night before?—"Brandon and I went out to dinner for our date, and the waitress—her name was Sarah Jane." Lydia flinched, remembering the woman's suggestion to get a romantic dessert. Had that been a dig at her ex? Was he even her ex? Lydia felt herself spiraling.

Clark spoke before her thoughts could go too far. "Lydia, that could be a complete coincidence; you do realize that, don't you?"

"But here's the thing, Clark. This woman, when she was waiting on us, she was—well, for lack of a better word, pissed off."

Mary and Martha both wrinkled their noses, as if synchronized, in response to Lydia's vocabulary.

"She kept staring at Brandon, and then she made this weird comment about whether we wanted to order some dessert. How romantic it would be to order dessert. And then, well, this is probably nothing, but . . ." Lydia trailed off, embarrassed by her other point in defense of her assumption.

"No point in being coy now, Lydia, dear," Fran told her.

"Well, when she first came to our table, she had her T-shirt knotted on the side, like you see the waitresses do at Rosetti's all the time." Lydia paused, waiting for the group's affirmation of her observation, then continued. "But when she came back with her main courses, the shirt was tied, not at her side, but at her waist, and much higher. I could see her belly button."

The M's grimaced further, and Lydia made a note of the fact that *belly button* was apparently even more uncouth than *pissed off*.

"The way she tied the shirt, her stomach was right about eye level for Brandon, but he never looked, not even once. I mean, I looked more than that. He stared straight ahead, as if a bear was next to him and he had been warned not to make eye contact."

Cynde guffawed.

"But if she was his wife and they were separated or whatever, no wonder she was winding him up, trying to ruin our date. She even made this weird comment about him liking extra ketchup with his fries. It makes so much more sense now. No wonder he kept acting like she was invisible. He was so uncomfortable, but I just chalked it up to first-date jitters."

"We should talk to her," Clark decided.

"Oh sure, Clark. We'll go find this woman who none of us knows and say, 'Hey, I heard your secret husband was murdered. Was that your fault?'" Heather replied snidely. It was a bit harsh, but the young shop assistant had a good point.

"Interesting counterpoint, Heather. Thank you for that insight. Still, I might find a need to have dinner at Rosetti's tomorrow."

Cynde nodded, "Yes! Great idea, Clark. Now, what about the Laniers? They knew Brandon best."

"I just had dinner with them tonight," Lydia told the group. "They said the police had been by, but they were reading together all of last night, I guess planning for the store's anniversary party." Lydia made sure to look away from Cynde as she said the last part.

"You can't be thinking Wade has anything to do with this sordid business?" Mary asked.

Lydia quickly clarified, "No, no. I just meant they didn't have any idea what had happened. No theories. They didn't even want to discuss it . . . but . . ."

The group waited.

"April did ask to talk to me tomorrow," Lydia confided.

Cynde looked excited, "Ask her about Sarah Jane!"

"Um. Okay," Lydia agreed, unsure how she would broach the topic but unwilling to disappoint Cynde.

Fran stood up and addressed the group, "Listen, everyone. Lydia has been through a lot. Thank you for coming to the class tonight. Let's leave your shirts here and finish any details after the weekend. I'm getting in the long-arm quilting machines first thing in the morning, so you will all have to come over and see them next week. And we'll host a craft night and see if anything has come to light. How about that?"

"Oh my word, is it really ten o'clock?" Martha asked, looking to her friend and doppelgänger for confirmation. Mary simply nodded, and the two women rose to leave.

Clark hastily stood up, adding, "Please allow me to escort you both home."

Lydia thought again that Clark might be a little fussy, but he was also kind enough to make sure the women got home safely, and gentlemanly enough to save them from asking.

And with that, the three headed toward the stairs and out of the shop, leaving only Cynde, Fran, Heather, and Lydia behind.

"I think we all need some sleep," Fran said, turning to her two employees. "I'm going to drive in early in the morning to receive the quilting machines, but after that, I think I'm going to go back to The Laurels and rest. We'll keep the store closed to shoppers tomorrow. Maybe I'll come into town in the afternoon for a treat at PeriDough."

Fran smiled. Lydia knew her friend loved the local shop's handcrafted donuts. She also knew Fran looked even more exhausted than she did, which was saying something. A few weeks ago, Fran had decided to move to her family's mountain house, The Laurels, on Cherry Log Mountain, full time, renting out her apartment in Peridot to Lydia. It was a long, windy drive going up the mountain roads. Maybe that was all—it was tiring her friend out. That and the shock of Brandon's violent death. Maybe.

"If you need anything, Fran, just let me know," Heather offered, without making the same offer to Lydia. She still had not won the young woman over.

"I'll be in touch, girls. I've got to get you up to The Laurels sooner rather than later," Fran added, referencing the mountain house by its family name. Lydia was hardly a girl, but she found it comforting, nonetheless.

Lydia had expected Fran to pull her aside, to have a moment with her without Heather. Even if it was just to tell her everything was going to be okay. That was the Fran she knew, always going out of her way to comfort others, especially Lydia. Tonight, however, Fran simply followed Heather out the front door, calling out for Lydia to lock up, without even glancing back.

As they walked out of the shop and into the evening air, Lydia thought again how Heather and Fran, so wildly different, seemed so in sync as they walked away and into the streetlights of the square, farther in the distance. Turning, Lydia left that wonder for another day and headed to her apartment, just as she told herself that her friend was tired, not cold. She wanted to leave all of that for another day.

Charlie barked in excitement when she opened the door. Fair enough—he had waited more than long enough for a walk that evening. Lydia looked for Baby Lobster, just glimpsing the cat's tail as she scurried from the kitchen to the bedroom. Was her new pet still unsettled? It would have to wait since Charlie was doing his urgent walk-me-now dance.

They headed down to the patch of grass in the center of the town square, near the magnolia that Sergeant Simpson had waxed lyrical about in what seemed like another lifetime. She had to give Charlie credit; he was efficient, and they were headed back to the apartment in no time.

Lydia tried not to look at the crime scene tape that still covered Brandon's apartment door. She also tried not to make any noise near Jeff's door. Back inside, Lydia looked over her patterns, wondering if sewing would help to calm her mind, but the enormity of the day crashed down on her all at once, and she left her patterns on her sewing table and got ready for bed.

Charlie circled at the foot of her bed, finally flopping into a contented pile, and fell immediately asleep. Baby Lobster seemed less sure about the sleeping arrangements. She stalked around the bedroom, seemingly dismissing each option as she came upon it. Then, the cat nudged an empty box sitting outside of Lydia's closet. It had held some garment notions she had ordered, since Measure Twice wasn't stocking them just yet. While Lydia might love the elastic, buttons, and quirky labels that came in the box, it turned out that Baby Lobster simply loved the box. Her orange and black splotches filled the box, and Lydia could hear faint purring. Maybe she would make Baby Lobster a little quilt for her box. Was that too much? Too crazy cat lady? Lydia shook her head and smiled. She had nothing to prove. Mentally, she added a cat-sized quilt to her never-ending list of sewing plans.

The animals were happily asleep. Why wasn't Lydia? All day, she had maintained, to each person that asked, that she was sure the police would figure it out, would catch whoever had killed Brandon. She was safe in her apartment. Wasn't she?

Chapter Eight

Lydia ran her hand along the display of Liberty Fabrics. At over forty dollars a yard, the fabric made her eyes water both from the luxury of it and also the price.

But instead of just feeling like silk, the fabric felt wet. Had she gotten the fabric dirty somehow? She would definitely be charged for it, and she was really planning more on daydreaming than purchasing.

Really wet. Was there a leak in the ceiling?

Charlie licked her hand again.

The glorious and storied British department store, Liberty, disappeared and was replaced by her bedroom in Peridot and Charlie waiting, not very patiently, for his morning walk and breakfast.

Lydia got up and got dressed quickly. She shook some kibble into Baby Lobster's bowl and got Charlie ready for his walk.

As she headed to the park, she prayed for an uneventful morning. Thankfully, once she arrived and gave the park a quick scan, Clark was nowhere to be found. Lydia let out a breath she hadn't known she had been holding. She didn't want to be anyone's confessor that morning.

Still, the park wasn't quite empty, even though it was way before any out-of-towners would arrive. Lydia could see Heather's bright-red hair from a distance, as the young woman bent and twisted, clearly doing some early morning yoga.

That was what Lydia should be doing. Graham had wanted them to do hot yoga together. Lydia hated sweating even more than she hated cheap polyester fabric. It was a nonstarter. It was a shame she couldn't count sewing as cardio.

Heather noticed her and rolled up her mat and came over, drinking water and wiping her brilliant red hair off her face. Why did some people look good even when they clearly felt exhausted?

"Hey."

"Hey."

The two women looked at each other as Charlie rolled happily in the rough grass, scratching his own back.

To be fair, Lydia thought of Heather more as a girl than a woman, even though she was twenty-five. The pale skin, fiery red hair, and trendy yoga clothes felt so young to Lydia, especially when she looked down at her own worn-out bike shorts and mismatched socks.

Lydia liked Heather, but she always got the feeling that Heather simply tolerated her. Then again, Heather had walked over to her first, and Lydia knew she could be just a little sensitive at times. What had Graham called her? A snail without a shell.

"Lydia?"

"Sorry, what?"

"I asked how you're holding up," Heather said, taking another long drink of water.

See? That was nice. Lydia was reading too much into the young woman's somewhat flat affect.

Heather waited for Lydia to speak, her chin tilted up and her lips pursed. Just like Fran would do, sometimes, when she grew impatient with Lydia in the store. It was weird how people came to mimic each other.

"I'm okay, I guess, all things considered."

"That was brave of you to come teach the class last night," Heather said, fiddling with her yoga mat.

Brave? "Oh well, the police said they don't think it's, like, a random maniac or anything, so they said I could still do things and go places." Why was it that the more Lydia wanted to sound articulate, the less articulate she became?

"I didn't mean it like that," explained Heather, now crouching down to rub Charlie's belly. "I think it was brave of you to show your face."

Lydia lost whatever response she had been forming. Brave to show her face?

"Anyway, I need to get going. Can't stay out in the park all morning. See you around," Heather added as she walked off, her small body moving quickly and gracefully.

Charlie got back onto his feet and started to pull her toward home. Lydia followed his lead, lost in her thoughts.

She'd been so relieved not to see Clark, and now she wished she'd run into her acerbic friend instead. What had Heather been implying? Did the others suspect Lydia? She had been so certain the night before that only Sergeant Simpson doubted Lydia's version of events. Now she wasn't so sure.

They had made it back to the apartment, and Lydia gave Charlie his well-earned breakfast. April had agreed to meet a little after noon at the shop. It was only eight now.

Measure Twice was closed. What would she do for the next few hours? PeriDough stayed open, but she wasn't in the mood for a donut or for the friendly owner, Kaleigh's, inevitable questions about Brandon. Of course, all the churches were doing their thing, but other than that, the town seemed to take the idea of a sabbath pretty seriously.

Although after the first service each Sunday, at ten AM on the dot, the M's did open up the church consignment shop, Blessed Again, they ran it as volunteers. It was a clever system. The M's could claim they were still serving the Lord since it was a church charity shop, but they also monopolized any shopping done before noon.

Lydia loved the thrift store, the hunt for quirky, forgotten knickknacks.

That decided that: she would go when the store opened and get a belated hostess gift for April.

But that still meant she had two hours to fill, and her conversation with Heather had left her feeling ill at ease.

Normally she would bake or sew, but for once, she didn't want to do either.

It was time to call in the big guns. Lydia found the remote and turned on an international baking competition. Then she went into her kitchen, got out her favorite vintage Pyrex mixing dish, and set about making herself a serious stack of pancakes.

Plate in hand, she sat on her couch, slowly working away at her mountain of pancakes. Wade could keep his brisket extravaganza; Lydia didn't believe in a life without carbs.

She watched as polite baker after polite baker managed culinary miracles in the face of impossible odds and stone-faced judges.

That was all she wanted. A life where the greatest danger was a soggy bottom or a split crème anglaise.

*   *   *

When Lydia woke up, the TV screen read, "Are You Still Watching? Y/N." At least she had put the plate half full of pancakes down on the coffee table before she had fallen asleep. But as she was about to get up, she saw the real miracle: Baby Lobster asleep in her lap, purring quietly.

Glancing up at the wall clock, Lydia realized it was almost eleven. If she wanted time to pick out a present for April, and maybe find something for herself, at Blessed Again, she would need to leave soon. Baby Lobster adjusted herself in her sleep, cuddling even further into Lydia's lap.

"Okay, sweetheart," Lydia said softly. "Thank you for the cuddle, but I have to go," and with that, she shifted the cat onto the empty side of the couch. Baby Lobster had cuddled with her! What would be next? Charlie and Baby Lobster, cuddling with each other? That was probably too much to hope for, but she did it anyway.

*   *   *

The walk to Blessed Again was hot and sunny, which made the crime scene tape on her building seem even more out of place.

Lydia tried to push the implications of the tape from her mind. She needed a gift for April. As she opened the door to the thrift store, she tried to think only of her friend, who loved gardens and worried far too much.

Just like Measure Twice, Blessed Again had a small bell on the front door that jingled as she entered. But while Measure Twice smelled of fabric, dust, and the lavender potpourri Fran kept in the backroom, Blessed Again smelled like something older: a mix of silver polish, old books, and what Lydia swore was the smell of doll's hair, the weird scent of childhood keepsakes so often brought to the shop.

As always, Mary and Martha were at the front of the shop, behind an ancient wooden desk, drinking sweet tea out of Depression-era glass goblets. The desk also held an outdated register and a bowl of jelly beans, Mary's only vice.

Lydia waved to the two women and headed down one of the dimly lit corridors of the shop. While Fran always had music playing at Measure Twice, often country music from the golden age, as she called it, Blessed Again was always quiet.

Even though Lydia knew the M's loved working at the shop, they probably thought music would make it seem a little too much like fun and not quite enough like service.

As always, Lydia kept an eye out for Pyrex. Graham had never wanted anything to do with Lydia's vintage Pyrex. Why use secondhand mismatched bowls and serving dishes when Williams Sonoma had so many classier and more expensive options? He'd gotten his way, and their Buckhead kitchen had been classy and expensive, and so, so boring.

Lydia had held on to her Pyrex collection, and now that she had her own apartment, she looked at the shelves of Blessed Again with hopeful eyes. Maybe a turquoise Cinderella bowl with the Amish print? She tried not to jinx herself.

But she also wanted to find something for April. She couldn't shake a sense of foreboding from that dinner. Even though she tried to blame the mood on Brandon's death, there was something else, something darker than grief at that table.

April had made such an effort with the dinner, even setting the table with fresh flowers. That might work for an idea. Lydia looked at the shelves of vases. They took over the whole back left corner of the shop. Most were cheap clear vases, the kind that came with delivery flowers. But as was always the case with Blessed Again, there were plenty of hidden gems if you took the time to look.

After a few close calls, Lydia settled on a medium-sized vase decorated with wildflowers and small strawberries. Pleased with her find, Lydia gave herself a bit longer to roam the aisles. One whole bookcase was devoted to just sets of salt and pepper shakers. Lydia had never imagined a market for such specific housewares, but she loved to see the new additions: cute dachshunds, a Peter Pan and his Wendy, and then two hotdogs with slightly off-putting grins.

Leaving the grinning wieners behind, Lydia looked at the display of coffee mugs. Mary and Martha insisted that the price stay at fifty cents a mug, and she had already taken more than a few back to her apartment.

Smiling, she picked up a mug with a stressed-out cat that said "Everything is fine." She would stick with the vase but was tempted by the mug for April. She wished she could convince her friend that everything really was going to be okay. She wished she could convince herself.

Lydia put back the mug and headed to the front of the store, presenting the vase to be purchased.

As the M's wrapped up the vase, they looked at each other conspiratorially.

"Is this for your new place?" Mary asked kindly with just a little too much interest.

Two sets of shrewd, blue eyes looked at her. Sergeant Simpson could learn a thing or two from these women when it came to asking questions.

"This? Oh no. You know me, I'm a sucker for Pyrex. This, um, this is for April. April and Wade had me over for dinner last night, and I wanted to get her a thank-you gift. I thought, with her lovely garden, a vase for her flowers might be nice?"

Why did Lydia say the last bit as a question? Something about Mary and Martha made her feel like she was in trouble in school. Not big trouble, but trouble, nonetheless.

Mary and Martha's searching looks softened at the mention of a thank-you gift.

"Well, of course, dear. What gardener doesn't appreciate a nice vase for a hostess gift? I'm sure April will appreciate"— Mary looked down at the half-wrapped vase—"your creative choice."

Oof. Leave it to the M's to make a compliment sound like a subtle insult. Or wait, was that an insult that sounded like a compliment? Lydia wasn't sure, but she was sure neither of the women would've wanted that vase as a gift. Noted.

"Now, how is April, the poor dear?" Martha added. There it was. Lydia knew there was a reason they were paying so much attention to her.

Martha followed the question with two distinct actions: she poured Lydia a glass of sweet tea, and then she went and flipped the store sign to "Closed," shutting and locking the door. Lydia resigned herself to the oncoming interrogation and sat down on a spindly needlepointed chair near the register while accepting the proffered tall glass of sweet, sweet tea. Wincing slightly as the sugary drink hit the back of her teeth, Lydia tried to answer the question honestly. "Well, I think April is okay, all things considered. Certainly shaken, but Wade must be a real comfort."

"Yes, Wade. They don't make men like Wade anymore, do they?" Mary mused. "Poor April has certainly had more than her fair share of trials, but God only gives us what we can stand."

At this, Martha lowered her gaze and nodded, as if responding to a moment in a sermon, and then added, "Two unexpected deaths. Truly such trials."

Lydia momentarily choked on her sweet tea, certain she must have misheard Martha. But Martha just looked serenely at Lydia, forcing her to ask for clarity. "I'm sorry, Martha, did you say two? No one was with Brandon; you know that, right? I was the one . . . well . . . I found . . . It was just Brandon, not two people."

Mary let Lydia struggle through her question and then explained, "This is not poor April's first brush with adversity. Peridot is a beautiful place, but not without its tragedies."

"Wade is not a local boy now, not from Peridot. Still, a great man, a real hero. But not a local boy. April, though, is Peridot born and bred. As was her first husband, Beau."

Lydia could have sworn Mary looked a little smug. First husband? Lydia knew the shock she felt must be clear on her face.

"Beauregard came from a fine family. His daddy's daddy's daddy was a judge in town, and they have always done right by Peridot—you can be sure of that."

"Um, sounds like a great guy. The divorce must have been hard on April."

"Lydia, that is what we are trying to tell you. There was no divorce. April found Beau, dead, in their kitchen one Sunday morning before church. He just keeled right over and died, waiting for his coffee, if you can believe it," Mary looked at Martha, as if, however many years later this was, they still couldn't believe it.

"Oh my Go—goodness." Lydia caught herself before she used the Lord's name in vain in front of His loyal M's. "How horrible for April. What did he . . . what killed him?" Lydia asked, finishing the last of her sweet tea.

Martha refilled her glass, and Mary continued, "Now, you know we're a small town here. Old Doc Tribble—he's gone home to his maker—he declared it a natural death. Beau was strong like an ox, but none of us ever know our time, now do we?"

Lydia thought about Brandon, collapsed on his desk, blood running down his neck to his arm, his hand still holding a pen. Had that been his time?

Mary felt Lydia's attention wandering, so she offered more salacious details, adding, "April was devastated. At first. We would never gossip," Mary said, nodding in time with Martha, and Lydia stifled her laugh, "but it did raise a few eyebrows, how quickly April found happiness again."

"You mean Wade?" Lydia asked, trying to keep up with the twists and turns of the conversation.

"Now Wade—Wade is a hero. And a credit to Peridot. I knew his mother's people, all fine people, lived a few towns over, for generations. Used to farm cattle . . ."

Mary looked in danger of telling Lydia the history of cattle farming in the Peridot area, so Lydia prompted her back to the topic at hand, asking, "So Wade has lived in North Georgia his whole life? I hadn't realized that."

"Oh heavens, no. He moved away first chance he could. Plenty of fine young men need a little more than North Georgia can offer someone at that stage of life. The Laniers followed him, sad to say. Sold the farm, sold the house. Last I heard they all lived in Atlanta. Which I'm sure is just fine for them. At least Wade saw sense and came back to the mountains."

"Wade is a fine man. But people will talk. We certainly do not gossip, but people will talk," Martha added, looking at Lydia as if she had just said Wade was a secret agent, or provided some other revelation.

Lydia stared back, utterly baffled.

"I'm not saying that April killed her first husband," Mary clarified sanctimoniously, which Lydia took to mean that was exactly what she was implying.

"But if she had, and Brandon had found out somehow, well."

The two women nodded at Lydia, looking quite pleased.

"You think April killed Brandon to hide the fact that she murdered her first husband?" Lydia spat out, unable to hide her incredulity. "April? Our April?"

"Oh good heavens, no! But it is strange, all the same. Well, the good Lord never gives us more than we can bear, isn't that so, Martha?"

"Indeed, Mary, indeed."

And with that Godly non sequitur, the conversation was over. Mary flipped the sign back to "Open," and Martha took Lydia's glass to wash out in the small sink at the back of the store.

She had been dismissed.

"Thank you again, ladies," Lydia said as she left the store, but their attention was already turned to a couple that walked in, happy to find a store open in the quiet town on a Sunday morning.

Lydia walked slowly around the square, from Blessed Again to Measure Twice, holding the vase in her hands.

She had clearly offended the M's, and Fran had made it clear that you wanted the two women on your side at all costs. But none of it felt right, least of all the idea that April was a killer.

Or was Lydia fooling herself?

She thought back to her last conversation with her friend.

Lydia had assumed at the time that April had wanted a chance to grieve. Wade clearly adored her, but he was also so, well, military in his bearings. April probably wanted a good cry and some cookies, Lydia had figured. Was there anything to the wild theory the M's had offered? Had April been guilty, not grieving?

Chapter Nine

Before she headed to Measure Twice, Lydia lingered in front of Clark's storefront. The Pampered Pantry had a fair claim to be the fanciest shop on the square. While the PeriDough bakery reveled in its down-home, no-frills style, Clark aimed for something more refined with his small shop. Plus, she thought as she checked the time, he opened at noon on Sundays.

Since she had rushed out of Blessed Again, Lydia had a little time to kill before she met up with April. Why did people say that? Kill time. Lydia shuddered. She would be more careful with her language moving forward. Or at least, she would try to be. Too often, she spoke before she thought.

The small bell tinkled as Lydia pushed the door open and stepped into The Pampered Pantry, immediately sighing in relief as the air-conditioned air washed over her. It was hard to believe that Blessed Again and The Pampered Pantry had basically the same skeleton, as buildings went. Whereas the thrift store felt cavernous and disorganized, like a maze of dust and treasures, The Pampered Pantry was a brightly lit wonderland of neat, labeled displays.

Lydia walked slowly over to the first staged table, this one set with muted plates and proudly displaying a variety of pestos. Picking up the nearest, Lydia read the label: sunchoke pesto with artisanal walnut and sun-dried heritage tomatoes. Huh. She flipped over the lovely, small glass jar. Fourteen dollars? Lydia fumbled the jar before placing it gently back in the display.

Clark walked over, announcing as if for no reason, "Wonderful, isn't it? Part of our brand-new pesto sampler. All twelve varieties. A total steal. What is more refreshing on a hot day than a nice pesto?" Clark asked, straightening the jar that Lydia had briefly considered.

Looking at the newspaper-wrapped bundle in her left hand, Clark wrinkled his nose slightly, asking, "How are Martha and Mary this fine summer day?"

"Good. Same as always, really. They truly are indefatigable."

Clark smiled. "I do appreciate your vocabulary, Lydia. You might be, well . . . you may hide your light under a bushel, as we say, but you really are quite sharp."

"Thanks," Lydia responded, aware that he hadn't exactly complimented her. That was just Clark's way. A little barbed, a little intense. *Not unlike a very expensive pesto,* Lydia thought. A little went a long way, but at the same time, there was nothing else that quite did the trick. Clark was truly one of a kind.

"Did you find one of your Pyrex treasures?" Clark asked, gesturing to the bundle. A snarky one of a kind, maybe.

"Not today. This is a vase for April. She and Wade had me to dinner last night, and I wanted to thank her. But I thought maybe you could suggest something else to pair with it?"

"I wouldn't say a secondhand vase from a charity shop is a traditional thank-you gift for a hostess. But I am sure she will appreciate the gesture. You know," Clark added, walking deeper into the store, clearly expecting Lydia to follow, "we have new cheese sets that came in this week. Just darling."

Lydia thought about her plate at dinner the night before. Fancy hors d'oeuvres didn't seem their style. She shook her head no.

Clark kept walking, making small noises of approval and disapproval as he moved throughout his store, almost as if he were arguing with himself.

"Now, isn't this just the ticket," he said, more to himself than Lydia, holding up a silver wine stopper in the shape of a little bunny. Lydia smiled and thought to herself that April was a little bunny. It was perfect. Then she thought about how much wine April had drunk at dinner. Her smile wavered.

"Clark, that is perfect," she said out loud, realizing she had kept Clark waiting on a response.

Clark and Lydia walked to the back corner of the store, where the cash register sat, staffed by one of the shop's workers. Clark waved the young man away, toward a group of day-trippers who had just walked in and were loudly discussing their upcoming visit to a local vineyard.

"Travis, be sure to mention the new toast points we're carrying," Clark admonished, as the young man walked away, leaving them alone for the moment.

As he rang up the wine stopper, Clark asked quietly, "Listen, Lydia. What I said about Brandon yesterday . . ."

Had it only been yesterday that they had talked in the park? What was the opposite of killing time? Time seemed to stretch on forever this weekend.

Lydia brought herself back to the moment and realized Clark was waiting on a reply, so she offered, "Of course, Clark. Of course. You had no idea. Fran was just saying to me the other day that feelings can get, well, heightened when you live in a close-knit community"—that sounded nicer than *small town*— "and I can understand why you were so hurt."

"Heightened. That is just the word for it. Precisely. Who would know that better than Fran?" Clark's smile twisted in pain for a moment. "Peridot is a blessing, of course, but it certainly is close knit. I am so glad we understand one another," he continued, passing the receipt for her to sign.

What exactly was she admitting to understanding? She looked back at Clark, but he was looking down at a picture frame next to the register. A framed picture of a dog she assumed was Rutty.

"What a beautiful dog," Lydia offered.

"He was. He was perfect," Clark replied tightly.

Clark stepped around to join Lydia and escorted her briskly out of the store.

"Has April said if they're going to keep Turn the Page open?" Clark asked as they reached the door.

April hadn't said anything about closing the shop. In fact, it seemed like they were going ahead with the anniversary event, even in the wake of Brandon's death.

"I think so," Lydia replied, unsure what Clark was getting at.

"Interesting." With that, Clark saw her out the door, closed it, and turned sharply back into his store.

Lydia let the heat of the day wash over her after the oasis of Clark's shop.

Well, that was strange. Had she learned anything new? Maybe? What had Fran really meant when she had talked about the deep resentments of a small town? Clark had hated Brandon, even if he had also asked her to keep that to herself. But why had he asked about Turn the Page?

Looking around the square, Lydia wondered about the businesses she saw each day. The larger town of Peridot had its bleak strip malls and dollar stores. But here in the square, there was a sense of a thriving community. Every storefront was charming and well presented. Tourists milled about, pointing at various displays.

Still, she knew from Fran how hard it was to make a profit, even with a prime spot in the square. Apparently, the prettiest parts of Peridot could still be a challenge for the people who called it home.

Lydia thought back to dinner the night before.

What had April said to her? *"About Brandon. We need to talk."* But Lydia had no idea what April had meant. Lydia should have kept her mouth shut at the dinner. Knowing April, she was probably appalled she had called Brandon pushy, and wanted a chance to recant. Or maybe there was another side to Brandon, one that only April had seen? It felt far-fetched to imagine, but then again, murder in Peridot had seemed impossible only a day before.

Fran had given April a key to the store before Lydia had met either of them, a gesture of one fellow shop owner to another in a town that could get hit with bad winter weather and other small disasters, so Lydia figured April would be waiting for her in the classroom. Not only was April never late, but she was also hardly ever just on time, instead arriving at least five minutes early. Lydia had originally chalked it up to Wade's military background, but even when April went somewhere without her husband, she showed up early, rushing as if she were unforgivably late.

Maybe Lydia should have gotten her that cat mug, after all.

* * *

Lydia held the wrapped vase carefully as she opened the front door to Measure Twice, the bell ringing to announce her arrival.

Why did walking into a quiet room feel so menacing still? What had happened with Brandon was the worst moment of her life, but it was a complete and utter aberration. This was Measure Twice. This was her new home. She tried to shake off the frisson of fear and straightened her back.

She breathed in deeply. Lydia loved the smell of the store: lavender, fabric, and dust. Maybe a note of fabric softener? The immediate comfort she felt reminded her of how she always felt in bookstores. A bookworm her whole life, Lydia saw a room full of books as a room full of adventures waiting to happen. Now a room full of fabric offered the same promise. Lydia ran her hand along some of the bolts, imagining what she could sew. Her list of projects was also longer than her list of completed tasks, but Lydia loved the dreaming phase, holding a new fabric in her hand and conjuring up a set of napkins or a comfortable pair of overalls.

The strong morning sunlight filled the room through the large windows at the front of the store, which looked out on the square. Sample quilts hung from the walls, and now that Lydia had gotten to feel at home in Peridot, she could easily point out which bore Mary and Martha's distinctive hand stitching.

Lydia spun the large thread display, watching the colors rotate. She checked the piles of notions set up tantalizingly near the checkout. Each had the Measure Twice logo on them: pin dishes, small rulers, clover clips . . . dress shears.

She should move those.

There it was again, that terrible sense of foreboding. Brandon. The dress shears. Brandon's death frightened her enough, but there was something else, something more sinister, because a sewing tool from the shop had been involved. She had bluffed about it to Jeff, but truth be told, Lydia could not think of a single reason for dress shears to be in Brandon's apartment, much less plunged into his neck.

This wasn't the time to feel bad for herself, though. April had been through so much more. Brandon was her close friend, and if the M's were even partially correct, this was far from April's first brush with a traumatic loss.

A "creative choice" of a vase from Blessed Again and a fancy wine stopper weren't going to fix anything, but at least maybe Lydia could just be a kind presence and a good listener.

April had said she would be in the classroom, looking at the new long-arm quilting machines.

Fran was so excited about the machines. She swore up and down to Lydia and Heather that they were the answer to

Measure Twice's financial prayers. Heather and Lydia, however, were unconvinced.

Before she had started sewing, Lydia had had no idea such a machine even existed. She thought, naively, that quilts were made on the machines she saw in stores like Measure Twice: nice compact Singer or Brother sewing machines that could be lifted by their trim, little built-in handle. Fran burst that bubble quickly. It turned out that the quilt *top* was made on a regular machine, and the backing too. But then the top and backing were put on either side of the batting, the soft cotton that made a quilt so cozy. Then, a long-arm quilting machine was used to sew all three layers together. It was not for the faint of heart, the machine as large as a couch, with a handle like a steering wheel to control the powerful, movable needle.

Not only were long-arm quilting machines hard to find, but they were also expensive. Really expensive. Thousands of dollars expensive. But Fran knew how to use one, and she was sure if they had a few of the machines in the store, they could generate some revenue. People would pay to have their quilts finished. People might even pay to learn how to use the machine themselves.

Lydia was excited to see one in person for the first time. In the past, she had mailed out quilt components to long quilters around the Southeast. Now she could see it all done in-house.

Walking down the stairs to the classroom, Lydia called out to her friend.

No one answered.

Then she turned the corner into the large space of the classroom and saw the disaster.

All three brand-new, expensive machines were tipped over, crashed onto the floor. Fran would be livid. And devastated. At the same time. This was the last thing Fran needed.

Who on earth would trash a quilt store? What had Cynde said the day before, about Brandon maybe having secrets, being involved with drugs?

Had some desperate addict ransacked the shop looking for cash? But no, the first floor was pristine. And what thief would target a quilt shop for loot? Was it kids, some sort of dare? Lydia knew it was hard on the young kids in Peridot. Cute mountain towns might lure middle-aged shoppers from the big city, but they could also feel boring and stifling for the kids who lived there. But two random acts of violence in the same building on the same weekend? What were the odds? And where was April?

At first, Lydia assumed April had left to get help. April was in her fifties, and it would be impossible for her to right the tipped-over machines. Lydia wouldn't be able to lift them on her own either, but she walked closer to try to figure out where they would start when April got back. Did these things have handholds somewhere?

Wait.

Wait.

April was under the machine, asleep.

How on earth did April manage to fall asleep underneath a tipped-over machine the size of a golf cart?

She hadn't. Because she wasn't asleep.

No blood. That was the next thing Lydia noticed. When she had found Brandon, there had been so much blood. Now, it was like a prank gone horribly wrong: April crumpled under a toppled-over machine. She was too still. Lydia knew she had to check for a pulse, but she also knew she wouldn't find one.

Crouching down next to the machine, Lydia threaded her hand through the machinery and lightly touched April's wrist. Still warm. No pulse. But still warm.

Lydia knew what to do this time. There was no door to the classroom, so she simply walked back up the stairs to the break room and sat down. Shaking, she pulled out her phone and the card Sergeant Simpson had given her at the station.

"Peridot Police Department, how may I direct your call," a pleasant voice asked Lydia.

"Sergeant Simpson, please," Lydia replied, her voice strangely calm.

"This is Sergeant Simpson speaking," came the warm, gruff voice she knew too well at this point.

"It happened again."

"What's that now?" he replied.

"I found another body."

"Miss Barnes? Is that you? Now just talk me through what is going on, won't you? Are you in danger?"

She heard quick activity in the background.

"I am going to send a car over for you, okay? Just stay put, and when my officer gets there, we'll get you over here and figure this all out. Do you need a doctor? Any chance you've been hurt?"

"No."

* * *

Lydia sank into the long paisley couch that dominated the back wall of the break room. It was ugly in a way that became pretty, in Lydia's opinion. Part of her mind wandered, imagining a dress made from the same fabric as the couch. Lydia bought as much of her fabric as possible at Measure Twice, of course, but when she needed something a little stranger, she headed to Fabric Universe, a discount warehouse just south of Atlanta.

She had mentioned Fabric Universe to April once, in a bid to get her interested in sewing. Unlike the others who all sewed something, April would admire what others made, but never tried to sew herself.

Where had they been when they talked about Fabric Universe? Getting donuts at PeriDough? Looking at knickknacks in Blessed Again? Lydia couldn't remember, and suddenly all she wanted was to remember. She was crying. When had she started crying? Why hadn't she ever gone to Fabric Universe with April?

Suddenly, it clicked. It had been one early trip to Peridot, when she still lived in Atlanta. They were in what was now Lydia's apartment but was then still Fran's main residence. It was spring, and the town square had been full of blooming azaleas.

April was explaining that she didn't sew, but that she still loved to look around in Measure Twice because Fran had such a great eye. Plus, she was always interested in what new craft books Fran had ordered.

Lydia and April had hit it off immediately, a former English teacher and a bookstore owner, so Lydia had felt comfortable pushing April about her reluctance to sew. April had admitted sheepishly that Wade ran their finances and liked to be frugal. Fabric could be expensive, and April was too worried she'd ruin whatever she made to be willing to risk the cost.

That was when Lydia had told her about Fabric Universe, a sprawling warehouse that sold only remnants, fabric destined for the landfill, as well as leftovers from larger orders, canceled lines, or photo shoots. Everything at Fabric Universe cost $2.99 a yard instead of between twelve and twenty dollars a yard like the fabric they stocked at Measure Twice.

"Come with me," Lydia had pleaded. She had told April all about her ritual, the diet lemonade from a drive-thru chain restaurant, a true crime podcast, coming home with bags and bags of random, glorious fabric that barely cost a thing.

April had demurred and Lydia had let her. She didn't want to force a new friendship. She should have tried harder.

Sergeant Simpson found Lydia in the back room, on the ugly couch, weeping that she had not convinced her friend to go shopping one spring day, months prior. He gestured the other officers down the stairs and came to sit next to her.

"Are you hurt, Miss Barnes?" he asked softly.

"No."

"Okay, that's a good thing. You know I'm going to need to talk to you about this, right, miss?"

Lydia nodded, trying to stop crying. Why was it the more she wanted to stop crying, the harder she cried?

"I need to take a look at the scene. So, this officer here"— a man in uniform walked up as Sergeant Simpson gestured at him—"is going to walk you over to a patrol car, and we are going to get you back to the station. Then, in no time at all, I will be there, and we can sort this out. All right?"

Lydia wanted to scream. Nothing was all right. Instead, she nodded and stood up, following the man in uniform.

Where was the vase? The silly wine stopper? It didn't matter, did it?

When the police car pulled up, Lydia was surprised to see Luke, or Officer Eisen, as she was probably meant to call him.

The first uniformed man opened the car door, because this was a patrol car with real doors, not a Jeep in the middle of the night. Because this was her second discovery of a murder victim, not her first. Brandon was dead. And April was too.

Luke, she still thought of him as Luke, was quiet as he drove her back to the station. No talk of *Dungeons & Dragons*, no friendly questions about her new life in Peridot.

Lydia suddenly wanted to tell Luke about Fabric Universe, wanted to explain to this young cop that she had meant to take April to a warehouse full of remnant fabric. Had planned to get drive-thru diet lemonade on the way. She had to press her mouth shut to stay quiet.

Finally, they arrived.

Neither of them had said a word for the entire drive.

Another officer opened the door and led her into the station. Everything had been gentle thus far. But Lydia still remembered what the sergeant had said before: *"The next time we talk, it might be a very different conversation."* Now she would find out exactly what that meant.

Chapter Ten

Lydia wanted to be offered a cup of tea. All her beloved British murder mysteries had convinced her, at some point, that tea was the answer to tragedy. But she wasn't in some cute country town, dealing with a poisoning at the Christmas fête. She was in Peridot, in September, and she had just found a body for the second time that weekend.

Thankfully, even cops in Georgia seemed to agree that sugar and caffeine were good for shock, and when she walked into the interrogation room, a nameless officer came and placed a large cup of sweet tea on the table between her and Sergeant Simpson.

Technically, she supposed, the station had air-conditioning. Otherwise, the heat would have been unbearable. But the room felt warm and still, heavy.

"Miss Barnes."

"Sergeant." Lydia waited. She knew that Sergeant Simpson thought she had killed Brandon. Or at least thought she made a good main suspect. Now, instead of returning with new leads and other suspects to offer him, she had returned having discovered another murder.

"First things first, Miss Barnes. You are not under arrest at this moment. Do you understand?"

She nodded.

"Good. Now, walk me through your day, if you would."

Just like last time, she thought.

"Well, I slept in this morning, woke up around ten. I took Charlie down to the park for a quick walk and then went home to make breakfast." She paused, trying to gauge how detailed he wanted her to be. Did she need to mention Heather?

"Right. I made pancakes, had some coffee, and, um, I watched an old episode of *The Great British Baking Show*. Then around ten, I headed over to Blessed Again to look around. I had planned to meet April at the store a little after noon, and wanted to find her a present. I also went to The Pampered Pantry. I got two gifts. To thank her. I had dinner at her house last night."

"Can anyone verify that, Miss Barnes?"

"Oh. Yes, I talked with Mary and Martha at Blessed Again, and I talked with Clark Putnam at his shop." She didn't know the M's last names, she realized with a start. But Sergeant Simpson didn't ask.

"Thank you, miss. Now, why meet Mrs. Lanier at Measure Twice?"

"Well, April had said she wanted to talk, and Fran had just gotten in the new long-arm quilting machines, but she wasn't going to open the store for customers, so I thought we could look at the machines and have a little bit of privacy."

"Was it locked when you arrived?"

"No. Fran gave April a key ages ago, just as a neighborly thing, like if a storm came and someone needed to get into the shop and Fran wasn't there. I assumed April was waiting for me in the classroom, where the long-arms were."

"Tell me about these machines, if you will, Miss Barnes."

"Long-arm quilting machines. Sewists use them to finish quilts, to basically sew all the layers together. They're pretty expensive, but Fran has been really excited about them. Although now . . ." Lydia stopped talking, overwhelmed by how much was ruined.

"Are they dangerous?"

"The quilting machines? I mean, you wouldn't want to stick your hand under the needle or anything, but I wouldn't call them dangerous. They aren't supposed to fall over."

"But they did." This wasn't a question.

Lydia's glass was empty.

"Someone must have tipped them over. Whoever . . . whoever hurt April must have . . ."

The tears were coming back.

Sergeant Simpson tried to keep her talking.

"You came downstairs and saw the machines pushed over. Then what happened? Please be as specific as you can."

"When I saw April, I went to her and felt for a pulse. But there was no pulse. And I couldn't get to her body because she was trapped under the machine. And I couldn't lift the machine because it's too heavy. And I couldn't . . ." The tears won out, and Lydia couldn't finish the sentence.

Sergeant Simpson took over, asking, "You crossed over, felt for a pulse, and upon realizing she was deceased, climbed back up the stairs and called my office? Does that sound correct to you?"

"Yes, sir," she managed to get out between sobs.

"For the second time in one weekend, you went to see someone and found that person dead. Not just dead, murdered. Correct?"

"Yes, sir."

"How does that strike you?"

"Excuse me?" Surprise helped Lydia hold back the tears.

"How does that strike you, Miss Barnes? Two dead bodies in about that many days. In a town of less than seven thousand people. I know you're new to Peridot, but let me make this clear to you. We have our share of DUIs, petty crime, domestic situations that have gotten . . . bad. But murder? We haven't had a murder in this town in years. Now, two people have been killed. And as far as I can see, they have one thing in common: you."

Lydia stared at the man with the mustache, this older, tall, gruff-looking policeman that had joked in the shop only the day before with Fran.

"I want you to explain something to me. Do you think you can do that?"

Lydia nodded, always the good student. Even in her own interrogation, she wanted to get an "A." Even now.

"Mr. Ivey was killed with . . ."

"Dress shears."

"Dress shears. And Mrs. Lanier was killed by a quilting arm"—Lydia didn't correct him—"and these are both from the shop where you work. I pride myself on knowing this town, Miss Barnes. And here is what I cannot understand. If you did not kill these two people, someone is going to a lot of trouble to make it look like you did. Does somebody in Peridot hate you, Miss Barnes?"

"No." But even as she said it, Lydia heard the uncertainty in her voice.

She realized how pathetic she must look, her sundress smeared with tears and sweat, her already wrinkled face worn from two nights of fear and worry. She had pulled her dark hair into a high bun, but half had already fallen out, dropping around her face, limp in the heat.

Maybe he pitied her. She wasn't sure.

"We will be in touch with more questions shortly, Miss Barnes, but for now you can go home. But let me be very clear. Do not leave town. Am I understood?"

Lydia didn't want to say she had nowhere to go, so instead she just nodded and followed him out of the room and out through the station.

This time, there was no casual ride home from an off-duty officer, no Jeep with the doors off to whisk her back to her apartment. Instead, Sergeant Simpson walked her up to an older gentleman in uniform and simply said to the man, "Hank? I am going to need you to drive Miss Barnes here home."

"You got it, Sergeant," replied Hank.

"Now, as for you, Miss Barnes. Clothes in the bag and right to an officer. You know the drill," he added, handing Lydia another evidence bag. "We will be talking again. Soon. Don't go anywhere. Anywhere at all."

The sound of the door to the station opening caught her attention, and she looked up to see Fran walking in. She tried to catch her friend's eye, but Fran just looked pointedly at the floor and shook her head, and Sergeant Simpson cleared his throat, waiting for a response to his orders. Why was Fran ignoring her? Why couldn't she even look at Lydia?

The sergeant asked, "Do you understand me?"

Lydia nodded and turned to follow Hank, who was already walking toward the front door of the station. Where was Lydia going to go, anyway? She would have gone straight to Fran, maybe asked to stay at The Laurels. But Fran was acting . . . surely, she didn't think that Lydia . . .

The officer was looking at her. Had he just said something?

"Sorry, Officer . . .?" Lydia trailed off. She had no idea what his last name was.

"Hank. Hank is fine," he answered, not unkindly, as he walked toward a patrol car and opened the back seat door.

Why did that name sound familiar? The lizards! Didn't Brandon say that an older man named Hank was part of the group that went looking for wildlife? The group that met in the Walmart parking lot. Suddenly, she wanted to tell this officer about her hellbender nickname. But she caught herself, finally taking in the cracked black vinyl of her seat and the partition, slid open so she could communicate, that separated her from Hank.

She was being driven home in the back of a police car, Lydia reminded herself. And this time, in the middle of the day, on a Sunday, right through the center of Peridot's town square. Lizard nicknames were a lost cause.

Hank chatted amiably as he drove her, sharing facts about the town as they went to her apartment. Lydia found she could only focus for short amounts of time, so she would come to attention to find him talking about wildly different topics. At least Hank seemed to require no response or engagement from Lydia, which right at that moment felt like an extraordinary kindness.

Pointing to the park, Hank said something about ponies. Then Lydia thought she heard the word *elephant*.

"What was that?" she asked, her curiosity winning out over her shock.

"Well, that was before your time," Hank clarified. Which, of course, clarified nothing for Lydia, who had not been really paying attention.

"Really?" she asked, hoping that would prompt him to offer more information.

It worked.

"At least ten years ago. But the children loved it." That made no sense to Lydia, but she nodded and waited, remembering from her years of teaching how useful silence could be.

"Geraldine Terry. What a woman. God broke the mold."

This was going to be painful. Lydia waited.

"She owned the ponies, of course. A few of the ponies were white, and that was really what made it. The dyeing did it."

"Huh?" Lydia squeaked, breaking her own vow to try to be silent in order to encourage Hank. Someone killed ponies?

"Geraldine dyed the white ponies all sorts of rainbow colors, and—well, the little girls could just not get enough, lining up for their favorite color. Her pony rides at the Apple Festival were legendary. That was just Geraldine. And she told me, she did, that one time a woman called her and said, 'Geraldine, I do so love your pony rides; could you get me an elephant?' Would you know it, Geraldine just says, 'I had the number of an elephant guy and sorted that lady right out!'"

Hank filled the police car with raspy laughter.

Geraldine Terry knew someone who could get you an elephant. That was the takeaway, as far as Lydia could figure.

Lydia couldn't bring herself to laugh, but she did smile.

Peridot never stopped surprising her.

And to be honest, Lydia would love to see rainbow ponies at a fair. She started to imagine sewing cute little fairy wings and magic wands to sell at the fair, for the little girls lining up for her imaginary ponies. She could sell starter stitch kits as well. Lydia dove headfirst into her planning.

"Miss, I don't mean to overstep," Hank said roughly after he finally stopped laughing. Was he going to ask her to play some board game too? Was she ever so slowly losing her mind? It sure felt like it. "Could I offer you a spot of advice?" he asked, not making eye contact.

"I am sure the sergeant told you to stay in town," Hank said, and Lydia nodded, "because we are a long way from figuring out what is going on here. But you're new to town, I've heard?" Lydia nodded again. Kaleigh at the bakery had been there for at least a decade, and the M's still referred to her as new in town, so Lydia felt like she had a long way to go. Lydia wasn't even Southern. That probably added at least another five years until she would be considered anything other than a new arrival.

"Do you have yourself a gun?"

"Excuse me?"

"All things considered, you should consider having a gun on hand," Hank said calmly.

The police car had been stopped outside the shop for the length of the conversation, and people walking by were starting to peer in, wondering what called for a patrol car in the town square.

"It seems to me that people near you keep ending up dead. If I were in your shoes, I would want to meet that danger armed. There is a good, reputable gun shop in Franklin, if you need a recommendation. I know a guy."

Lydia almost wanted to ask if it was Geraldine.

"Oh. Great. Thanks. Sure. Okay," Lydia stammered as she got out of the police car. Hank nodded and drove off. Lydia watched the car loop through the town square and head back to the station. The town square was busy, holiday visitors walking happily on the brick-lined paths, looking at the restaurant windows, debating their lunch choices.

The police were busy outside of Measure Twice, but just like with Brandon's apartment, people looked curious, but not afraid. Why would they? Sergeant Simpson had made it clear to Lydia that Peridot was not a place where people felt afraid.

As Lydia dug through her bag to unlock her door, she heard Jeff come out of his apartment.

"Hey there, Lydia. Was that a police car you just got out of? Any news about who they think killed Brandon?"

Lydia silently cursed her bad timing and tried to come up with a response that wasn't just bursting into tears.

The best she could do was say, "Hey, Jeff."

"Why are they taping up Measure Twice? Do they really think the killer got that, um, those shear thingamajigs from the shop? Are they taking prints? Scary, isn't it? All of this in our little building," Jeff added, but he didn't look scared; he looked excited.

She had to tell him. It would be weird if he found out later and realized she had kept it from him. Or what if he saw it as lying?

"The police are at the store because April Lanier was murdered in the classroom. Today. And I found her body."

"Whoa," Jeff responded.

"Yeah." Lydia put her key in her lock and tried to bring the conversation to an end.

No such luck.

Instead of taking the hint, Jeff walked toward Lydia.

"You know, Lydia, I meant what I said before. You really might be safer staying with me. You would have to board your pets, of course. Can't have them traipsing all over the trains! I would be more than happy to sleep on the couch and let you have the bedroom, Lydia. I just want you to be safe. Can't be relying on things like this now, can we?" And with that, he reached out to her.

At first, Lydia thought he was brushing a leaf or something similar off her shoulder. But instead, Jeff reached his hand right to the point above the neckline of her dress. His fingers brushed against her skin as he pinched her pendant and flipped it over, switching it from the plain silver side with her initials to the enameled side showing Saint Christopher carrying Christ across the river. His fingertips were cold and dry against her hot, sweaty skin.

She shivered.

"Wow." Lydia tried to keep her tone neutral. Surely, he wasn't trying to be creepy. "Thanks for the offer, Jeff, really. I feel perfectly safe in my own apartment." Lydia winced since that wasn't actually true.

Thankfully, Jeff seemed to take her at her word.

"If you change your mind, Lydia, just say the word. I'll keep you safe. You can be sure of that."

Lydia looked down and noticed that Jeff was rubbing his fingers against his thumb. The fingers that had just touched her chest. Ugh.

"I am sure the police will have this solved in no time, but thanks," Lydia pushed at her door.

"Unlikely!" Jeff exclaimed, turning back to his own apartment.

Lydia felt a weak smile. She pictured Jeff saying "Inconceivable!" instead of "Unlikely!" Her neighbor looked so much like Vizzini from *The Princess Bride* that she'd done a double-take the first time they'd met. Just once, she had tried to make a joke about the movie with Jeff, but he had stared back, blankly, before informing her that he had little time for contemporary cinema. Lydia didn't want to admit to him that she was worried it was unlikely too. And she was feeling less and less safe in her apartment. But Sergeant Simpson had told her to stay put, so she would stay put. And even though she was scared, she still wasn't quite frightened enough to take Jeff Johnson up on his offer. Too many trains. That was all it was, she told herself. And she almost believed it.

Chapter Eleven

B ack in her apartment, Lydia told herself she should go let the others know. They needed to know about April. That April was dead. But she couldn't bring herself to explain what she had seen—not again. Not yet.

Fran knew, but she didn't want to talk to Fran. Not after seeing Fran ignore her in the police station.

Besides, the others would hear soon enough. Would they think she did it, like Sergeant Simpson clearly did? Sergeant Simpson! That reminded her that she said she would give the police her clothes. Surely she could shower first?

Charlie danced around her feet, tail wagging, blissfully unaware of how her life was unraveling. Lydia bent down to pet him while casting a glance around for Baby Lobster. Then she heard a muffled meow. Lydia looked at Charlie as if the dog could tell her where the cat was.

Then she tried to follow the sound of the cat, like a location ping on a cell phone.

Like most sewists, Lydia had a healthy pile of scraps under her sewing desk, stored in an old laundry hamper. She didn't have a plan for the small pieces of fabric, but she also couldn't bring herself to simply throw them out. So, they waited, under the desk, for a project that could use such small, irregular pieces.

The pile had been disturbed, but Baby Lobster was not hidden in the basket, like Lydia had hoped. Where was that cat? Then Lydia remembered the pattern she had been cutting out on the floor of her bedroom. She was still working on convincing Fran to carry more dress patterns in the shop, so when she wanted a new pattern, Lydia sometimes went the PDF route.

Just the other day she had seen a new pattern she just had to try: Friday Pattern Company's Wilder Gown.

After purchasing the PDF version of the pattern, she had printed it off on the shop's printer and then taken it home to assemble. It was a weirdly calming but laborious process. First, she trimmed the bottom and right sides of each piece of the pattern; then she lined up the pages, taping them together as she went. Once the whole pattern was taped together, and for some patterns this was over sixty pages' worth of pieces, she traced her size and cut out the pieces.

Surely, Lydia had closed the bedroom door when she had left that morning. Surely. That was Cat Ownership 101. Close the doors. Close the bathroom door, or your cat will shred the toilet paper. Obviously. Close the bedroom door, or . . .

Your cat will find the half-finished pattern, try to play with the Scotch tape, somehow wrap her body in that tape, and run howling around the room, dragging the entire tape dispenser behind her in her distress.

The pattern was in tatters, of course, but Lydia had no one to blame for that but herself. Besides, she had a bigger fish to fry.

Her cat, her very cute but also incredibly hostile cat, was covered in Scotch tape.

Lydia took a deep breath and tried to remember the advice from Cynde the night before. Crouching down, a safe distance from the cat-tape hybrid, she called, "Psspsss psspsss psspsss."

Baby Lobster stopped howling and looked at Lydia. Okay, that was a start. Lydia kept calling the cat, but at the same time, she turned and walked into the living room, leaving the bedroom door wide open.

For a moment, Lydia was reminded of Greek mythology: she was Orpheus, trying to lead Eurydice out of the underworld without turning around. Then she heard Graham, in her head, calling her a nerd. She squinted for a second, telling that voice to skedaddle, and focused on coaxing her miserable cat out into the living room.

Every sewist knows one of the key rules of sewing is that you only use fabric scissors for fabric, so Lydia quickly dismissed that option, but she needed scissors, nonetheless. Baby Lobster stayed at the threshold to the room, as if to say, "I will come this far but no farther," while Lydia hunted for and quickly found her snips, the small scissors sewists, knitters, and other crafters kept for tight fits and small jobs. It was time to snip her cat free.

Lydia felt the sweat on her back. Who knew cutting a cat out of tape would be such a workout? Probably everyone; that was an easy guess to make. What amazed her was how little Baby Lobster struggled. Once she realized what Lydia was trying to do, she sat still, not making eye contact, but not fighting her either. *And boy, does Baby Lobster know how to fight,* Lydia thought, remembering back to the volunteer's oven mitt–covered hands.

As she worked, snipping at the tape, Lydia sang the only song she knew by heart: "Rocky Raccoon" by the Beatles.

The job was completed with no blood drawn, but the cat did look like she had picked a fight with a box fan and lost, patches of hair missing or cut far too short all over her multicolored body. *Actually,* Lydia thought as she tried to wipe the sweat from her face, *Baby Lobster looks just about how I feel.*

Lydia's phone rang, freeing Baby Lobster from the impromptu serenade.

"Lydia, dear."

Lydia exhaled a breath she hadn't realized she had been holding. Fran wasn't going to completely ignore her.

"Fran."

"Lydia, I am leaving the police station. We need—well, we need to talk about what happened. The group is going to want to know. Wade knows. I saw Wade here. But the rest. Well. Of course, we can't meet at the store. I am going to call Cynde and have her gather everyone at PeriDough. Can you come? Can you come and tell us all what happened?"

"Of course I will, Fran. I'm so sorry."

Neither woman said a word. The silence lengthened.

"Can you be at the bakery in half an hour?"

Lydia was still wearing her clothes. The ones she said she would bring straight to the police. This was hardly going to make her look any better. Sighing, Lydia stripped and placed her clothes in the bag from the station. Then she showered, as hot a shower as she could possibly stand. Too overwhelmed to enjoy a handmade outfit, she threw on an old college T-shirt, from her undergrad years at Kenyon, and a pair of jean shorts.

For a moment, Lydia stood in front of her bedroom mirror, pulling her hair back into a bun. She was forty. A little heavy. Wrinkled from smiles as much as from the sun. She had made peace with what the mirror told her in the past few months. But today, even her green eyes looked washed out, her normally pink cheeks sallow. She looked almost as bad as she felt.

When she left her apartment, she stopped by Measure Twice, handing her bag of clothes over to the first officer she could find, hating that she felt a strong sense of déjà vu. She walked quickly to the bakery, trying to outpace the looks from the officers that seemed to follow her every step.

Thankfully, PeriDough was just as welcoming as ever, no matter how terrible Lydia felt. The shop was all done in green and white, with a Formica counter and padded stools. To the left of the counter, a clear glass window let shoppers view the donut-making process. To the right of the counter were a few tables where the regulars sat with their morning papers during the week. "Bakery and Café" seemed like an overstatement to Lydia, since they really just did donuts. Well, donuts, quiches, coffee, and sweet tea. Coffee, not even lattes. But honestly, everyone just called it PeriDough, anyway.

Kaleigh let Lydia into the bakery, even though PeriDough technically closed at three PM on Sundays. Fran had called over and explained that Measure Twice was now a crime scene, and Kaleigh, always a den mother, had offered caffeine, sugar, and somewhere for the group to be.

Lydia watched as her friends walked into the shop.

Fran came in first, brisk and businesslike, and walked right past Lydia, without giving her one of her standard, brief, one-armed hugs, and sat down at the large table Lydia had already staked out. Fran stayed silent. Where was the warmth Lydia had heard on the phone?

Kaleigh came over with a tray and an old-fashioned pot of coffee. The regulars had their mugs on the wall next to the register, and the table already had little creamers and a large sugar dispenser, glass with a silver lid.

"Here you go, Fran, all we had left today. I am just so sorry. About April. The shop. I know . . ." Kayleigh looked down at the platter of donuts on the table, lips pressed together. She shook her head slightly, her tight braids bouncing, and changed the topic.

"So y'all have some cinnamon-sugar donuts, some old-fashioned ones, and today's special—the Hummingbird." Kaleigh pointed at a purple-frosted ring donut. "Darrel came up with this one; It's our vanilla frosted with some blackberry added."

All three of them looked at the platter. Kaleigh held a breath but then let it go slowly. Lydia wanted to prompt her, to ask her what she was thinking, but instead she picked up a hummingbird donut from the platter and took a large bite.

Thankfully, the donut was delicious.

Kayleigh put a large keychain, anchored with a huge hot-pink pom-pom, on the table in front of Fran, adding, "You just take your time, Fran. Lock up and drop the key back to me on your way home, won't you?"

Fran nodded just as the door opened to reveal Mary and Martha walking, with enviable posture, into the bakery.

The two women simply nodded in Kaleigh's direction and sat down opposite Fran and Lydia at the table.

Kaleigh gave a tight grin to the two women and readied herself to head out. Lydia watched her as she left, realizing how little she knew about PeriDough's owner, even though she made an almost daily pilgrimage to the shop for the donuts. Lydia knew Kaleigh owned the bakery. She knew Kaleigh's husband, Darrel, created the new flavors and baked goods that made the spot so popular.

How long had PeriDough been on the square? Darrel was local—she knew that from the M's—but was Kaleigh? She didn't think so. Kaleigh seemed to be extra kind to Lydia, as if to say, "I know how it feels to be new here." Why hadn't Lydia at least asked her where she was from? What could Kaleigh tell her about finding her way in this adopted town?

"What do you think, Lydia?"

Lydia snapped back from her wonderings about Kaleigh, asking, "What do I think of what?"

"What happened to April? Could it have been an accident?" Clark asked, munching on a piece of dried seaweed. He may have condescended to join the group, but as Mary would say, the devil would ice skate to work before Clark ate a donut. Fran had obviously told the group what had happened, and they seemed to be choosing curiosity as a coping mechanism. No small talk this time. She couldn't blame them. She was self-medicating with donuts.

Did Clark have a point? Lydia flashed back to the shop, April crushed and still under the long-arm machine. Could it have been an accident? Those machines were so heavy, and April was so small. Lydia shook her head and Clark looked at her expectantly.

"No. No, I just don't see how it could have been an accident. I mean, even without . . . even if you don't think about . . . even if you ignore what happened to Brandon, I saw April. She was crushed under that machine. Someone pushed it on her. I'm sure of it."

That's it, Lydia thought to herself. She was sure of it. Just like she was sure that Measure Twice was the right place for her. That Peridot was her new home. That she was going to eat another purple donut . . .

"She was terribly clumsy."

"Mary, sometimes April slipped when the sidewalk freezes in the winter. Clumsy doesn't explain ending up underneath a huge machine built not to fall over. Long-arm quilting machines are designed to be stable," Fran replied sharply.

Heather added, "Which means April was murdered. Brandon was murdered. Two people in Peridot have been murdered in the past two days. And Lydia found them both." The young woman's face was hard to read, but she was right.

"And I'm still the main suspect," Lydia admitted.

The comment quieted the group, but Clark rallied, saying, "Well, then, it is simply all the more important that we figure out who is doing this. For Lydia's sake. For our own, if there really is a crazed murderer in our little town."

Lydia could tell Clark thought the last comment would lighten the mood. It did not.

"What do we know so far?" Fran asked, trying to get the group to stop imagining a murderer at their doorsteps that night.

"Well, Sarah Jane is out of the running, at least, right?" Cynde asked the group. "Maybe you could be so mad at your estranged husband that you kill him, but why on earth would she kill April?"

Clark assumed his most comfortable role, that of devil's advocate, and replied, "What if she thought Brandon had some sort of a fling with Lydia *and* April? April and Brandon did spend a lot of time together at the bookshop, after all," he added, looking pleased with himself.

Heather replied quickly, "Wasn't April about twenty years too old for him?"

"Love doesn't always follow the rules," Fran quickly replied to Heather, who looked chastened in response, though Lydia thought Heather had made a good point.

"Still," Lydia jumped in, "even if Sarah Jane was convinced that they had been having an affair, why would she kill April after she killed Brandon? Wouldn't killing Brandon have been enough?"

The group sat in silence, considering this angle.

Clark rebounded quickly. "Fair point, Lydia," he admitted with a tilt of his head toward her. "Maybe this is more about April than it is about Brandon?"

"Oh, come now. Who on earth would want to harm April?" Fran exclaimed.

"Well, I guess that rules out the spurned-lover angle," Heather added.

"Not quite, Heather," Mary replied, looking knowingly at Lydia.

"Lydia, you understand, of course," Mary continued.

"What?"

"With all that you have been through with that scoundrel of a husband," Mary finished.

"Oh, right. I guess you could consider that a love triangle." Once more, Lydia fought against the memory of her diet lemonade on the floor. Her cheating ex was the opposite of a secret with this group. They had all, to varying degrees, helped her through those first few days of shock and grief as her marriage had crumbled. Did the M's think that April and Brandon had been . . . were a . . . had an . . .

"Do you think that April was cheating on Wade with Brandon? And he killed them both?" Heather spoke up again, adding, "Don't they always say the husband did it?"

"Heather. Wade is a hero. He was awarded one of the highest honors the military bestows. I fail to see how a man who risked his life, who was injured in the act of saving others, could possibly be considered a . . . could possibly be considered guilty of such a crime," Mary snapped, unwilling to go so far as to even utter Wade's name and the word *murder* in the same statement.

Martha chimed in, equally offended by the suggestion, "And he is a pillar of the Peridot community, working with those fine young men each weekend."

That only confused the group, who waited for Martha to offer a clarification she had no intention of providing. The women sat with their mouths pressed in two matching thin lines. Gossip about potential murderers might be allowed, but besmirching an American hero was a bridge too far.

Cynde saved the day, explaining, "Oh, you mean the ROTC cadets. Wade trains the ROTC cadets on the weekends. You're right, he would have been with them. Otherwise, surely he'd be in jail by now?"

"Heather, we think no such thing about Wade. Of course, we hate to speculate at all about people's private lives." Lydia heard Heather choke back a laugh at the truly absurd claim, but Mary didn't notice. "But suppose this Sarah Jane was still in love with Brandon?" Martha nodded her agreement. "Suppose she knew Brandon was moving on . . ." Martha kept nodding, but Lydia interrupted their routine.

"It was one date! I hardly consider that moving on!" she declared, wishing for the millionth time she had never agreed to have dinner with Brandon in the first place.

"Oh, not with you, Lydia. With April. Sarah Jane, riddled with jealousy, murdered them both."

There was a downbeat of silence, as if Mary expected applause. Even more strangely, for a moment it felt like the group might indulge her and clap. The world truly was upside-down.

"But April had wanted to meet with me. She said there was something about Brandon. She wasn't acting like someone who had just lost a great love," Lydia countered.

"Well, if it wasn't this Sarah Jane, who was it?" Clark asked.

"I hate to even think this, but is there a chance that April killed Brandon and then killed herself? Maybe Sarah Jane had nothing to do with it. Maybe April loved him, and he didn't want to be with her. What if she couldn't take it?" Cynde asked, not quite making eye contact with the table. Cynde looked heartbroken by her own theory. The rest of the group turned to look at Lydia.

"No, Cynde. No. I saw her. There is just no way she pulled that machine down on herself. It had to be someone else," Lydia clarified, trying to reassure her friend.

"It wasn't an accident. It wasn't a love triangle. It wasn't suicide. How do you explain it?" Heather weighed in.

"And how on earth will we ever open up the shop again?" Fran asked miserably.

"We need to do better than this, people. And we need our shop back." Clark turned to Fran. "We won't let this cast a pall over Measure Twice. We simply won't." But Fran seemed more concerned by his promise than comforted.

Lydia liked his enthusiasm, though, so she shared her most absurd theory, asking, "Do you think Jeff could have something to do with it?"

"Jeff's Trains Jeff? That Jeff?" Cynde asked, clearly taken aback.

"I'm probably just being ridiculous. He gave me a ride to get Baby Lobster and seemed really interested in Brandon's murder. Weirdly interested."

"Baby lobster?" Clark gasped, almost choking on his ice water. "What does a baby lobster have to do with anything?"

"No, no, I adopted a cat yesterday. A cat named Baby Lobster."

Clark looked at her as if that clarified nothing.

"Go on," Cynde said, encouraging Lydia to move past the cat.

"Jeff told me that he wants to set up a brick-and-mortar shop but that finding real estate on the square was really hard."

Lydia tried not to notice as Cynde flinched.

"What if Jeff is trying to drive Turn the Page out of town and take over their place on the square?" she asked, but as soon as Lydia said it, she heard how absurd it sounded.

"One of your neighbors killed the other so he could have a better way to sell toy trains?" Heather asked, incredulous.

Yep. It sounded absurd.

"What if he likes her?" Clark asked, perking up.

"What if who likes who?" Cynde retorted.

"*Whom,*" Mary corrected.

Clark let a little huff of impatience, "What if Jeff likes Lydia? He saw her go on the date with Brandon. Then he killed Brandon out of jealousy."

"Even if that worked—and it seems like a stretch—that doesn't explain what happened to April," Cynde countered.

"What did April say to you last night, Lydia?" Clark asked.

Lydia scrunched up her face in concentration, trying to remember what had turned out to be her last words with April.

"She said, 'I want to talk to you. About Brandon. Something has been bothering me. I just need to talk it through with someone.' Or something close to that," Lydia hedged, not completely trusting her memory.

"That could mean anything," Clark replied. "Maybe Jeff killed Brandon, April somehow knew about it, and Jeff killed April to cover it up."

"But the police keep investigating Lydia," Heather pointed out. "If he likes Lydia so much, why is he pointing the finger at her?"

That brought the conversation to a standstill. No one else wanted to say that all the evidence pointed at Lydia, but they couldn't ignore it either.

Lydia heard small gasping noises and was shocked to realize Martha had started to cry. While the others had tried to forget their grief, Martha had been overwhelmed.

Fran noticed too. "Listen, everyone. I'm glad we could be together. These are some good theories. But they will keep. This is a lot to process, so I suggest we head home for the day. The store is a crime scene now"—Fran's voice cracked, and she paused to regain her composure—"but I will let you all know when I can open it again. For now, I think we should all go home. I will stay behind and lock up PeriDough and drop the keys off to Kaleigh, but let's call it a day."

The group stood up to leave, Clark repeating his kindness from the night before as he stepped up and offered an arm to each M before walking them home.

Cynde looked at Fran. The look lasted long enough for Lydia to notice. What was that about? Heather tapped Fran on the shoulder, breaking the moment.

"Fran, do you need any help?"

"No, Heather, but thank you for offering. I don't know what I would do without you."

The young woman glowed with the praise. Lydia told herself not to feel jealous.

"Why don't you two girls come up to The Laurels tomorrow after lunch? I would love to show you both around the place. And we can talk about how to move forward with the store."

Heather smiled, which made Lydia realize how rarely that happened, and replied, "That sounds great, Fran. Lydia, I can drive." With that, Heather left.

Now it was just Fran and Lydia in the bakery.

"Lydia, dear, do you have plans for dinner?"

"Tonight? No." Lydia stopped short of saying that her last two dinners had ended in murder for the other person.

"Why don't I stop by in a bit with a pizza from Frank's? There are things we need to talk about. Things better said in private."

Chapter Twelve

B ack home, Lydia felt heavy from the heat and the donuts she had eaten with the others while they played amateur detectives.

She wanted to call Sergeant Simpson, to offer him some other suspect, some other name to put at the top of his list. On Saturday, Fran had convinced her that everything they knew was just normal small-town tensions. What did they know now? A lot of nonsense about love triangles. Her own absurd theory about Jeff. She had nothing to tell the officer. No name to offer in place of her own.

The tears came hard and fast. For the first time that weekend, Lydia made no effort to stop them. She just cried. It was what her mom used to call ugly crying, where she would hiccup and sputter. But when the tears finally slowed, she felt a little better.

Lydia heard the doorbell and Charlie's barks at the same time. She wiped her face with the bottom hem of her college T-shirt and went to the door.

Rubbing her cheeks with her hands one more time for good measure, Lydia let her friend in. Fran would know immediately she'd been crying, of course. Lydia had no poker face, and Fran wasn't easily fooled, even if she had bothered to try. Still, she didn't want to look totally bedraggled.

Fran walked straight to the small kitchen and sat down, opening the pizza box she had brought with her.

One moment earlier, Lydia would have sworn she wasn't hungry. But faced with a cheese pizza from Peridot's own Frank's, Lydia felt ravenous. Which, she suddenly remembered, meant hungry like a raven. Were ravens known for eating a lot? What was the difference between a raven and a crow?

"Why don't you have the last piece, Lydia, dear."

She looked up and realized that she had eaten more than half of the pizza while wondering about birds, never even offering Fran a drink.

"Oh no, please, you have it. Can I get you something to drink?"

Lydia opened her fridge, embarrassed that she didn't really have much to offer Fran in the way of beverage choices. Even in her twenties, Lydia hadn't been much of a drinker, but having already celebrated her fortieth birthday earlier that year, she had found herself reaching for a cocktail even less often.

"Um, would you like some lemonade? Or, um, some water? I should have gone over to Clark's shop and picked up something nice to drink. I'm sorry, I just—"

Fran interrupted her rambling apology, "Lydia, dear, water is fine. As you well know. Neither one of us needs to be muddled tonight—not with all that has happened. Come sit down and eat this last piece. Otherwise, it will go to waste."

Lydia did as she was told. Why was it such a relief to follow orders when they came from someone like Fran? Lydia let the thought pass, deciding it didn't need an answer just now. All that was needed were cheese and carbohydrates.

"Listen, Lydia. I know the group was throwing around theories about who did this. But really, we are the ones who need to figure this out. You and me. First our dress shears, now the long-arm quilting machines in our actual store. These murders have far more to do with Measure Twice than I am okay with. Why us? I keep asking myself, and I can't come up with an explanation. I don't know what Sergeant Simpson said to you, but he made it clear to me today that this all looks very suspicious. And very, very bad for Measure Twice."

That was a lot for Fran to say at once, and she looked exhausted from the effort.

"Sergeant Simpson went further than saying it was suspicious when he talked to me, Fran. He told me I'm their number-one suspect." Lydia cleared the table of the empty pizza box as she said the final part, afraid to look her friend in the eyes.

"Ha!" Fran barked. "No need to waste our breath on that. The sergeant is a nice man, but he has lost his way on this case. Ignore him. Who do you really think did this? Do you really think it was that neighbor of yours, Jeff?" Fran asked quietly but with intensity.

"To be honest, at first I wondered if maybe it was Wade. Like Heather said earlier, on all my crime shows"—Fran knew how Lydia loved to watch mysteries and true crime shows like *Dateline*—"the husband is the first suspect and more often than not the actual villain. But he had an alibi for Brandon's murder; he was with April that whole night. So that would mean that someone else killed Brandon, and he killed April? And I don't see how there could be one, let alone two killers in a town like Peridot."

At that, Fran and Lydia both looked out the window at the side of the apartment as if they could see out to the town square. The first time Lydia had seen Peridot, she had wondered for a second if it were a movie set, that was how picture-perfect her new home felt. Now she wondered how many murderers lived nearby.

"Plus, the M's pointed out that Wade wasn't even in town when April died. He does the high school ROTC class, and I think he had a bunch of kids out running on the track at the college campus that morning. I don't know what to think, Fran; I really don't."

She looked at Fran.

"What *do* you think?" Lydia asked, knowing that Fran hadn't really shared her honest opinion over donuts at PeriDough. She had listened and asked questions, but it wasn't clear what she believed. Now, more than ever, Lydia needed to know what her wise friend really thought.

"Lydia, dear, I am going to be honest with you. I have no idea. And I'm worried that if we can't figure out who did this, a cloud of suspicion is going to hang over the shop. If we have an answer, then the town can grieve and start to heal and move forward. No one will punish us for a terrible event. But if there is a sliver of doubt that it has something to do with the store"—Lydia appreciated the euphemism her friend used instead of saying, *"No one will want to shop with us if they think you're a killer, Lydia"*—"if the shop stays connected to what has happened, I'm worried it will ruin me." Fran paused, blushing. "I hate to talk about my own worries when two people are dead, but Measure Twice is barely staying afloat as it is. I have put everything I have into the shop, Lydia. If it fails, I have nothing left."

It was without a doubt the most emotional confession from Fran that Lydia had ever experienced. She looked at her friend with fresh eyes. Fran was wearing what Lydia thought of as her summer uniform: a shapeless, sleeveless cotton dress with a row of wide buttons running from the neckline to the hem. Sometimes, Fran mixed it up and layered the dress over a plain cotton T-shirt. Sometimes, she went fancy and wore a cardigan over it.

Fran never wore makeup, and her straight gray hair was short, cut like a cap close to her head. One of the first words that always came to mind when Lydia looked at her friend was *capable*. Fran seemed ready to handle whatever needed to be handled.

Fran wasn't arrogant, like Lydia's ex-husband, who was quick to explain what someone should've done or should've known. And she wasn't fussy like Clark either, with detailed instructions and painfully precise advice. Fran just dealt with things.

Ordered the wrong quilt batting? Let's call the distributor and see if we can sort out an exchange. Embroidery thread not selling? Ask Heather to design a cool new window display and make sets to sell at a discount.

Catch your husband cheating on you in your bed? Come to Peridot, Lydia; rent this apartment, and work at my shop. Fran handled things without drama and without any expectation of fanfare. Lydia had been so worried about clearing her own name that she hadn't really considered what the case meant for Fran.

"Fran, you're exhausted. You've lost two of your friends and here you are, making the time to feed and take care of me. Of course, things seem impossible right now. But I promise you we will keep Measure Twice going. And we will figure out who did this to Brandon and April. And when you go back to The Laurels, take a bath and go to bed. You're scared. We're all scared. Heck, Hank even told me to get a gun!" Lydia offered, hoping to snap her friend out of her funk.

"Who did what, now?"

"After they, um . . . questioned"—Lydia didn't want to say *interrogated*—"me at the police station earlier today, they had some guy named Hank drive me home. Do you know him?"

"Oh, Hank. Everyone knows Hank," Fran replied less than helpfully.

"Well, Hank pointed out that people around me seem to be getting killed, so I should make sure to have a gun," Lydia explained, as if Hank had suggested she get full body armor as well.

"That is worth considering, Lydia, dear. But you're right. I do need a good meal and a hot shower. I am not thinking straight." Fran paused and chuckled, even though Lydia wasn't sure what the joke was.

"Some maniac is out there, hurting people," Fran continued, in a more serious tone. "Hank has a point, Lydia. I have a gun at The Laurels. You should think about getting yourself one."

Fran knew Lydia hated guns. How scared was she?

"I am exhausted and want to get home before it's too late. I don't like driving on the twisty mountain roads in the pitch dark," Fran added as she walked toward the door. "You stay safe,

Lydia, dear. I used to think nothing bad could happen in Peridot. I don't know what to think anymore." Then, with a short, tight hug, Fran was gone.

* * *

Even though Fran had said she was going to head to bed early, Lydia still felt too awake to follow suit. She washed the few dishes from dinner and then went and sat in her living room. She could watch television, she supposed.

Lydia turned on the TV, hoping to take comfort in *The Great British Baking Show*, but the smiles of the bakers felt too discordant. She flipped over to a documentary on an Arctic ice expedition. Too depressing. She turned on a comedy special, but the laughter was worse than the smiles had been. No TV, then.

Grabbing her rotary cutter and large cutting mat, Lydia went to work on a new sewing project. Normally, Lydia listened to true crime podcasts while she sewed, but that was obviously not an option tonight. Instead, she worked in silence.

Sewing wasn't magic. Lydia knew that. But sometimes it felt like magic. Growing up, Lydia had always been curvy. Or womanly. Or voluptuous. Or whatever other term people gave to a body that never fit in the low-rise jeans of her youth.

Lydia had shopped in the women's section as a teenager, then in the plus section as a woman, fighting against what felt like a conspiracy to drape her in beige and gray tents. She wanted to be a rainbow, she wanted to be artsy and bohemian, but it seemed the fashion world had decided skinny people could be quirky and curvy people could just as well blend into the industrial carpeting. There were ways around it, of course, a few brands here and there, but it took time and patience, things that Lydia had always felt were in short supply in her life.

This pattern was a new one, the Zadie jumpsuit, and Lydia had picked out purple linen. It wasn't an advanced pattern, but it was complicated enough to keep her mind from drifting. For a few hours, Lydia just sewed, pinning hemlines, adjusting waist ties.

When the jumpsuit was finished, she left it on the sewing table, too tired to even try it on. Sewing had worked to distract her, but it had also worn her out after a day that was the longest she could remember. It was time to go to sleep.

After another long, scalding hot shower, Lydia put on her pajamas and climbed into bed. She looked at her bedside table, stacked with murder mysteries and books of poetry. The idea of reading about murder for fun turned her stomach, and she certainly didn't have the peace of mind she preferred to have when reading poems. Like the TV, her books were no comfort.

Normally, Lydia would tackle a tough time falling asleep by dreaming of patterns. Or even better, dreaming of patterns she could convince Fran to sell in the shop. But she was sick of patterns, and as she fell asleep, she wasn't thinking about fabric. She was thinking about murder. In her dreams that night, murder followed her.

Dream Lydia went about her day, working at the shop, walking Charlie, talking with friends, but it was a horror movie, not a comedy. Something was stalking her, waiting just out of frame, menacing. Dream Lydia would rush and open doors, peer quickly around corners, sure she could spot the threat. Again and again, there was nothing there, but her fear grew.

She opened an unknown door. It was Fran. Bleeding. Fran was dying. She rushed to try to reach her friend, save her, but the door crashed in her face. She heard Heather laughing.

Lydia sat straight up in bed, looking for the door. It took her a moment to realize she was not in the nightmare. No Fran, no Heather. But the crash was real, so what had made the noise?

Once she turned on her bedside lamp, she realized it was just what cat owners apparently called "the zoomies." In her nighttime Olympics, Baby Lobster had knocked over a tall pile of books. Nothing to be afraid of after all.

Lydia looked at the books scattered across the floor and then at her unrepentant cat. Crouching down, she started to stack them again, telling herself she needed to make a trip to IKEA when she wasn't a murder suspect.

How was that something she would ever actually say about herself? A murder suspect. Glancing at the book in her hand, Lydia realized it was the book of poetry April had given her when she had gone over to her house for dinner, the last time she had seen April alive.

Sitting on the floor of her bedroom, under the judgmental gaze of Baby Lobster, Lydia opened the book and started to read.

Chapter Thirteen

Even though Lydia wanted to press "Pause" on her life, Charlie still had his expectations. Mornings meant a walk.

Yawning, Lydia turned on her coffee maker and shook some kibble into Baby Lobster's bowl on the kitchen floor. The cat, which she needed to start thinking of as *her* cat, padded softly into the room.

After her bad night of sleep, she needed coffee before the walk, so she told Charlie to be patient and waited by the machine as the carafe slowly filled. Breathing in the scent of fresh coffee, she picked up the poetry book she had started to read the night before.

AWOL. That seemed like a strange title. Lydia didn't have any family in the military, but the phrase sounded familiar. She watched the coffee drip and considered getting out her phone to do some research. Then it hit her: absent without leave— AWOL. That sounded like something that would get a soldier in a lot of trouble. Why use it as the title of a book?

Flipping through the pages, she was struck again by Joe Stanton's talent. The poems were short and stark, rendering time in war through short snapshots. No wonder April had wanted him for the book party.

Finally, the coffee maker beeped, and Lydia filled a travel mug and got Charlie ready for their daily constitutional.

* * *

They walked to the park, listening to the sound of sprinklers watering yards before the bright sun would scorch the wet grass. Part of Lydia hoped to see Clark that morning, but more of her was relieved to round the corner and see only empty benches. No Heather. No Clark. Great.

At only nine in the morning, it was already hot. Lydia reminded herself, as she wiped the beginning of sweat off her brow, that at least it was bound to be a little colder than Atlanta. Now there was a pros-and-cons list she was not ready to make. Atlanta had hotter weather and her ex-husband. Peridot had an amazing new life for her and two murders. In both of which she was the main suspect.

Lydia shook her head as if she could clear her thoughts that easily, like some sort of human Etch A Sketch. Charlie looked up at her expectantly.

"Oh, sorry, buddy. No treats."

"Lydia?"

Lydia knew that Charlie could not speak. Still, the park had been empty one second ago.

"Lydia?"

This time the voice came attached to a person—the last person Lydia expected to see.

"Wade? Wade, what on earth are you doing here?" Lydia asked a little unkindly. Realizing how cold she sounded, she tried to smile in his direction, though it felt, as she attempted it, more like a grimace than anything comforting. What was wrong with her?

Thankfully, Charlie came up to Wade, tail wagging, delighted to see him. At least one of them was acting right.

Lydia turned to Wade. "Wade, I don't know what to say. I'm so sorry. Are you . . . are you holding up okay?"

Wade nodded, his eyes red, and repeated back to her, "I'm holding up okay."

Without agreeing to it out loud, they both walked toward the nearest bench and sat down, still not speaking.

Charlie lay down on the concrete near Wade's feet and lazed in the sun. The park was still empty. Everyone who lived in town had left for the long weekend, but it was still too early in the morning for the day-trip explorers to have arrived from Atlanta.

Heather and Fran had planned so many deals and promotions for the holiday weekend. Lydia knew the same had been true for Turn the Page. Hadn't April said something about it last week? Or had it been Brandon at dinner? She couldn't keep her memories straight. How could they both be gone? Eventually, the stores would have to open again, or at least Measure Twice would. Would Turn the Page even stay in business? Would Wade leave town?

The silence stretched out, filled with the hum of summer bugs and distant sprinklers.

"April." Lydia and Wade said the name at the same time, and both stopped abruptly.

"Oh, go ahead, sorry—what were you saying . . .?" Lydia trailed off.

"April really liked you, Lydia," Wade continued, still looking at the ground.

First her conversation with Clark and now this. Lydia was starting to feel like a priest offering the strangest form of confession, as Wade continued speaking but still refused to make eye contact.

"Did you get to talk to her? Did you at least get to talk to her before . . ."

Lydia shook her head no.

"It doesn't matter. I know that. It was a stupid hope. I thought maybe you could have cheered her up, gotten her to stop worrying about the stupid . . ." Wade bit on his lip, swallowing whatever word he had been about to say. "The stupid book party. I wanted to think that in the end she was happy. Before." Wade bit his lip again, this time as if to bite back tears. "Lydia, I have saved so many lives." Wade paused as if seeing his Purple Heart before them in the hazy morning air. "So many. Why couldn't I save the one that mattered the most to me? I know you were the one to . . . the police told me that you were . . . I just want you to know, Lydia, I don't blame you."

"Oh. Thanks?" Lydia answered, but it sounded like a question. It felt like when Heather had said she was brave. It sounded like a compliment but felt like an insult.

Wade stared off in the distance. "The truth is," he confided, "that I blame myself."

"What? Why?" Lydia had not expected this from Wade, but when she turned to face him, he was still staring out into the empty park.

"My wife, Lydia. My only employee. Whoever did this destroyed the people that meant the most to me. And without them, I don't know if I can keep the shop open. Someone is destroying my life. Someone hates me, Lydia—that's the only sense I can make of all this. So. I blame myself." Wade turned and coughed awkwardly into his elbow.

Was Wade crying? Lydia was normally comfortable with emotions; some, like Heather, might even argue she was too comfortable with emotions. What had Heather said once? *"I'm like an M and M that's all candy and no chocolate, and Lydia, well, you're all chocolate, no candy."* Heather had been right, of course. But suddenly, Lydia desperately wanted Wade to stop crying. He was supposed to be grilling and talking about his ROTC cadets, no blaming himself for the worst tragedies possible.

Worse, Lydia knew there was another way of looking at the murders. Sergeant Simpson had made that abundantly clear.

She owed it to Wade to tell him. Lydia tried to sit up a little straighter and quickly said, "It might not be about you, Wade. The police think that maybe someone is targeting me, so you shouldn't blame yourself, because it might really not be about you—I mean of course it is, but the police think maybe someone is trying to frame me, so you could blame me, I guess. You could."

Wade turned to face Lydia, but she looked at the ground. Would he yell at her? Walk away in disgust?

"You?" was all he said.

Lydia nodded.

"The police think someone is trying to frame you?" Wade sounded incredulous.

"Well, the police said, um, someone is trying to frame me, or, um, I did it. Because, because of all the connections to the shop. The sewing scissors. The long-arm quilting machine. But Wade, please know, I would never . . ." Lydia ran out of words to say. How do you convince someone that you aren't a murderer.

Thankfully, Wade interrupted her sputtering, kindly saying, "Lydia, I know you didn't do this. I know that. You loved April. Just like I did." Wade paused and squinted toward the sun. "And I don't blame you—not really. It just hadn't occurred to me, to be honest, that someone might be framing you. It all felt so personal. But if that's what the police think . . ."

"Yeah," Lydia added lamely.

"Who would want to frame you, Lydia?"

At least Wade seemed less distraught, Lydia thought. But how could she answer that question?

Wade looked at Lydia with hope in his eyes, as if she could offer him a handhold on the slippery slope of his grief.

"Well, at first, I couldn't think of anyone. I mean, I just moved here. But if I had to say someone, the only person I could think of is . . ."

The silence stretched out.

"Yes?" Wade prompted.

He deserved her honesty, even if she hadn't told anyone her suspicions. Not even Fran. Lydia only had one theory, and she had tried to bury the idea, even from herself. But she couldn't do that any longer.

"Heather," Lydia admitted.

"Heather?"

Wade really wasn't holding up his end of this excruciating conversation. Lydia elaborated reluctantly. "I think it's been a little hard for Heather, with me in the store. She hasn't really warmed to me, and I think my ideas bother her, and Fran has been paying more attention to me, so . . ." She heard the sound of Heather's laughter from her dream the night before.

Lydia waited. She wanted Wade to tell her that she was being ridiculous, that clearly this was the work of some maniac, not anyone they knew. That Heather might be cold and distant and unpleasant, but he knew for a fact that Heather actually really liked Lydia.

"Fran does really adore you," was all Wade said, which was exactly what had Lydia worried.

Fran was the best thing that had ever happened to Lydia. But what if that meant that Lydia was the worst thing that had ever happened to Heather?

Maybe her luck really was that bad. Like walking in on her husband, in the bed they shared, with her teaching assistant, not doing any kind of teaching. Like quitting her job for that same husband and then having nothing to hold on to when her life fell apart. Bad things happened to Lydia. What had Fran said to her? *Your luck isn't bad, honey—just uneven. That poor excuse of a man—you got a good deal on an expensive lesson. No kids. Just take Charlie and call it a loss. You were meant to find your way here, Lydia, and this is your home now. Your good luck is just getting started.*

Fran had no idea just how wrong she was. Lydia's vision blurred, and it took a minute for her to realize she had started to cry. The tears were silent but thick, sliding dramatically down her cheeks.

Wade pressed for more details, asking, "You really think it could be Heather? Did she know where you would be? When you found Brandon, when you went to see April?"

Lydia nodded, still crying.

"Lydia, this is serious. You might be on to something. She had a motive. She knew where you would be. She had access to the store, to the supplies. Why didn't I see this sooner? Have you told the police?"

"No. I mean, I don't really think Heather . . ."

Wade waved his hand, as if to dismiss her point. "Are you going to see her any time soon?"

"We're having lunch today at Shenanigans before we drive up to Fran's mountain house," Lydia admitted sheepishly.

"You think she might be framing you for a double murder, and you're having lunch with her? Driving with her? Why on earth would you do that, Lydia?"

Why, indeed? Lydia tried to explain her thinking to Wade, even though she didn't really understand it herself. "I don't have a car, and Fran invited us up to the Laurels, and it all seems so absurd. Heather offered to drive me, so I offered to treat her to lunch. Besides"—Lydia tried to laugh—"what could happen to me at Shenanigans?"

Wade looked directly at Lydia, and she felt the full force of his military career. This was a man who made decisions. He saved people, Lydia remembered, thinking again of his purple heart.

"This is nothing to laugh about, Lydia. Shenanigans is fine, of course, plenty of witnesses, but you're planning on being alone in a car with Heather? Even if there's only a sliver of a chance you're right, how could you consider something so dangerous?"

Lydia had no answer. Thankfully, Wade kept talking, "Lydia, I'm not trying to tell you what to do, okay?"

She nodded, even though part of her desperately wanted Wade to tell her what to do at this point. He looked so solid, so reassuringly capable.

"But I am going to ask you to promise me something. Do not let Heather know that you suspect her. I don't want you to spook her into doing something . . . into hurting you, Lydia. Okay?"

She nodded again.

"Tell her you suspect someone else. Convince her, Lydia. And if you can, find another ride up to the mountain, okay?"

"Sure, Wade, I'll do that. I'm sure Heather has nothing to do with this, but you're right. Better safe than sorry," she added through her tears.

Wade let out a big sigh, adding, "Exactly. I'm glad you were honest with me. Please take my advice. Better safe than sorry, Lydia." He stood up to leave.

"Wait. Wade. Who do I tell her I suspect?" Lydia knew she sounded pathetic, but she felt pathetic too.

"Lydia. It doesn't matter. Just don't tell her the truth."

And with that final command, he patted her on the back and then stood and walked out the park, looking like a soldier drilling, his gait perfectly timed, posture perfectly straight.

Lydia took a moment to stop crying. She knew she must look a mess. Her eyes hurt; her nose was running. She was so hot and so sad. Standing up, she called to Charlie and started the slow walk home, feeling like a boat that had slipped its mooring in the night, and in the morning found itself lost at sea.

Chapter Fourteen

S itting in the summer sun, hearing Wade's advice, had left Lydia both sweaty and overwhelmed. When she got back to the apartment, she poured some water for Charlie and went straight to the shower.

As she got dressed, she considered the day ahead of her. First, she'd meet Heather for lunch at Shenanigans, and then Heather would drive her up to The Laurels since Lydia still didn't have a car. Heather. What would she say to Heather?

She looked around her small bedroom, trying to distract herself, and remembered the make she had finished the night before.

Lydia knew some sewists who really relished the small details, laboring over perfect hemlines and neatly turned-out corners. That was not Lydia. At all. It never had been. She didn't love details when it came to any part of her life. It used to drive Graham crazy, the sheer number of things she either forgot about or never even tried to remember in the first place.

She looked at the jumpsuit sitting next to her sewing machine. Were there still threads to be trimmed? Certainly.

Could it use a good press? No doubt. Was Lydia going to wear it as is? Absolutely.

The deep violet linen felt cool and clean against her skin. Lydia let out a long, loud sigh. Then she looked in her bedroom mirror and did a little shimmy. Yep. The jumpsuit was just right, no mods (as sewists called modifications) needed.

The smile on her face faded as she thought over Wade's advice.

She had felt terrible even admitting her suspicion to Wade. Yet she couldn't quite shake it either. It wasn't time to meet Heather yet, but Lydia felt jumpy and ill at ease. This was ridiculous. She was wrong, and it was her fault that Wade now suspected Heather as well. She just needed to talk to Fran, that was all. Fran always sorted things out.

Thankfully, Fran picked up on the first ring.

"Lydia, dear. Is something wrong? Are you still planning to come to The Laurels?"

"No, nothing is wrong. Nothing more than everything, I guess," Lydia hedged, forcing an awkward laugh.

"This has been hard on all of us, Lydia. No one expects something like this to happen to them. Especially not in a place like Peridot. But we have to trust the police and be patient."

"I know, I know. Still, if we could figure out who did this, we could help the police, right?" Lydia silently willed Fran to agree with her, to come up with a plan to catch a suspect. Wade's advice wouldn't matter if Fran could figure out who the real killer was, someone who wasn't Heather.

"Lydia. Dear. It's all good and well to gossip about theories when we are all together at the shop or the bakery. That is a part of small-town life, the dissection of any major event, the desire to put yourself in the middle of the action. At the end of the day, however, we are not the police. Do you understand that, Lydia? You have to let this go." Fran's voice was flat and controlled, which somehow seemed worse to Lydia than if she had yelled at her.

"But Fran, you said we needed to figure out who did this, to save the store!" Lydia heard her own voice rising, growing louder.

"I know what I said, Lydia. And no matter what you think, Measure Twice is my store. I will handle it."

"Of course, it's your store! Fran, I just—"

"Measure Twice is my store. Maybe these . . . tragedies . . . maybe they ruin the store. It is what it is. But that is my burden to bear, Lydia, not yours. You need to let the police find the killer. Stop snooping. Stop guessing. Just stop. You need to let me handle this. I've had a good run as it is. Nothing lasts forever."

"What does that mean?" Lydia's voice had grown quiet.

"Just what I said, Lydia. Let it be. I'll see you this afternoon with Heather."

"About that, Fran. Could you maybe come pick me up? I don't want to bother Heather . . ." Lydia sounded forced, even to her own ears.

"Lydia, Heather is happy to drive you, and I have matters to take care of up here. I'll see you both later this afternoon."

With that, Fran ended the call. Ended the call? She hung up on Lydia.

Lydia had been walking around her apartment while arguing with Fran, and now she dropped to the couch with a graceless thud.

Charlie, sensing her distress, came and curled up next to her, placing his nose on her leg. Even Baby Lobster came a little closer, perched on the opposite edge of the couch, a show of distanced solidarity.

Lydia patted Charlie on the head, trying to soothe herself as much as the dog. Then she started talking to him, too overwhelmed to keep her painful thoughts to herself.

"Charlie, I just don't understand. Sergeant Simpson said, 'Find me another suspect.' Fran said, 'We need to figure out who did this, so the shop stays afloat.' But now she wants me to leave it to the police? What on earth did she mean by 'nothing lasts forever'? We're talking about Measure Twice! Her baby! The most important thing in her life. The most important thing in my life. In what universe does it make sense for us to just 'let it be'?"

Charlie looked up at her, but he had no insight. Because he was a dog, Lydia reminded herself. She had called Fran for clarity. The phone call she imagined played out in her mind.

"Fran, I'm so worried about everything that's happened. What if we can't find the killer?" Lydia would be worried, tearful.

Fran would reply, calm and encouraging, "We are not going to let that happen, Lydia, dear. When you come up to The Laurels today, we are going to sit together and figure this all out. I have a hunch I know exactly what's going on. Then we will go straight to that sergeant and tell him exactly what is going on right under that mustachioed nose of his!"

Lydia would have weakly chuckled. That was what should have happened. Instead, Fran had told her to stop digging, to sit and be quiet and leave it all alone. Fran had basically told her, the shop is not your concern. What had happened to her fairy godmother who had offered this whole new life? Wade said that Lydia was Fran's favorite. But hadn't she known Heather longer? How far would Fran go to protect that prickly, red-haired young woman. What if Lydia was right about Heather, and Fran knew it too.

The call that was meant to shake off her concerns only made them louder in her mind. She felt tangled and caught in her own worries and fears, rather than relieved and a little embarrassed, like she had expected.

It was time to meet Heather for lunch. She needed another suspect for the murders, but she had no idea who she could offer as a decoy to Heather.

Back out on the sidewalk, that sun burned even hotter. At least it was a short walk to Shenanigans, Peridot's only live music venue. While the bands and open mics were only in the evening, the place opened for lunch and served a nice selection of sandwiches and salads.

When Fran had invited them to The Laurels, Heather had offered to drive Lydia, well aware that Lydia didn't have a car. Lydia, trying to show her appreciation, had offered to buy Heather lunch beforehand as a thank-you. Now the timing felt frightening.

Stepping into the venue, it was easy to find Heather. Her red hair lit up her table in the corner of Shenanigans. It always struck Lydia as strange that Heather's hair was so bright, but her pale face was almost always close to a scowl. Still, Lydia walked up, pulled out her chair, and tried to make her own smile as convincing as possible.

As Lydia sat down, she noticed that Heather was sewing on some hexies, the small six-sided pieces of hand-sewing that could be used for English paper piecing. Basically, EPP let the sewist bring a quilt wherever they went, perfect for moments of stolen time, stitches done between other tasks. Lydia loved it. Smiling awkwardly, Lydia pulled her own hand-sewing out of her bag. That was one of the many advantages of having sewing friends: No one judged you for sewing wherever and whenever. And Heather was her friend, Lydia reminded herself unconvincingly.

Without looking at the menus, Heather said, "I already know what I want. Are you ready to order?"

Placing her pouch of hexies on the table, Lydia opened the menu.

It was just for show since she already knew what she would order. But it bought her some time to think of how she wanted to approach Wade's advice. Who could be her decoy?

Heather concentrated on her hand-sewing, and Lydia took a moment to look around the restaurant.

The whole restaurant was made of one large rectangle, with a narrow side facing the square and the bulk of the venue extending back farther than was first expected. One long side of the room was the old-fashioned wide wood bar, backed with myriad shining bottles. Directly opposite was the stage, just large enough for a small band. In between were clusters of tables and high-tops, all seats easily turned toward the stage in the evenings.

At night, the place would be packed, but for lunch, they had a little elbow room, which Lydia needed for what she wanted to say next.

A waiter came by for their order, and Heather asked for the avocado toast, while Lydia ordered the Serenade Salad with fried chicken. She knew fried chicken more or less negated the purpose of a salad, but she had given up those worries in her thirties. Plus, she needed fortification for what lay ahead.

After they gave their orders, Lydia dove in.

"I saw Wade this morning," Lydia told Heather quietly, worried that they could be overheard.

"How was he?" Heather asked, nonplussed.

"He said he was 'holding up okay,'" she replied, doing the air quotes with her fingers, "but I'm not sure I buy it. Which is totally understandable. The thing is, Heather, he asked me about April."

Heather just looked at her. If the others were a little too eager for details, Heather more than balanced them out with her nonchalance.

"Wade said he blamed himself. He thinks someone is out to punish him," Lydia admitted.

"That's ridiculous. What did you tell him? I hope you didn't walk him through the nonsense of Jeff and Sarah Jane and crimes of passion," Heather replied at full volume.

This was Lydia's chance to show Heather she didn't suspect her.

"No. No, he really wanted to talk about what I think is going on. We talked about how the whole thing seemed to come back to the shop."

Heather raised one eyebrow.

Lydia internally cursed herself. "Obviously, neither of us had anything to do with it . . ."

Heather's other eyebrow shot up as she asked, "Are you serious?"

Lydia shook her head. She had lost control of the conversation. Was she serious? About what? How could she get this back on track?

Their food arrived, but Heather didn't eat, staring instead at the sewing in her lap. Lydia ate her salad in the tense silence, hoping Heather would elaborate on her earlier question.

Finally, Heather looked up, and the anger in her eyes startled Lydia. "You. Can. Not. Be. Serious."

Every word out of Heather's mouth sounded like its own sentence. Heather wasn't yelling, but this intense over-annunciation was almost more alarming. Lydia was still lost.

"Heather, I don't under—"

"Who even *are* you?" Heather cut across her words, never raising her voice but also making no effort to whisper. "You show up here, with some sad-sack story about your perfect little life getting all messed up. And what happens? Fran rescues you. You're an adult, Lydia. And Fran had to rescue you. Not only that, but she gave you a whole new life."

Even though Heather spat that last sentence at Lydia like an insult, Lydia completely agreed with her.

"I know, Heather, I didn't—"

Heather railed on, undeterred, "She gave you a job. A place to live. Friends. And what have you done for her? You brought your demon of a cat to her apartment. You never shut up about your stupid ex-husband. You push and push to teach classes no one needs. You barely even know how to sew. Now you accuse her of being a murderer? Killing two of her friends? Her *friends*, Lydia. Hers. You. Can. Not. Be. Serious."

Lydia's cheeks grew hot. She could only guess that her face was turning bright red. Everything Heather had said was true. Fran had saved her, given her a whole new life. But she didn't think that Fran was the killer!

"Heather, I just—" But before she could explain that she didn't think Fran had anything to do with the murders, Heather started again.

"You just what? Think Fran did it? That's insane. You want to know who I think really did it, Lydia? You want to keep playing amateur detective? How about I call over everybody in here and tell them what I think?"

Heather was getting louder and louder as she went. Other tables were starting to sneak glances over to them. Lydia wanted the floor to open up and swallow her.

"You."

Lydia looked up at Heather. Was she asking her something?

"*You* did it. That's what I think, Lydia. Why else would you come in here with some absurd distraction, trying to get me to doubt Fran, of all people?"

Lydia gasped. Heather was half right. It *was* supposed to be some absurd distraction. But it was never supposed to be about Fran.

Heather plowed on, "Everyone knows what a basket case you are about that ex-husband of yours. Going on and on and on about how you walked in on him with that other woman. How many times have we all heard that story? What happened, Lydia, huh? Did Brandon tell you that you sound like a psycho? Did you try to kiss him goodnight and he laughed at you? So, you stabbed him with dress shears? And then what? April found out? Tried to convince you to go to the police and turn yourself in? That's what April would do, wouldn't she? Too sweet and dumb for her own good."

It was Sergeant Simpson's theory all over again, but this time said with cruelty.

Heather's avocado toast sat uneaten as she packed up her sewing.

"Don't come to The Laurels. Don't call me. Trying to make me doubt Fran? I might have just suspected you before, Lydia, but now I know. Fran is the best person I have ever met. The only mistake Fran ever made was being nice to you. She should have sent you packing right back to Atlanta where you belong. Fran is too good a friend for someone like you. You know who the villain is in this story, Lydia? It. Is. *You*." And with that, Heather stood up and walked out of the restaurant without a single backward glance.

After Heather had left Shenanigans, the waiter came to the table. The poor kid—Lydia thought of anyone under twenty as a kid—had clearly been waiting to bring the check. Who knows, he might even have been listening to the whole conversation. How was this story going to make the rounds on the Peridot grapevine? Lydia immediately pictured Mary telling Martha she had heard that Heather slapped Lydia right in the face, if you can believe it.

The waiter was still hovering. Lydia tucked her credit card into the bill holder and did her best to avoid eye contact.

Lydia had no proof against Heather. Just a theory. Everyone had theories. Sergeant Simpson had been more than clear about his particular theory. And now so had Heather. Only Fran hadn't doubted her innocence. Fran had assumed Lydia was innocent, even though she had found both bodies. Even though everything pointed to Lydia, Fran had never wavered. But Heather was about to tell Fran that Lydia had more than wavered, that she had practically accused Fran. Lydia had made a mess of everything.

Well, not everything. Now she didn't have to worry about being alone in a car with Heather. She didn't have a ride to the Laurels, and more than that, she knew she couldn't show her face there after what had just happened.

Her cheeks felt hot, even in the cool air-conditioning of Shenanigans. She had to leave, and she had to tell Fran she wasn't coming to The Laurels. But Lydia didn't want to call Fran yet. When she walked out of Shenanigans, she went catty-corner on the square to the old-fashioned fudge shop. Lydia wasn't a huge fan of fudge, and when she wanted something sweet, she tended to bake something herself or head over to PeriDough. But she didn't want to see Kaleigh or anyone else that she knew, so she headed to the fudge shop.

Garrison's Chocolates and Sweets was an institution in the square, selling all sorts of handmade indulgences with a Peridot spin on them. Fran had told her that in the winter they sold flavored hot chocolates with snowflake marshmallows that town visitors would drink while riding around the square in a horse-drawn carriage, all under the Christmas lights that would festoon the buildings. Fran had promised her the most magical Christmas of her life that year.

Would she see it for herself?

As she waited in line, Lydia heard whispering. Her friends might be willing to pretend she wasn't a suspect—scratch that, the *main* suspect—but clearly other people had no such qualms. Maybe news of Heather's devastating rant had already hit the street. Lydia held her head high and tried to think about her next sewing project.

The jumpsuit felt wonderfully comfortable, plus it had pockets. Maybe she would make another one? She could ask Fran about that new linen. No. She couldn't.

"What can I get you?"

The voice interrupted her fabric and guilt-filled daydreams, a voice she vaguely recognized.

"What would you like?" the woman repeated, gesturing to the glass display cases of chocolate treats.

"Sarah Jane," Lydia said before she could stop herself.

The woman at the counter reeled back in surprise.

"Hi, I'm Lydia Bar—"

"I know who you are," Sarah Jane said, interrupting the introduction.

"Right. Could I have two pecan turtles, please?"

"Sure," Sarah Jane answered, her mouth ending in a closed, thin line. As Sarah Jane selected the two chocolates, Lydia tried desperately to think of what to say next.

"That'll be five fifty-six," Sarah Jane said while handing over a small white paper bag with the two caramels.

Lydia handed her a ten-dollar bill, and as Sarah Jane rang up the purchase, she called to the older man behind the ice cream counter, "Hey, Bill, I'm going to take my break."

Taking her change, Lydia walked slowly to the door as Sarah Jane took off her apron and met her, both walking together out into the hot summer sunshine.

* * *

Since it was the Monday of a long holiday weekend, court was closed, so there was no chance of running into Cynde on her usual bench. Lydia steered them in that direction, sitting on the first open bench next to the towering magnolia. What had Sergeant Simpson said about magnolias? They were older than bees?

"So," Sarah Jane interjected into Lydia's worries about very old bees.

"So," Lydia replied, turning to take stock of the waitress who had actually been married to her date.

Sarah Jane was pretty. Really pretty. Lydia had noticed it that night at Rosetti's, but she hadn't really paid attention, focused instead on how the date with Brandon was going. Now she paid attention.

The first thing that hit Lydia was that Sarah Jane looked awfully young to be divorced. Lydia was forty and looked it. Sarah Jane could have been a youthful thirty or a weathered twenty-two—it was too hard to say.

Her bright blond hair was pulled tightly back into a high ponytail, and her sharp-featured face was made all the more striking by heavily applied makeup. Lydia thought for a moment about her own morning "makeup" routine: moisturizer and a little mascara when she was feeling fancy.

Sarah Jane, on the other hand, must have a whole routine, judging by her lipliner, eye shadow, and blush. Her blue eyes stood out brightly behind the black eyeliner, though her cheek-bones, already sharp, seemed even more so under the copious amounts of blush. In a different version of reality, Lydia would have asked how she kept from sweating off all that makeup. Instead, in real life, Lydia needed to ask her about her dead ex-husband.

"You were the one who found him," Sarah Jane said.

It wasn't a question, but Lydia still nodded.

"And you found April Lanier too."

Again, not a question. Again, Lydia nodded.

"Sorry if I was rude the other night," Sarah Jane added.

Lydia was so confused by the change in direction that she almost couldn't remember what Sarah Jane was talking about.

Either not seeing her confusion or not caring, Sarah Jane continued, "I hadn't expected Brandon to come in the restau-rant on a date, you know?"

And suddenly, to Lydia, Sarah Jane looked painfully young.

"We broke up years ago. We just never got around to mak-ing the paperwork final. I was probably dragging my feet a bit. But we weren't together. I shouldn't have been surprised. He had every right to be on a date . . ."

Sarah Jane trailed off.

Lydia tried to comfort her, explaining, "For what it's worth, it was hardly a date. Fran, um, my friend Fran just wanted me to get to know some folks in town. Really."

Sarah Jane looked relieved. But Lydia was too curious to stop there, "None of us knew that Brandon had been married."

"Yeah. Well. We were high school sweethearts. Got married right after graduation."

Now that Sarah Jane had started to tell her story, the words came quickly, spilling out in a jumble.

"It was a shotgun wedding, you know. Brandon knocked me up spring of senior year, and my daddy demanded he do right by me. He would have anyway. Brandon is—was—a good man. He said we would be a family. And it wasn't his fault. And it wasn't my fault."

Lydia waited and didn't ask any of the questions in her mind.

"When she . . . we lost her . . . and I wasn't pregnant anymore, it was real hard on Brandon. He had such big dreams, you know? And here he was, still in Peridot, the last place he wanted to be. He had his book to write, and I guess that saved him. He wrote all the time, filling up pages and then burning them in a barrel in the backyard when he didn't like them. He wrote, and I stayed out drinking with friends. We got through it, I guess, but not together. We didn't even last a year."

Sarah Jane had given this whole monologue without looking over at Lydia.

"I thought maybe," she continued, still gazing straight ahead, "I thought maybe with him up here in Peridot, if I were around, maybe we could have another chance."

Sarah Jane ran her fingertips under her eyes, trying to keep any tears from messing up her makeup. Lydia noticed her bright-red nail polish from the other night was chipped and flaking off.

"I should have let him know I was in town. I was too embarrassed. I wanted to just run into him, see if he was as happy to see me as I was to see him," Sarah Jane admitted, fiddling in her purse for something. As she pulled out her vape pen, she asked Lydia one question: "Was he still writing?"

"Yeah. Yeah, he was. He said he was working on the next great American novel," Lydia replied.

Sarah Jane smiled. "I'm so glad," she said between drags on her vape pen. "Thanks for letting me know. Sorry if . . . sorry I was rude . . . or whatever the other night—" Sarah Jane's phone alarm interrupted her stammered apology. "Listen, my break is over. But can I ask a favor?"

Lydia had only disappointed or upset people lately, so she grabbed at a chance to do something for this lost young woman from the chocolate shop.

"Sure, sure, Sarah Jane—ask away."

"If you find his book, I really want . . . *need* to read it. Promise?"

"I promise," Lydia replied, even though she had no idea how to make good on her word.

Sarah Jane tucked her vape back in her bag, reapplied her lipstick, and walked back to the fudge shop. As she opened the door, she turned and gave Lydia a small wave.

It was a short walk from the bench to her apartment, but Lydia walked slowly, weighed down by the heat and the last few hours. The wide brick-paved sidewalks of Peridot Square made for easy walking, and the whole well-organized town center seemed to mock Lydia's own confusion.

Measure Twice might be closed, but the square was still full of day-trippers up from Atlanta for a getaway in the mountains. Hikers moved as a pack, strong legs carrying them to the outfitters for new gear. Local college girls laughed their way to the boutique, a flutter of sundresses and uncomfortable shoes.

There was crime tape around the shop and Brandon's apartment, but even Lydia had a hard time believing it meant murder. Of course, visitors assumed it was just a break-in or something else not that frightening.

What was she doing, promising people things? She had made a mess out of her own life. Heather would be on her way now, to tell Fran about the lunch, her suspicions, the whole disaster. She had to call Fran.

"Hey, Lydia, dear. Are you on your way with Heather? I was thinking we could have a little dessert this afternoon. Nothing as fancy as what you make, but maybe some ice cream? I don't know if I told you, but there's a caretaker up here on the mountain, Mr. Williams, and he brought me some local honey with lavender in it. I was thinking it might be good on some vanilla ice cream. Maybe with a little—"

"Fran."

"Yes?"

"Fran, I'm really tired."

"Of course, of course. What you have been through. What we have all been through . . ."

"If it is okay with you, I'm going to stay home this afternoon. I'll come see The Laurels another time."

"Absolutely, Lydia, absolutely. The house isn't going anywhere. Why don't you get some rest and call me tonight?"

Such a kind response. Because that was Fran.

"You still there, dear?"

"Sorry. I'm here. I'll call you later."

"Take care." And with that, Fran was gone.

* * *

Still holding the phone in her hand, Lydia walked to her apartment. She needed to sleep. It was only Monday. Friday night, she had put on a nice, newly made green dress and her best Birkenstocks, and she had gone to dinner with a younger man who worked at the bookstore nearby. It had all the makings of a Hallmark movie, that dinner at Rosetti's. Now it was Monday, and that younger man, the next great American author, was dead. Her friend April, nervous and eager to please, trying to bring poetry to Peridot, in love with her husband enough to eat a dinner of only brisket—her friend April was dead too.

Everyone, it seemed, had a bit of a motive. But only a bit. Cynde resented Brandon. Brandon had Clark's dog put down. Sarah Jane still loved her ex. Jeff only loved trains, but Lydia still couldn't discount him. Even the M's had insinuated that April was to blame for everything somehow. But no matter how she moved the pattern pieces across the fabric, she couldn't make it fit. Sergeant Simpson was right: she was suspect number one. And if she told him her theory about Heather? He would probably laugh her out of the police station. Or would he just arrest her right then and there?

Imagining herself in handcuffs, Lydia opened the door, noticing that Charlie was weirdly quiet. Was he asleep on her bed? Normally, the sound of her key in the door would bring him to the door, asking for a walk. Maybe he felt as tired as she did.

She leaned against the door, eyes closed, enjoying the blast of the air-conditioning. Her electric bill was going to be unpleasant. But worth it. Why hadn't Charlie come to the door? She opened her eyes.

"Wade?" Lydia tried to keep the surprise out of her voice but failed. She knew he was grieving, but why on earth was he in her apartment? More to the point, why was he sitting at her sewing table? Was he going to offer to drive her to the Laurels?

Time slowed.

Why was he at her sewing table, holding her rotary cutter, the sharp blade out and shining in the sun?

Chapter Fifteen

"Wade! What on earth are you doing here?" she added, her voice now sliding from surprised to angry.

"Hi, Lydia. You're back early," Wade said, smiling. He was handsome. There was no denying it. He wasn't Lydia's type; she liked her men a little more bookish and quirkier, but she knew Wade's broad shoulders, thick brown hair, and easy smile would charm most women. He had charmed April.

Right now, however, the smile wasn't charming; it was creepy. Even creepier, he was wearing gloves—blue latex hospital gloves.

Before Wade could continue, Charlie barked from her bedroom, and Lydia moved farther into the apartment on instinct, worried about her dog. As she moved toward the bedroom door, Wade stood and, more quickly than she would have thought possible, crossed behind her, locked the door, and turned to face her, one gloved hand still clutching her rotary cutter.

"Lydia," Wade said, as if they had simply run into each other at the bakery, "I think you should have a seat. We should talk." And with that, he gestured at her couch.

Lydia did the math quickly. She was five feet five and around two hundred pounds, so she wasn't exactly a slip of a woman. But Wade was at least six feet four and probably north of two hundred and fifty. Plus, he clearly lifted weights, while Lydia considered folding fabric her own version of cardio. Add he had a rotary cutter in one hand, and she only had her phone. If he wanted her to sit down, then she would sit down. So, she did.

She glanced at her hand, wondering how quickly she could dial 911, but Wade followed her eyes and snatched her phone. While still watching her, he set it on the ground and smashed it with a heavy, booted foot. He kicked the broken pieces out of the way and started to speak.

"I thought you would be home later. I thought you would be at Fran's. I'm sorry we're going to have to do it this way." Wade's shoulders raised in a shrug, as if they were talking about who would make the pasta salad for a cookout.

"Do what, Wade?" asked Lydia, still angry, even as she started to realize the gravity of the situation.

"You're going to die, Lydia."

Lydia shook her head as if she had water in her ears.

"I'm so sorry, Wade. I think I'm still in shock from everything that's happened. What were you saying now?"

"Lydia, you're going to die." Wade said slowly, like a teacher explaining something to a kindergartener.

"Why?" she responded, close to but not quite yelling. She didn't want to upset Wade, but the whole situation was so absurd she was having a hard time responding the right way.

"Oh, Lydia, haven't you figured it out yet?" How could someone so threatening manage to also look condescending?

Lydia hated Wade in that moment more than she had ever thought it possible to hate anyone. But he was still talking. "You did it. You killed Brandon because he spurned you. You killed April because she figured out you had done it and was going to turn you in. And now you're going to skip town, after leaving a note, confessing the horrible things you've done." Wade smiled, gesturing at typed-out note he had left on her sewing table. He had thought of everything.

Heather would believe it, after their argument. Of course. That was the whole reason he had encouraged her to doubt Heather. It only made Lydia look worse.

"And boy, are the police going to look hard for you, little Lydia." He ran his tongue against the corner of his open mouth.

"They won't find you, because you will be dead and sunk in Marsden Lake, but they'll look, and we'll all be sad and shocked, and somehow life will continue, and the town will heal, and everyone will take care of me, a widower who invited a murderer to his house for dinner. How tragic."

Lydia felt the blood drain from her face. She grabbed at her couch and gripped a throw pillow covered in pink unicorns, one of her first sewing accomplishments, made with Fran's patient help.

Fran. The shop. Unicorns. Lydia steadied herself. Wade hadn't won yet.

"I thought the dress shears were a nice touch, to be honest, if a bit much," Wade added, shaking his head as if reproaching the scissors for being an imperfect murder weapon.

"Brandon was easy, really. Once he started writing, he was dead to the world. Ha. Pun intended!"

Was Wade enjoying this? Lydia tried to smile in appreciation of the joke, anything to keep him talking.

"I had a key to his place, you know, for emergencies. He trusted us. Of course. Why wouldn't he? I just opened the door, walked in, and stabbed him in the neck, turned around, and walked out. I didn't lock the door. I wanted you to find him. I thought it would take a little longer. I didn't expect you to be quite so desperate, Lydia, walking over to see him again after your little dinner date. Pathetic. But it worked out even better!" Wade smiled at her with his lips slightly open, his tongue moving across his teeth, back and forth, back and forth.

Lydia didn't think she could feel any more scared, but the tooth-filled smile made her fear burn even more sharply.

"How did you know he would be there? What if we had still been at dinner? Or what if he had invited me in?" Lydia asked, genuinely curious, even in her dire circumstances.

Wade smirked. "Invite you in? Please. I don't know why Fran thought this 'date' was going to work to begin with, but it certainly wasn't going to end with you being invited in. A woman your age? Who looks like, well, who looks like you? Not a chance. Everyone knew he was taking you to Rosetti's. It wasn't exactly a secret. I just waited in my car, parked over by Shenanigans, and waited until I saw him go into his own apartment. Alone. Just like I knew he would. Lost in his own world, writing away."

That was it, wasn't it? Wade thought he knew everything. If she was going to get out of this alive, and she was, she told herself, she needed to appeal to his arrogance. That was the key.

"Wow, that was clever," she said, awkwardly even to her own ears.

Wade lost his smirk. She had misstepped. She had to get him back to bragging.

"I mean it. It wouldn't have occurred to me to just wait like that. And it never occurred to the police. They were so sure I did it. I guess they still are."

That helped. Wade seemed mollified and started to talk again.

"Of course, they are, Lydia. I led them right to you."

"But Wade," Lydia took a risk and pushed him a little further, "why kill Brandon at all?"

She held her breath. Would he end it now, lash out and slice her throat with the rotary cutter? Or would he wait to kill her, drag her out of the apartment, and sink her in a lake like he said?

"Oh, Brandon needed to die," Wade said as if starting a lecture to a slow student.

Lydia exhaled. Her luck had held. At least for now.

"He thought he was smarter than me. With his fancy class. I told him, I can find authors for the store, but, no, Brandon had to find his own poets." Wade said the last word with disgust.

"Poets? This is about poetry?" Lydia exclaimed before she could help herself. Her mom always used to say, when Lydia was growing up, that her mouth would get her in trouble. She had no idea how right she would turn out to be.

"One poet. Joe Stanton."

Before she could stop herself, Lydia's eyes went to the book April had given her, still sitting on her kitchen counter.

"Yes," Wade said, following her eyes, "that Joe Stanton. I told April I would find a poet, but she let Brandon do it. He insisted, saying he knew just the guy, a military guy. You heard her—she thought it was great, supporting another veteran."

Sensing Lydia's confusion, Wade continued. "I served with him. Joe Stanton. We served together, and he knows how I left the Marines. I was dishonorably discharged."

He waited for Lydia's reaction, but she just raised her eyebrows, forcing him to continue. "I don't expect a civilian like you to comprehend what I'm saying. But I'll try to explain it so that you can understand. I did not earn a Purple Heart in Kosovo. I deserted my unit and was dishonorably discharged. Joe could have told April if he had come here and found out. He would have recognized me immediately."

"That sounds embarrassing, Wade, but I still don't understand why anyone needed to die."

"Embarrassing? If Joe had found me, Lydia, I would have been tried in a court of law for stolen valor. The military does not appreciate someone pretending to have earned a Purple Heart. Stolen valor means prison time. I could have gone to prison, Lydia. Do you understand now? Joe Stanton was going to come to Peridot and destroy my life. April would know it was all a lie. Everyone would know it was all a lie."

For a moment, Lydia felt a pang of sympathy. Then she remembered herself: She was in her own apartment, held hostage by a murderer who had killed to cover up his lies and his shame. She didn't feel sympathy; she felt revulsion. But if she let that show, it might be her last mistake.

"I understand now, Wade, what was at stake for you. Your whole life."

Wade nodded, too engrossed in his own tale to notice if Lydia's voice rang false, as she was afraid it would.

"It is all Brandon's fault. I tried to convince him that Joe Stanton was the wrong call. But he wouldn't listen. He got suspicious. April would still be alive if it wasn't for Brandon. All he had to do was keep his big mouth shut. But he couldn't. And he has no one to blame but himself.

"He had already told her. You can see, Lydia, can't you, why April had to die too? Brandon might have ruined my marriage, but I could still have had my life. I could have had the bookstore, my place in this town, my reputation, my work with the cadets. April admitted that Brandon had told her about his suspicions, that he had started to connect the dots, had what she called 'concerns.' I thought I had done enough, killing Brandon, but he had told her before I could eliminate the threat.

"But that was what made April so amazing. Anyone else would have simply gone to the police. She should have gone to the police. Instead, she told me. She told me that Brandon said all these lies about me. Never, not for one moment, did she believe any of it." Wade let out an exhale and smiled like an old-time movie star thinking, "What a gal!"

Lydia wanted to vomit.

"That night, after you left for your stupid class"—Lydia flinched while some part of her also understood insults hardly mattered at this point—"April told me the whole story. How Brandon had reached out to Joe. Heard some things that 'concerned' him. He had pulled April aside at the store and started digging. How much did she really know about my past? Had she ever met anyone I served with? Seen any pictures? He insinuated I was a liar, Lydia. A liar!"

He was getting angrier. This was not what Lydia wanted; she wanted to keep him calm and keep him talking.

"What did you tell April?" Lydia asked, hoping to bring Wade back into storyteller mode.

It worked.

"I told her what I had always told her. Real soldiers didn't brag. Real soldiers don't talk about war. That was all. But then she started to ask the wrong questions, Lydia. The wrong questions."

"But what about the cadets?"

Wade stared at her.

Lydia knew it was pointless to dig for more details, but she also knew that the longer she kept Wade talking, the more time she had to plan some sort of escape. If Wade was talking, Lydia was alive. She wanted to keep it that way.

"You said that when April died, you were training the ROTC cadets at the college," Lydia reminded him. At the time, she had found it a convincing alibi and so had the police.

Wade laughed. For a moment, Lydia felt like it was all a horrible dream. She had fallen asleep at Wade and April's house over her ridiculous plate of meat. Wade was laughing at her. Because that was the sound of her friend, Wade, laughing at a joke, a gaffe of Lydia's.

Then she felt the sweat running down her back. Nope, this was not a dream. Wade was laughing as she tried to understand how he had gotten away with murder.

"Lydia, Lydia, Lydia. They're kids! Kids who think they know what it means to serve." At this, Wade laughed harder, wiping at his eyes. "You know what you say to a kid like that? You say, 'Cadet, I am going to need you to say I was here yesterday. Can you do that, cadet? Can you follow a direct order, cadet?' *Ha!* They eat it right up. Think they're a part of something important. It's almost too easy—it really is."

"Okay, so you weren't with the ROTC kids, but I still don't understand how you killed April," Lydia said aloud, and added silently to herself, *Keep talking, Wade, keep talking.*

"I'll admit, killing April was harder, because . . ."

Lydia expected Wade to talk about his love for his wife, but he quickly continued, "I had already committed to framing you, and I had to keep the ruse going. That was trickier. But you know April—such a trusting soul. The night Brandon died, she fell asleep reading, and it never occurred to her that I could have left the house. That it could have been me. Who killed him. Even with Brandon dead, she still confided in me. She still shared all her plans with me. It was simple, once I really put my mind to it. April made it easy, really, when you think about it. I just followed her to the store. She left the door open for you, of course. Always too trusting, our April."

Again, Wade smiled, showing his teeth.

"She was tired, and it was easy enough to get her to rest her head on the table. Then one blow to the back of the head with a tire iron. Simple. Tipping over the machine, now that was hard, but I wanted it to be in your store when she was waiting for you. It always had to point to you, Lydia. And it did.

"They already suspect you, Lydia. All this is going to do is confirm their suspicions. And you know how the police love to be right. We can't deprive them of that, now, can we? We all know you're a talker, Lydia. It makes sense you would want to leave a note, saying you are so, so sorry." Wade made an exaggerated sad face at her, then smiled again.

"Poor Lydia, overwhelmed with guilt, confesses and leaves town, never to be seen again."

Lydia couldn't think of anything else to say, any more questions to ask. A whole life of talking too much, and now when it mattered, her brain was empty. She tried to stall for time.

"Wade, no one is going to believe that."

"What choice do they have? You know yourself that Simpson is grasping at straws. No one wants to believe we have a killer in sweet little Peridot. I'm giving them the answer they already want. You're the easiest solution, Lydia. The only solution."

"What about Heather?"

"Ha! You really believed that, didn't you? Heather had an alibi, Lydia. Her whole knitting group, making hats for babies, or whatever. Only an idiot would believe Heather was the murderer!"

Lydia laughed and then clamped her hand over her mouth. Perfect—she would die laughing at the wrong moment. Too fitting. Wade was right, she really was an idiot. Then she realized how quiet the apartment was. Charlie had stopped barking. She didn't feel like laughing anymore. She felt like crying.

"It's all on you, Lydia. Has been from the start. Sergeant Simpson can spend the rest of his life looking for the woman who tricked him and got away. You'll be dead, of course, at the bottom of Lake Marsden. It won't hurt, Lydia. I promise. One quick hit with the tire iron, and then it goes over the edge of the boat with you. It all fits. It's almost beautiful," Wade added, stepping toward her. She was out of time. It was over.

"What about my pets? No one is going to believe I ran away without them, Wade. You know that," she added, close to pleading.

"You want to take your pets? You want your little dog and stupid cat to end up at the bottom of a lake with you? That is more depraved than I expected from our sweet little Lydia, I can tell you that. But you know what? You make a good point. No loose ends. Time to get your pets and leave town, Lydia. Forever."

It had worked. Wade pushed open her bedroom door.

Charlie came out first, barking, but quickly went up to Wade, his tail wagging.

Wade looked at Lydia and pulled out a piece of bacon from his pocket, giving it to Charlie. So that was why Charlie seemed to like Wade so much at the park. Bacon. Clearly Charlie wasn't going to get them out of this mess.

Lydia sent up a silent prayer to God and to the M's, figuring they had God's ear if He wasn't inclined to hear from His wayward Lydia just at that moment. Charlie was happily waiting for a walk, as if he believed everything was going to be okay. But not Baby Lobster. Baby Lobster padded over to the couch and took stock of the room, turning her little cat face around as if doing a survey. She saw the fear on Lydia's face. She saw the rotary cutter in Wade's hand.

Wade was talking, telling Lydia to get the leash, bragging about the bacon trick, but she barely heard him, watching instead as her cat crouched against the sofa cushion, coiled like a spring.

Lydia would later admit that she couldn't say for certain how much the cat understood the situation. But that was just something she said to other people. In that moment, Lydia had no doubt. Baby Lobster, still raggedy from her run-in with the Scotch tape, knew Lydia was in danger. And she knew, in her weird, scratchy Baby Lobster way, that Lydia had saved her, taken her home, and loved her. Now it was her turn.

"Okay, it's go time, Lydia. Lydia, do you hear me? Get a leash for that dog and whatever you need for that . . ." And with that Wade turned to face Baby Lobster.

And Baby Lobster launched. As if from a slingshot. Hissing, feet first, claws bared. With the most beautiful precision, that cat landed right on Wade's face.

Lydia had hoped the cat would cause some sort of chaos, buying her time to try to escape, but this was more than she had even prayed for.

Wade dropped the rotary cutter and grabbed desperately at the cat, lurching about the living room as his screams filled the small apartment.

Chapter Sixteen

Wade stumbled away from the door, cursing and yelling. His huge hands clamped down on the cat, desperately trying to pull her off. Baby Lobster looked comically small against his large hands, but she had dug her nails into the soft flesh of his face and was holding on for dear life.

Lydia darted to the front door, unlocked it, and ran straight outside and down the stairs, bursting onto the main street of Peridot like a maniac.

Sergeant Simpson caught her by the shoulders as she ran smack into him, sobbing for someone, anyone, to call the police.

"The police? Calm down, Miss Barnes. I *am* the police. Miss Barnes, take a deep breath," the last of these statements was said as a command and Lydia immediately stopped wailing and took a breath. Teacher voice was powerful, but she guessed cop voice was even stronger.

"He's upstairs. Baby Lobster got him," she tried to explain, still breathless and gesturing up to her apartment above the store.

Sergeant Simpson looked at her, clearly worried she was having some sort of episode, and asked, "What's this about a lobster, miss?"

Before she could answer, her apartment door slammed open, and Wade stumbled out onto the walkway just as he finally pulled the cat from his face and flung her away.

Lydia held her breath but quickly released it as Baby Lobster landed on her feet and hissed at Wade. Then she padded back into the apartment, as if nothing had happened. That cat was indestructible. She had left claw punctures on Wade's neck and both cheeks, and blood ran down his face like a terrible version of tears. He didn't have the rotary cutter, but he was still wearing his gloves, the blue latex shocking against his otherwise casual weekend outfit.

Lydia stepped behind Sergeant Simpson and shouted, "He did it! He killed them! Brandon *and* April. And he tried to kill me!"

Wade froze, and for a moment, it felt like time stopped. Lydia had heard people say that before. About their weddings, the moment they were fired, or some other expected major life event. She hadn't really believed them. She did now.

No one moved. No one spoke.

"Get back here, you little . . .!" Wade screamed.

But Sergeant Simpson cut him off, yelling up to the walkway, "You okay there, Wade?" as if Wade weren't bleeding, screaming, in latex gloves in front of Lydia's apartment, about to call her a name the M's didn't even know existed.

The truth hit Lydia hard, and judging by the look on Wade's face, he had been smacked by the same realization. Maybe, just maybe, if he had come out of her apartment and claimed to be the victim, then maybe he would have had a chance to keep up the pretense, to sell his version of events. But that is not what had happened. In the heat of the moment, he had let the mask drop. He looked like he wanted to kill her, and everyone could see it. Especially Sergeant Simpson.

Lydia moved behind the sergeant. She knew, logically, that Wade was no longer a threat, but that did not stop her from shaking in fear.

"Wade, buddy, why don't you have a seat right there on the walkway. That's right. Just have a seat. Let's all calm down for a minute." And with that, he freed his walkie-talkie from his belt and called in backup.

While they waited, Sergeant Simpson gestured Lydia over to a bench, all the while keeping his eyes on Wade and his hand on his gun holster.

Looking at Sergeant Simpson, Lydia pointed at her apartment.

Shakily, she asked, "Can someone . . . will someone . . . my dog . . . my cat . . ."

"Don't worry about that, Miss Barnes. I will make sure your pets are taken care of."

She slumped down on the bench, relieved and out of words to say.

Lydia had no idea if the rest of the police came quickly or slowly. Time didn't matter anymore. She just sat, staring at the Measure Twice storefront window until it was time to get back into a patrol car yet again and head back to the station—yet again.

They must have cuffed Wade and dragged him away at some point, but Lydia never looked up to where he waited for the police, and once she was in the patrol car, she never looked back.

But even though she tried to pretend he didn't even exist, she could still hear him hollering.

First, he was shouting that they had the wrong person. Why weren't they arresting Lydia? Couldn't they see she had attacked him? That got him nowhere. Then he stopped shouting and used his most official military voice, demanding to see who was in charge, threatening to have people fired, asking them if they knew who he was, how he had served his country.

Lydia wanted to cover her ears with her hands, but she couldn't seem to get her hands to cooperate. Lies. It was all lies, always had been.

Finally, he tried pleading. The last she heard of Wade's booming voice was a plea to be gentle with the man who had just lost his wife.

As they drove out of the town square, she could just make out the words, "I've been through so much."

How broken did a person have to be to lie like that? Just a few hours ago, Lydia would have heard that and been completely convinced.

She pressed her forehead against the window of the police car and looked at the back of Sergeant Simpson's head. The car smelled slightly of aftershave. Did people still wear aftershave? Where did they even sell aftershave? Lydia tried to imagine but found her mind falling short. She was too tired and too scared to delve into the mysteries of Sergeant Simpson's personal grooming.

Lydia knew déjà vu meant experiencing something for the first time but having it feel familiar. But was there a term for experiencing something for the second or third time and feeling like it was stuck on repeat? Just like she walked Charlie each morning, would she do this drive to the police station each afternoon? What a nightmare.

They rode in silence, but at least this time it was Sergeant Simpson driving her, and she didn't have to talk about *Dungeons & Dragons* or handguns. He didn't even mention the magnolia tree as they drove by, and Lydia was relieved. She didn't have it in her to wonder about bees right now or aftershave. Or how Geraldine whatever-her-name-was knew how to get an elephant. She never wanted to wonder about anything ever again.

* * *

Back at the station, Lydia didn't wait to be shown into the interrogation room this time. She just walked straight in, sat down, and put her head in her hands. Sergeant Simpson followed her in.

Third time's a charm? The rule of three? Good things come in threes? She chuckled quietly.

"Now, what exactly is funny, do you think?" Sergeant Simpson asked.

Lydia swallowed her laughter and brought her face out of her hands.

"Hi, Sergeant. Nothing is funny. I just keep ending up in this room. Have you seen the movie *Groundhog Day*? It's this nineties movie with Bill Murray . . ."

224

She was rambling and she could tell. Sergeant Simpson just pursed his lips together and raised one very bushy eyebrow.

That man could give a master class in wordless communication. She shut her mouth, hoping he would say something, but he just waited, raising that same eyebrow a touch higher.

Fine.

"Wade killed Brandon. And Wade killed April. And Wade was going to kill me."

Now it was Lydia's turn to try her hand at facial expressions. Since there wasn't a mirror in the room, she couldn't be sure she was succeeding, but she tried to go for a look that said, *"See, I wasn't the murderer,"* but that was a lot to say with her eyebrows.

He relented. "It certainly seems that way. Can you tell me what happened today?"

What happened today. What had happened today?

"This morning, I took my dog, Charlie, for a walk in the park."

Sergeant Simpson nodded, clearly remembering her habit from the last two interrogations.

Lydia continued, "And when I was at the park, I saw Wade. I was—well, I was worried about him, losing April like that." Lydia felt a wave of nausea crash over her as she said the words. Wade hadn't lost April after all.

Sergeant Simpson waited patiently for her to continue, "Because I didn't know, at the time. Well, anyway, I sat down to talk to him, and Wade asked who I thought had . . . and I told him that I thought maybe Heather had . . ."

For once, Lydia had managed to surprise the gruff man sitting across the table from her. She wanted to be proud but was simply too exhausted to take any pleasure in his reaction.

"Heather Moulton? Now why on earth would you believe that?" he asked, dropping the now-expected "Miss Barnes" in his disbelief.

"I know, I know. I hate that I suspected her. Believe me. You cannot make me feel worse about this than I already do. You had asked me if anyone hated me. And well, Heather really doesn't like me . . ."

Lydia shook her head, thinking about how much worse that relationship would soon be.

"Wade told me not to let her know I suspected her. But I had plans with her. So, when I went to lunch at Shenanigans with Heather I tried to throw her off the scent and just made a mess of the whole thing. She thought I suspected Fran . . ."

Sergeant Simpson silently mouthed, "What?"

"I didn't! I just. And she was so mad. She read me the riot act. In Shenanigans. It was awful. After I got some pecan turtles. And talked to Sarah Jane. Then I called Fran and told her I wasn't going to come up to The Laurels with Heather. I didn't tell her why. I was too ashamed. I went home, and that's how I surprised Wade, setting up my staged flight from Peridot, after taking the blame for both murders." Lydia stopped, waiting to see if Sergeant Simpson had questions.

He remained quiet.

"Wade thought I would go to The Laurels and make a mess of all my friendships, leaving him time to stage my apartment, but I came back early and surprised him."

"And then what happened?"

At least Sergeant Simpson hadn't called her stupid. Not yet. "Well, I wanted to keep him talking so he wouldn't hurt me, and it worked; he kept talking and talking about why he'd killed Brandon and why he'd killed April and how he was going to drop my body in a lake where no one would ever find me."

Sergeant Simpson let out a slow, soft whistle.

"Yeah. I thought maybe he was going to kill me right then and there. But he wanted it to look like I had left town, so you would blame me and stop looking for any other suspects. He said he was going to kill me and sink me in Marsden Lake. But we had to leave the apartment first."

With that, they both fell silent. When she talked about the events of the weekend, Lydia could distance herself from the horror of what had happened to her, to her friends, to the town. But she had just said something that couldn't be a story, couldn't be told from any sort of distance. Wade had planned to kill her and sink her body in a lake, where no one would find her. They wouldn't even know to look for her. What would Fran have told her family? What would they have come to believe, talking it over at PeriDough? How long before the story started to make sense and the truth of who Lydia was wore away? It was bad enough to die. Wade had wanted her to be hated and then forgotten.

"But that didn't happen, now did it, Miss Barnes?"

Lydia pulled herself back from the darkness of her thoughts to answer him, "No. No, it didn't. I told Wade that no one would believe I left town without my pets. Thankfully, Wade agreed."

She continued, "I figured . . . I just adopted my cat—Baby Lobster? That's my cat's name. And she is, um, spirited. When he let them out of my bedroom to get them out of the house with me, she—the cat, Baby Lobster—well, you saw . . . she jumped right on his face and I got away. Wade had broken my phone, so I ran down into the street, looking for help. You were there for that part, Sergeant." Lydia managed a watery smile.

"Indeed, I was," he answered, returning the small smile with one of his own. "It would seem that I owe you an apology, Miss Barnes. I had this all wrong."

"Thank you?" Lydia replied, uncertain if she was meant to accept the apology or dismiss it as unnecessary. But something more than the intricacies of apologies from the authorities was bothering her.

"But what were you doing there?" she asked.

"What's that?"

"Why were you at my apartment? No one was taking evidence at the shop; I noticed when I walked home. You told me that I was your main suspect. That I was your *only* suspect. Were you there to watch me?"

Sergeant Simpson looked uncomfortable for the first time. "I know I told you that, miss. In terms of evidence, you were our only suspect. But. Well. It didn't sit right with me. And I have been at this long enough to listen to my gut when it tells me something is wrong. Wade's first alibi was April. And at the time, I had no reason to doubt that. But when April died, I started to wonder. Easy enough to get his wife to cover for him. Then for her murder Wade's alibi for that was some kids from the ROTC program he helps out with. Here you have a Purple Heart–decorated soldier in charge of some kids who are still doing math homework each night. Seemed to me like if anyone could figure themselves two false alibis, it would be Wade. So why was all the evidence pointing at you, Miss Barnes? It felt, well, it felt a little too easy. I decided to pay our friend Wade a visit. I was planning on heading over to the bookstore. But you got to me first."

"Yes. Yes, I did."

"I imagine you have a lot more you can tell me. Isn't that so, Miss Barnes?"

She nodded her head yes. There was still so much to explain. For a moment, she wondered if they would let her take a quick nap, just put her head on her arms on the table, close her eyes for a moment.

Sergeant Simpson was still talking. "But I propose that can keep until tomorrow. We have Wade—Mr. Lanier—here. He can answer our questions. You need to get a good meal and a good night's sleep."

Lydia wanted to hug the man. Was that illegal? She almost giggled. He was right, she needed food and rest as soon as possible. But . . .

"To be clear, though, Miss Barnes, you may not go home."

"But . . ."

"Your entire apartment is a crime scene. In fact, before you leave the station, we will have our forensic techs swab you for evidence. It's protocol, you understand."

Lydia nodded, even though she wasn't sure she understood at all. Where was she supposed to go now?

Chapter Seventeen

E ven though Lydia's apartment was a crime scene, Sergeant Simpson agreed to let her grab Charlie and Baby Lobster and a few things to tide her over, but he had also made it clear it would be a few days at least before she could go home for good.

She could ask Fran to let her stay in at The Laurels, but Lydia still felt ashamed about the whole conversation at Shenanigans, even if Fran had no idea.

Instinctively, Lydia reached into her bag for her cell phone, remembering a moment too late that it was shattered. And evidence. Two months ago, Lydia had shown up in Peridot, brokenhearted and lost. Now she stood in the police station, and it felt like all she had built in that time had washed away.

"Simon says, *Go!*"

Lydia startled and looked around her. Cynde was standing in the station, smiling at her.

"Simon who?" Lydia asked, confused and still lost in her own thoughts.

"It's a joke, Lydia. Because you're standing still in the middle of the police station. So, you know, Simon says you can walk now?" Cynde was speaking a little slowly. Lydia realized she must look a little absurd, even daft.

Lydia looked at her friend and asked, through tears, "Can Simon tell me what to do?"

"I don't know about that, but I sure can. Sergeant Simpson here called me and told me what was going on. He said you might want a place to stay tonight? I thought I might just swing by and see. Would you like to stay at my house tonight, Lydia?"

Why was everyone in this town so dang nice? Lydia started back into a shame spiral over how she had doubted Heather, but she realized that Cynde was waiting for an answer.

"Oh, Cynde, I would love to."

"You know, don't you, that I'm not much of a cook?" Cynde said, smiling.

Lydia let out a weak laugh, but she wasn't done asking for favors, adding, "Cynde, please feel free to say no. I don't mean to be rude. I know this is last minute. I'm sure you . . . I'm not trying to . . ." Lydia petered out.

"Oh, the pets!" Cynde interrupted. "Of course, bring the dog and the cat!"

She surprised Cynde with a long hug and then let her friend steer her out of the station and to her old beat-up minivan, which seemed better than a limo to Lydia in that moment.

The drive to her apartment was quiet. Cynde played her favorite band, the Indigo Girls, and Lydia tried to think of nothing at all.

Thankfully, Cynde offered to give Lydia a hand retrieving the pets. That meant that when Jeff popped out of his apartment to waylay Lydia, he got Lydia and Cynde instead.

"Lydia, it is so good to see you. So, so good. So good to see you. Wow."

Cynde tried to hide her confusion. She was new to Jeff's weird blend of friendliness and sleaze.

"I saw the police have been in your apartment. Lydia, I was right, wasn't I? This just proves it. Absolutely. You aren't safe. I'm sure your friend here"—he gestured at Cynde without asking for her name—"could take your animals. It's time for you to come stay with me. And the trains."

Jeff said the last line as it were the coup de grâce.

Cynde coughed to cover her laugh. Jeff ignored her, waiting on what he believed to be Lydia's inevitable acceptance of his invitation.

"Jeff, that's so thoughtful, really. It's definitely been a crazy day. I'll have to tell you all about it some other time. Simpson doesn't want me staying at my place, so I'm just getting Charlie and Baby Lobster and then heading over to stay with my friend, Cynde. But thanks so much for offering."

Even though Jeff only had a low circle of hair around his head at ear level, he swept his hand over the top of his head as if fixing his coif.

"I'll be here, Lydia." With that enigmatic claim, he turned and went back into his apartment.

Cynde made quick work of gathering the animals and a few essentials and led Lydia back down to the minivan. More Indigo Girls. More trying not to have any thoughts. And before she knew it, Lydia was walking into Cynde's house.

Charlie, clearly exhausted from the showdown with Wade, hopped onto Cynde's couch, brought his nose snug against his tail, and went right to sleep.

"Oh, I can . . . do you want me to . . . is it okay . . .?" Lydia felt like she was starting to forget how to speak like a regular person.

"It's fine—it is. He's had a hard day too, haven't you, Charlie?"

Hearing his name, Charlie snuggled a little deeper into the couch, making himself more than at home.

Baby Lobster was still in her carrier. When Lydia had gone to the police station, they had kept the pets at her apartment. They had also, she learned later, attempted to swab Baby Lobster's claws. Lydia hadn't witnessed the debacle, but she couldn't help but notice when she and Cynde had gone to collect the cat that a few of the officers had Band-Aids on their hands and were casting dark glances in Baby Lobster's direction.

Lydia leaned over and let her little hero free. Door open, Baby Lobster cautiously padded out of the carrier and into the living room. Holding her breath, Lydia waited for her cat to do something ridiculous or miraculous. Instead, the cat meandered into the kitchen, found a delivery box by the recycling bin, curled up, and followed Charlie's lead by falling fast asleep.

Lydia looked around the kitchen. It was spotless. The whole house was remarkably clean. Lydia glanced at the spice rack and had her suspicions confirmed: alphabetized.

"What are you in the mood for?" Cynde asked, admiring Baby Lobster fast asleep in her new home.

"Cynde, it's so nice of you to take me—well, *us*—in. I don't want to be any trouble. How about we do delivery? My treat?" Lydia had noticed the delivery menus tacked to the refrigerator and was pleased to see Cynde smile at the suggestion.

"Well, if you insist. How about the Amazing Wok?"

"Sounds perfect. Can I use your phone? I don't have my phone because—"

"Why don't I order? You go have a seat with Charlie while Baby Lobster settles in," Cynde laughed.

Lydia felt tears building. The simple kindness of someone else doing what needed to be done was almost too much. She nodded and went to the couch, hearing Cynde listing off an impressive number of dishes to the person was on the other side of the call.

Cynde finished ordering and came and joined Lydia on the couch. Casting a smile at Charlie, Cynde picked up the TV remote and turned on an old rerun of *House Hunters International.* They sat in companionable silence, waiting for the food to be delivered, while a couple debated the pros and cons of a series of beachfront villas in Puerto Rico. It was more than Lydia could have asked for and exactly what she needed.

The food came quickly, and the driver called Cynde by name as he handed over the heavy brown bag.

In no time at all, the small kitchen table was an impressive tableau of half-empty containers and entirely empty bowls. Lydia hadn't felt that hungry, but once the steaming hot Chinese food was in front of her, she showed no restraint. Not even any dignity.

Cynde understood that Lydia needed the comfort of comfort food, nudging more lo mein and chicken and broccoli into her bowl each time she emptied it. They ate mostly in silence, happily crunching and slurping their way through the many boxes.

Lydia could see the sign at the entrance of the square from the window in Cynde's kitchen, declaring Peridot's founding date and population number, the words all written in the bright green of the town's namesake gem. Lydia wondered if she could find a linen to match that shade.

"Will you stay?"

"What?" Lydia asked, pulling herself back from thoughts of Peridot-green outfits.

"With everything that has happened, will you stay in Peridot?" Cynde asked, not unkindly.

"Oh" was all that Lydia could manage as a reply.

She was embarrassed to admit to her friend that she hadn't even considered not staying.

Cynde busied herself cleaning up the meal, giving Lydia some time to think of an answer.

Weirdly, Lydia found herself thinking of her college days, when she had moved off-campus with a few friends. There were petty arguments about dishes and who paid for groceries, whose boyfriends could stay over, the normal struggles of having roommates. After one bad argument, Lydia had gone out with Graham and gotten drunk, which was unusual for her, and debated moving out of the apartment and in with Graham. Back in the apartment, she had confided in one friend that she had almost decided to move out. She had expected to be soothed, but instead her friend had simply looked at her and asked, "Why did you come back, then?"

Was that what was happening now? Was Cynde, always so kind, trying to tell her that she couldn't stay in Peridot anymore? Even though everyone would find out that Wade was the murderer, not Lydia, was that enough to let her back in? What had Fran said? Small arguments ran deep in close communities. What if Lydia was never really forgiven?

Lydia could feel the tears in her eyes.

"Hey, Cynde, thanks again for dinner and for . . . everything. I'm going to take Charlie on his nighttime walk, if that's okay with you?"

* * *

Charlie shuffled along slowly, clearly exhausted from the day, like Lydia. She looked at the sign for the town square, lit up in the summer dark, and then turned to walk down the side street Cynde's house was on, going the opposite direction. She couldn't bring herself to walk through Peridot tonight.

The side streets were quiet, but at least the air had cooled a bit. Was this her home? Lydia wanted to call Fran and then immediately felt ashamed. What right did she have to expect Fran to guide her through every decision in her life? Fran deserved better. Heather had been right about that, at least.

At least Heather would realize Lydia wasn't a murderer. Did that count as an upside? She thought back to that fight among her roommates so many years ago. She hadn't moved out. And weeks later, when she admitted to her friend how heartbroken the suggestion to move had made her, her friend had been stunned. Sage, that was her name. She'd been having a bad week and been annoyed, spoken sharply, that was all. It had never occurred to her that Lydia would take it to heart. They'd gotten pizza, laughed about it.

Back when she taught middle school, Lydia had had a knack for diffusing arguments, winning over jaded or difficult students. It was a point of pride. She told herself she could read people. But that wasn't really the case, was it? She could read kids, see the hurt or frustration behind their jostling and bragging.

Why was it so much harder with adults? Again and again, that weekend, she had thought she understood someone, only to be proven wrong. For one wild moment, she imagined asking Charlie if she should stay in Peridot or not. Didn't people do that—have animals bet on horse races or trade stocks? She could write down *yes* and *no* on pieces of paper and see which one he fell asleep on first.

She looked down at her beloved dog and saw he was close to falling asleep on the sidewalk. "Sorry, Charlie," she said, and she steered them both back to Cynde's.

* * *

Cynde's sewing room doubled as her guest room, and she bustled around the room, tidying up fabric and notions as she kept talking.

With most of the clutter tucked away in decorative baskets, Cynde opened the sleeper sofa. An ottoman nearby stored the bedding, and in the blink of an eye, Cynde had made up the bed and was explaining where the shower was and when coffee would be ready in the morning.

Lydia sat down on the bed, now cozy with one of Mary and Martha's distinctive quilts.

Cynde was still talking, but one look at Lydia, seated with her hands in her lap, staring into space, must have told her that her friend needed sleep, not the ins and outs of staying over.

"I'm going to let you hit the hay, but I just wanted to say, I figured you were pretty rushed when you packed, so I thought . . .," Cynde gestured at the lump of fabric on the pull-out bed.

Lydia reached out and felt the soft flannel. It was an old-fashioned nightgown, worn thin and faded, the floral design more a blur than a pattern.

"This is perfect—thank you, Cynde."

"All right, I'm going to . . ."

"Cynde?"

Cynde had stood to leave but now sat down on the edge of the pull-out bed. "Yes, Lydia?"

"Can I talk to you?"

"Lydia! Of course you can talk to me!"

"No, no. I know that. I can't thank you enough for having me, for having all of us here. I guess I just wanted to talk to you about something . . . something I'm ashamed of."

Cynde waited.

"Before. Before everything tonight. I thought that Heather was the murderer, and she was framing me. On purpose."

Cynde stayed silent, but her eyes went wide with shock.

With the admission made, Lydia began to weep.

Cynde rubbed her back, and finally Lydia stopped crying.

Cynde passed her a tissue and asked, gently, "Why on earth would you believe that about Heather? I'm not saying she's a warm and cuddly young thing, but a murderer?"

"I've been asking myself the same thing all day, believe me! The thing is. Everything that Fran has done for me. This new chance at life at Measure Twice. It felt . . . sometimes it feels too good to be true. The apartment. The job. The chance to teach the class. And the last time I thought my life was perfect . . . the last time I thought my life was perfect, my husband was sleeping with my teaching assistant, and everything I thought I had was a lie. A stupid, tacky, preppy lie." Lydia winced, thinking about her ex-friend, Emma Grace, in her perfect sundresses and headbands. She was nothing like Lydia. That was what Graham had really wanted. Not Lydia at all.

"Cynde, the last time I thought my life was too good to be true, I was right."

Cynde looked at Lydia and said, "I know that was horrible for you, Lydia. Heartbreak is . . . well, there is no greater pain than not being able to be with the person you love. I know that. But your ex? Your ex is a punk. A total punk."

The way Cynde said it made Lydia feel like Graham had just been cussed out. She smiled.

"But," Cynde continued, "Heather is not a punk. Heather is human—don't get me wrong. She can be awfully judgmental about my fabric choices." Cynde smiled. "Heather isn't perfect, but she's a good person. And so are you, Lydia."

"Lately it seemed like Fran was mad at me. She's been colder to me, and I thought maybe, maybe she was regretting making me such a big part of her life here. Maybe she knew Heather hated me. Maybe . . ."

Cynde nodded, "Lydia, that's what I am trying to tell you. People are complicated. I have known Fran for a long time. I think you might be right, that something is weighing on her. Now I mean in this is in the kindest way, Lydia, but even though Fran loves you and wants you to be happy, you aren't the only thing going on in her life."

Lydia tried to hide the hurt look she knew was on her face. Why could she never have a poker face?

"I'm not saying you aren't important to her. You are. So is Heather. But Fran has her own troubles. Have you asked her what's wrong, told her you noticed she's been off?"

"No." Lydia was embarrassed to admit she had done nothing of the kind. "I should have. I will now, if . . . do you think, when she finds out the mess I've made, that Fran will ever forgive me? That Heather will?" Lydia asked her friend.

"I know they will. But the question is, Lydia, when are you going to start forgiving yourself? I love living in Peridot. And I think you could love living here too. But a small town demands you to live with your mistakes and imperfections. I'm not trying to scare you off, Lydia. I just want you to think about it, okay?"

Lydia nodded, exhausted.

"But what am I saying? You don't need to think about anything tonight. Not after the day you've had. You need to sleep. And I need to get out of here so you can do just that. There's a shower in the bathroom through that door." Cynde gestured to a door that would lead to the en suite bathroom. "I'll see you tomorrow, Lydia. Everything will look better in the morning. It always does." With that final encouragement, Cynde rose and left the room.

Suddenly, Lydia was desperate to be out of her clothes, the clothes she had been wearing when she had found Wade in her apartment, the clothes she had been wearing when she learned the truth. She went to the bathroom and took a long, hot shower. After the first few minutes, Lydia sat down in the bathtub and let the water run over her until she started to grow cold.

Alone in the small room, Lydia changed into the nightgown and slid under the quilt. She heard the soft clink of Charlie's tags as he pushed his nose against the door Cynde had left slightly open and came into the room. He jumped on the bed, and as he circled and circled, Lydia thought about turning off the bedside light.

Then she heard the lighter steps of Baby Lobster padding toward the bed. Lydia hummed "Rocky Raccoon" as the hero of the hour curled up on the opposite corner to Charlie's, at the end of the bed, like a second sentry there to guard Lydia's sleep. *How am I ever going to fall asleep?* she wondered, still humming softly.

She flicked off the light and, without even trying, fell fast asleep.

No one died in her dreams that night. But she still had nightmares. Now in her sleep, dream Lydia walked the town square, stopping at the shops she had come to know and love. She stopped at The Pampered Pantry, eager to see what epicurean delights Clark had displayed in his window, but as she gazed into the window, Clark walked up and turned the sign from "Open" to "Closed."

Strange. Dream Lydia continued on, this time pausing at Blessed Again, hoping to see some Pyrex from outside the shop window. Mary and Martha came toward her, from inside the shop, and locked the door, turning the sign to "Closed," just like Clark had. Lydia kept walking.

Now she stood outside of Measure Twice.

She marveled at the new display. Fran and Heather had clearly used quilted letters to spell "Your Heart's at Home in Peridot," and then hung the letters across the window. It was a wonderful, scrappy, brightly colored love letter, not only to the town but also to sewing since Lydia knew those letter blocks were not a quick make.

Lydia went to walk into the shop to congratulate her friends, only to find the door was locked. Standing with her hand in the doorknob, Lydia looked up to see Fran and Heather flip the sign in the window to "Closed."

All night, in her dreams, Lydia walked past each shop in Peridot's town square, and each time she passed, the signs flipped from "Open" to "Closed," over and over, as the night wore on.

Chapter Eighteen

One week. It had only been one week since Labor Day Weekend. Since the worst weekend of Lydia's life. But as she walked Charlie down to the park, it seemed like the tragedy of that long weekend had taken place in another lifetime.

It felt good to be back in Peridot. Charlie delighted in his favorite spots, sniffing for longer, rolling around on his favorite scratchy grass. Sergeant Simpson had been right when he suggested she leave town for a few days once Wade was arrested.

It had been a hard phone call, explaining to her parents that someone had tried to murder her. They had insisted on catching the next flight to Atlanta and had even offered to book an Airbnb so that Lydia could come stay with her pets.

It had been nice to be spoiled and fussed over. Her mother baked and cooked constantly, while her dad maintained a firm belief that her ex-husband, who had absolutely nothing to do with the murders, was somehow to blame for the whole horrifying chapter. Her dad's logic seemed to be some sort of bizarre Rube Goldberg machine, where Graham cheating on Lydia led directly to Wade trying to kill Lydia in her Peridot apartment.

Her dad also thought she should immediately move back to New Hampshire. But Lydia didn't blame Graham for what had happened, and more importantly, she didn't blame Peridot. As nice as the short vacation with her parents was, Lydia found herself desperately missing her new home. When the week ended, she had hurried back.

Charlie stopped by the mailboxes clustered at street level near Measure Twice. While he sniffed, Lydia took a moment to check her mail, even though most of the people that had her new address lived in Peridot, so they didn't need to use it.

Surprisingly, a letter-sized brown package was thick enough to take up most of her mailbox. She checked the label, thinking it must be meant for the store, but she saw her name, clear as day. There was no return address. Lydia looked from the package to the window of Measure Twice.

Even though it was Saturday, a big shopping day, Fran had decided to close the shop. Technically, it was no longer a crime scene, but there were still tattered pieces of the crime scene tape, a terrible version of holiday decorations, stuck to parts of the building.

She had plans to meet the crew, as she thought of them these days, over at the PeriDough bakery in a bit. But she was so curious about the envelope, she sat down on a bench in front of Measure Twice, and opened the thick brown paper with her snips from her hand-sewing kit.

It was a manuscript for a book: *Stolen Valor* by Brandon Ivey. Well, not quite a manuscript, but enough to start pitching it to agents, perhaps. Lydia scanned the synopsis and then started to read. The first page dedicated the book to Sarah Jane.

She turned the page and held her breath as she read on, diving into the first chapter.

This was Brandon's NGAN, his next great American novel, at least the first three chapters. He had started it. He must have put it in the mail right after their dinner. Why not just hand it to her? Lydia wished she could ask him, biting her lip in frustration that barely covered her grief.

It was good. Quite good. And the main character was a veteran with a dark past named Cade. Wow. Brandon hadn't made much effort to disguise the inspiration for his protagonist. Lydia read on. If she hadn't heard it all from Wade, she would have been shocked beyond words. As it was, she couldn't stop reading. Charlie pulled at the leash, wanting to go home and have his breakfast, but for once she ignored him.

Cade was a veteran in a small town and had beguiled the locals into believing he was a hero. But in flashbacks that sliced through the chronological narrative, readers saw Cade as the soldier he had really been, abandoning his men in battle, leaving not with honors, but with the pall of dishonor and disgrace.

Lydia wondered how Brandon had planned for the book to end. Brandon knew Wade's secret, but he had had no idea what it would mean for him, or for April. After dinner, she would sit on her couch and read those first three chapters slowly, carefully. She owed him that. And tomorrow she would find Sarah Jane and fulfill her promise. Maybe Sarah Jane could find a future for the book her first love never got a chance to finish.

Charlie was still tugging, so Lydia relented and took him back upstairs to the apartment for his breakfast. Feeding Baby Lobster as well, Lydia placed the manuscript down carefully on her counter and wandered into her bedroom, trying to decide what to wear.

She had brought her sewing machine to the rental house with her parents and had made a new dress. This time, it was a linen-collared button-down shift. It was one of the more advanced patterns she had attempted, a Myosotis dress by Deer and Doe patterns, and she was pleased with the finished product, even if, up close, the buttons were a little wonky. The black-and-cream-checkered linen pattern slightly clashed with the bright pink vintage buttons, but that was Lydia's way of approaching color: hot pink was a neutral. It was perfect. She wondered if the M's would comment as she headed out to the bakery.

Like a human jack-in-the-box, Jeff popped out of his apartment as she neared the stairs.

"Hey there, Lydia."

Only one button undone today, but the silk shirt was covered in some fashion logo Lydia didn't recognize, though she had no doubt he would enlighten her at the slightest provocation.

"Hi, Jeff."

"Are you back to pack up your things, or . . .?"

"I'm headed to PeriDough, and I'm already late." It was only a white lie, she told herself.

"We'll have to talk later, then. I have an idea I want to run by you. A sewing idea," he added, catching her interest as she tried to squeeze past him to the stairs.

"You want to learn to sew, Jeff?" Lydia wasn't about to turn down a potential student, especially now that she knew for certain he wasn't a murderer.

"Ha! No! Of course not. But I was thinking about a little retail synergy."

"Excuse me?"

"Coozies."

"Excuse me?"

"Lydia, you should sew coozies. For my trains. Train coozies. Like they have for beers. That way, when I ship them, they stay pristine in their little fabric holder. And you get to sew something. Everyone needs a side hustle, Lydia. Even you."

Train coozies.

"Wow, Jeff. I'll definitely think about it. Thanks," she added, as she hurried to the street below, trying to hide her smile.

As she walked toward the bakery, she wondered when the weather would turn. Growing up in New England, September had meant sweater weather, warm drinks, and bright red and orange maple leaves. When she had moved to Atlanta, she was not prepared for how hot it stayed into September, a month she firmly associated with fall. Maybe here, in the mountains, her favorite time of year would come a little sooner than it had in the city.

She was imagining a long-sleeved version of her current make as she walked into PeriDough. Maybe flannel? That would be cozy.

And when she looked up, there they were, the same group, sitting at the same table, drinking coffee from the same mugs. Though, if she really paid attention, she noticed that the donuts weren't purple this time, but stuffed and glazed instead. And her friends looked different too.

It took Lydia a moment to realize why some of her friends looked slightly different that morning. Mary and Martha were there, looking the same as always. When Lydia imagined their houses, she pictured closets like the ones shown in superhero movies or cartoons: rows and rows of the same outfit, ready for the start of each new day. But instead of a black Batsuit, their closets would have smart sweater sets and pencil skirts in coordinating colors.

Then it clicked. Cynde and Clark were both wearing the Shirt No. 1 they had made in Lydia's sewing class the week prior. It was a silent but clear vote of confidence in Lydia's dream for Measure Twice.

Kaleigh came over soon after Lydia sat down, with a new tray of donuts.

"Hey Lydia, glad to see you back in town. I heard . . . well, I just wanted to say, I'm glad you're back, and you're okay. And Darrel has some new flavors I thought you might want to try."

That was Kaleigh in a nutshell, kind enough to reference what Lydia had been through, but also kind enough not to make Lydia relive it.

Lydia perused the tray of donuts as Kaleigh listed off the new offerings: "This is the special of the day, the Sweetheart. Darrel named it for me because it's made with fresh raspberries, my favorite!" Kaleigh blushed. "Then we have the regulars, cinnamon-sugar, old-fashioned, and glazed. Oh, and the jelly-filled is something new too. Muscadine jelly!"

Lydia raised one eyebrow, and Mary offered an explanation. "Muscadines are grapes, Lydia, that grow here in the South. They make a nice jelly."

"And wine," Heather deadpanned.

Mary did not deign to recognize that added use of the grapes.

Clark, however, brightened up at the mention of muscadine wine. "Exactly, Heather. Muscadine wine is really experiencing a renaissance. Rightly so, I might add. The grapes are wild with antioxidants. We're carrying a new, high-end line from Two Cousins Vineyard at the shop. Local really is best. Can't recommend it enough."

Who was he recommending it to? Unclear. Lydia nodded and replied, "Sounds great, Clark. I will have to check it out."

He smiled and ate a small sliver of a Sweetheart donut. Clark was eating donuts? What would happen next? A pig flying by the bakery's front window?

For a moment, the group was quiet, trying different pieces of donuts and drinking coffee. Then Heather reached into her bag and placed something on the table.

It was the Archer Button-Down Shirt pattern by Grainline Studio. Lydia recognized it immediately and choked up, thinking of Brandon, how she had imagined him as that pattern on their one date, but thankfully no one seemed to notice.

Heather smiled at Fran, then looked at Lydia.

"Lydia, I was wondering. Now that you're back in town, maybe we could try a harder pattern? You know, for the next class?" Heather gestured at the packet in front of her. She continued, "I know it's still hot out, but I thought we could start planning ahead for the fall, maybe talk Fran into ordering some of that flannel that Kauffman does?"

Heather moved some donut slivers around on her plate.

Lydia was stunned. But before she could say anything, Heather continued, "Also, I was thinking. A shirt like this needs great buttons. The . . . I mean . . . Mary and Martha often have great vintage buttons at Blessed Again. So, I went ahead and bought a bunch this week and did this," and at that Heather reached into her bag again and pulled out yet another surprise.

Small white cardboard pieces held sets of vintage buttons, all with Measure Twice written neatly at the top of the card and decorated with a small vintage ribbon. They were the sewing equivalent of perfectly presented candies. Lydia reached out before she could stop herself.

She picked a set of navy-blue buttons with gold anchors on them. All six were neatly displayed on the card and there was even a price sticker on the back. Heather had thought of everything.

"Wow! Oh wow, Heather. This is beyond cool." Though, judging by Heather's reaction, no one actually said "beyond cool" anymore. "How about we do a class in two weeks? I can walk you guys through making the shirt, and we can talk about what fabric to order this week. And then we can have the actual class when the fabric comes in. You know, Ruby Star Society just came out with this chore coat cotton fabric, with a really nice heft to it, you could . . ."

Fran cleared her throat and Lydia laughed. No one needed a lecture on new fabrics right at this moment.

"I'll pull up some options to show you guys. Maybe some nice shirting in case someone wants to make a smart dress shirt instead of a cozy one," Lydia added, looking at the M's, who smiled at the idea of something a little nicer than a flannel work shirt. Lydia had a feeling there was not one piece of flannel in their superhero closets.

The donuts were finished, coffee cups close to empty.

Lydia breathed in and looked down at the shirt pattern on the table and the cards of colorful buttons next to it. Then she looked at the handmade Shirt No. 1's worn around the table. They wanted her to feel at home. But they also probably wanted to know all the latest news; they were just too kind, or in the case of the M's, too well-mannered, to say anything about it.

Lydia let out the breath she'd been holding.

"When I got back into town, I went to the police station," Lydia started.

The entire table seemed to exhale, and then everyone leaned forward.

"Sergeant Simpson had invited me to stop by when he called me to say I could move back into the apartment." Lydia didn't mention that this time she got to talk to the stern older man in his office, not in the interrogation room.

"He was really nice and gave me a full update on the case. He said they had found a ton of evidence against Wade. It was Sergeant Simpson's theory that Wade was so sure he could frame me that he didn't really try to cover his tracks toward the end."

The whole table nodded in unison, and Lydia continued, "He did clear something up for me that had been—well, bothering me. I could see Wade creeping up on Brandon while he was writing, but how did he get April into place? Turns out it was gabapentin!"

"What?" Clark spat out. "Who was Gabby? What on earth are you talking about, Lydia?"

"Sorry. Let me slow down. Wade really wanted it to look like the murderer was connected to the shop—with Measure Twice, with me."

"Right. We got that. But who is Gabby?"

"Not who, *what*. Gabapentin is a sleep medication. See, Wade thought the long-arm machine would make the connection even clearer, so he drugged April's morning coffee before she came to see me. The police told me that April took gabapentin to help her fall asleep at night. Wade knew where she kept it, and it was easy enough for him to open the capsules, and he stirred twice her normal dose into her coffee. It was enough to make her dizzy and lightheaded, so when she got to the store she laid her head down by the machine, just like he had hoped she would. That let him attack her in a way that pointed back to me. He drugged her."

"Then why didn't the police tell us that immediately?" Clark complained, forgetting that the police had never told him a thing.

"Sergeant Simpson explained that too. Apparently, *CSI*, the TV show, is really misleading, and tests like that aren't quick. Plus, it didn't raise suspicion initially because she was known to be on the medication. Wade moved faster than the lab did, basically."

Clark nodded, appeased.

"Will you have to testify? In court?" This time it was Heather asking a question.

"Sergeant Simpson said that was likely, but he also said things like this move pretty slowly. Wade isn't going anywhere, thank goodness. He also said I needed to stay in the state, in case they need to interview me about something or whatever."

The table grew quiet.

No one had asked. Not yet. Was she back to stay? It was one thing to talk buttons, but it was another to put down roots in a town where she'd been a murder suspect.

"I told Sergeant Simpson he knew where to find me," Lydia shared, smiling. "I might have even suggested he try out a class," she admitted, raising her eyebrows mischievously.

Fran laughed out loud. "Merritt?"

"Huh?"

"Merritt Simpson in a sewing class? I'd like to see the day!"

Sergeant Simpson's first name was Merritt? "Merritt like a merit badge?" Lydia asked. It sort of made sense. He was like a big, grown-up Eagle Scout.

Mary stepped into the conversation, explaining, "Merritt, honey."

Lydia just stared at her.

Cynde added, "Two R's and two T's. It's a pretty common Southern name, Lydia."

"Oh. Okay. Merritt," Lydia said, drawing out the R's and T's, "Got it. I think I'll just stick with Sergeant Simpson. Anyway, I told him I'm staying put. Peridot is my home."

Everyone smiled, and the whole table seemed to understand that it wasn't really Peridot that Lydia was calling home. It was this group, at this table, at this bakery.

Fran stood up, bringing the informal reunion to a close. "All right, Lydia, why don't you stop by the store before you head back to the apartment? I'm going to open up Measure Twice for a few hours this afternoon; you can help me get ready."

Lydia nodded. Cynde came over and gave her a quick hug before heading out into the sunshine. Clark and Martha discussed a new proposal by the town for a fountain in the town square, of which neither approved, as they walked out together toward their shops.

"I'm going to head over to the hospital," Heather told Lydia. "I know you're not much of a knitter, but the hats are pretty easy to make. If you wanted to come sometime. Or whatever," she added, leaving the bakery. Heather had forgiven her, in her own way. Would wonders never cease? Apparently, the wonders were not ready to cease, because Mary had hung back as her friend walked briskly over to Blessed Again. She was holding a wrapped package that she must have stored under her seat while the group had chatted.

Shyly, she handed the package to Lydia.

"We're all glad you've come to Peridot, Lydia, dear," Mary said quietly, and then she walked out to join her sister, not pausing for a response.

Lydia looked at the package. Mary and Martha weren't rude to her. They probably weren't even capable of being rude. They weren't even capable of using a contraction, for all Lydia knew. Still, they weren't exactly friendly either, which made this sudden gesture all the more surprising.

That and the fact that it had Christmas wrapping in early September. Lydia made quick work of the Santa-covered paper and opened the brown paper box inside.

Her breath caught as she removed three nesting Pyrex mixing bowls in the almost impossible to find pink gooseberry color.

Each of her new friends had found a way to say they were glad she was back. Now it was time to get to work. Finally.

Holding her gift carefully, she walked with Fran around the square to Measure Twice. Peridot was busy with visitors, shopping and wandering between the stores. Lydia noticed the slogan T-shirts about mountains calling, and remembered Officer Luke and his game of *Dungeons & Dragons*. Maybe she would go this week.

"What are you smiling about?" Fran asked.

Lydia, embarrassed, fudged the truth by showing her the Pyrex bowls and just forgetting to mention her thoughts of Officer Luke.

"Mary gave you that?" Fran asked, clearly as surprised as she had been. Lydia nodded and they both laughed.

Their laughter stopped as they walked past Turn the Page.

"What will happen to the bookstore now?" Lydia asked. Wade had killed April and Brandon, but he had killed the bookstore too.

"Rumor has it Wade is selling it to cover his lawyer's fees."

"What do you think will replace it?" Lydia asked.

"Didn't you say your neighbor was interested?"

"Jeff? Poor Jeff. He has no idea I really considered him as a suspect for the murders. But I don't think there's any way to apologize for that. Even the M's don't have a protocol for saying, 'Sorry I thought you were a killer—turns out you're just super creepy.'"

Fran laughed and Lydia joined her, laughing harder as she imagined rows and rows of trains with their matching coozies.

When they reached the shop, Fran suggested coffee in the break room, even though they had both had their fill at the bakery. As she fiddled with the coffee machine, Fran kept clearing her throat but then saying nothing. Lydia waited.

Fran evidently had something she wanted to discuss, something she didn't want the others to hear. Heather must have told her about their argument in Shenanigans. When Heather had told her how Lydia had doubted Fran, what exactly had she said? Truth be told, Lydia didn't trust Heather not to make it even worse than it was.

She didn't know what Fran wanted to discuss, but Lydia realized she needed to be honest first.

Sending up a small prayer that she didn't make a total mess of it, Lydia decided to come clean with her fairy godmother, saying, "Fran, before you tell me anything, I need to tell you something. Before Wade"—and Lydia waved her hand around in a way that she hoped conveyed *tried to murder me*—"I told him that I thought Heather had killed Brandon and April."

Fran gasped but Lydia continued, afraid that if she stopped talking, she wouldn't be able to start again. "I convinced myself she didn't want me elbowing her out of the store you built with her, that she wanted me out of your life and out of Peridot, and she was willing to kill to do it." Lydia took a deep breath and continued. "It gets worse. When I had lunch with Heather, I didn't want her to know that I suspected her, and she ended up thinking—she thought I thought, she thought I was thinking . . . you killed April and Brandon. I swear I never did. But Heather thought I suspected you were the killer."

Whatever Fran had expected Lydia to say, that was clearly not it.

"Oh. Honey. Did she believe you?" Fran cut right to the quick.

"No. Not in the slightest. She set me straight. That's why I didn't come to see you that day. That's why I went home when Wade thought I would be at the Laurels. That's how I caught him—well—" And again she waved her hand in what Lydia was starting to rely on as her *he tried to kill me* shorthand.

There. It was done, said, out in the open. Now what would Fran do? Kick her out? Cancel her lease? Run her out of town? Did people still get run out of town? Probably, and Lydia felt like she was a good candidate for whatever indignity it entailed.

"Oh, honey. You really believed Heather hated you that much?" Weirdly, Fran didn't sound angry. She sounded sad. That was not what Lydia was expecting.

"Sweetheart, when are you going to realize you are loved?"

How could Lydia answer that?

Lydia remembered how Graham had left: he'd offered her a half-hearted version of "I'm sorry you had to find out this way." Then he'd moved out, found an apartment, gotten a lawyer, and set the paperwork in motion.

She had packed up her things, moved to stay with Fran in Peridot, and let Graham list the house. Graham's lawyers offered her alimony or a lump sum. The number had been fair—maybe not generous, but certainly fair. Lydia thought about alimony, getting a monthly check from Graham, a line of money tying them to each other down the years. For a few days, she thought maybe that was the path to take; maybe the Emma Grace debacle would collapse, and they could find their way back to each other.

Instagram put an end to that momentary stupidity with an *"Oh my God, ya'll, we're engaged!"* post from Emma Grace before the divorce was even technically final.

The next day, Lydia opted for the lump sum, with an understanding that she'd get half the value of the house when it sold. Then she blocked Emma Grace and Graham on every social media platform she could think of and tried to focus on her new life in Peridot. Graham didn't love her anymore.

Fran interrupted her memory by asking again, "Lydia, dear, when are you going to realize you are loved?"

Lydia didn't know what to say.

"Lydia, it feels like you have always been a part of the Measure Twice family. This is where you belong. We love you," Fran said. "Heather can be a little standoffish—I know that. But she loves you just like I do. We don't need to harp on all this . . . this darkness. We're still your family, and Measure Twice—well, that is a little more complicated."

Now Fran seemed uncertain how to continue. "Listen, I haven't wanted to worry you, but . . . but the truth is, I can't afford to keep the store open. I've pursued every angle . . . but when we had to shut down last week, and now with the part-time hours, it's just been too much of a loss, even though I still stand by it. It's been the right thing to do."

Lydia nodded.

Fran continued, "I hate to be the bearer of bad news, especially after all you've been through, but I think I'm going to have to close Measure Twice. For good."

Lydia couldn't find the words to reply.

After everything that had happened, all she had overcome, this was how it would end? Not with a bang but a whimper? Who wrote that? Lydia started to wonder. Frost? No. T. S. Eliot? That seemed right.

Fran could tell Lydia was lost in her own thoughts yet again. To bring her back to earth, Fran said something even more unexpected: "Or there is another option. I could sell."

"Oh. Do you know someone? Do you think they would keep Heather and me on? I mean, not to make this about me; I just—"

Fran laughed and said, "Lydia, dear, I could sell the store to you."

Lydia knew, of course, the expression that someone could be knocked over with a feather. Now she felt it. She was dizzy with surprise. But then she started to smile too.

Why not? She loved Measure Twice. She had some money. Of course, she could hear her father's voice efficiently listing all the reasons it was a terrible idea. Words like *overhead* and *deduction* and *risk* sounded in the back of her mind. There were a million reasons why not. There would always be a million reasons why not.

Lydia realized something. She could live in a world where she made mistakes. She could live in a world where, every Christmas, her dad brought up that crazy time she tried to own a fabric store in the Blue Ridge Mountains of North Georgia. But she couldn't, she absolutely could not, live in a world where Measure Twice didn't exist.

Fran had been watching her face the entire time. Lydia knew she had no poker face. So, she wasn't surprised to see Fran start to cry tears of joy.

She looked down at the coffee in her hands. Fran had the most beautiful mugs in the break room. It looked like a white mug dipped in an ocean wave. She took one more sip of coffee, and then she said, "Yeah. You could. You could sell it to me."

Acknowledgments

Always and forever, most of all, this book is for Andrew, Gemma, and Bowden.

Thank you to Dawn Dowdle, Faith Black Ross, and everyone at Crooked Lane Books for making my dream come true.

Thank you to Jane Simpson for the weekend on Cherry Log Mountain that started this story in my mind.

Thank you, Julie Pace, for teaching me how to be a writer.

Thank you, Diana Taylor, for teaching me how to sew. Fabricate Studios in Atlanta, Georgia, will change your life, folks.

Thank you, Cindy Blake, for teaching me how to believe in this book.

Thank you, Dad, for not letting me quit. And for all the coffee in the study hall.

To my very first readers, Missy Church, Jes Huggins, and Liz Blake, thank you for making my words better in every way!

Thank you to my family, Dad, Liz, Captain Mr. Risky Man, Jennifer, Frank, Diana, Rose, Jean, John, Eric, and Lauren.

Acknowledgments

Thank you to my friends who feel like family: Siena, Missy, Jes, Tati, Kathryn, Mary, Hanna, April, Darby, Sarah, Delaney, Christine, Liza, Jane, Maureen, Devon, and Rosie and Felipe.

Thank you to my sewing community, especially Lily and Cait, Leigh Metcalf at Topstitch, the kind workers at Fabric World, the wonderful designs of Helen's Closet, and the wise women of Tiny Stitches Quilt Shop, the South East Fiber Arts Alliance (SEFAA), and the Atlanta Sewing Center.

To all my wonderful friends in Atlanta, thank you for believing in this adventure.

To my blob fish—a promise is a promise.

To the dinner party of Ladd's baptism back in '21—I asked if you wanted your names in my book—ta da!

To Harry Styles and Kelli and Rori—here's to treating people with kindness.

To Liz Griffith—get ready for the world tour.

And finally, to the three authors who taught me to love mysteries—Agatha Christie, PD James, and Ann Cleeves—thank you for the books I will spend my lifetime reading and reading again.

Read an excerpt from

QUILTY
AS CHARGED

the next

MEASURE TWICE
SEWING MYSTERY

by MAGGIE BAILEY

available soon in hardcover from
Crooked Lane Books

CROOKED
LANE

NEW YORK

Chapter One

Friday

I t had to work. It was as simple as that. It had to work.

    Lydia Barnes' fabric store, Measure Twice, was in the red. Bright red. Each day she worked at the store, located on the cute main square of Peridot, an even cuter North Georgia mountain town, trying to win new customers, and each night she stayed up, bleary-eyed, and worried it wouldn't be enough. Every night as she struggled to fall asleep, Lydia scrolled through her Instagram, overwhelmed by the budgeting she still had to finish. Then one night, there it was. An invitation to a sewing retreat on the coast of Oregon. The retreat offered three days of good company, good food, and a chance to sew new clothes and learn new sewing skills. It was expensive, really expensive, and it looked incredible. Lydia wished someone would do something like that near her. Then it hit her. *She* was that someone. And her idea was born: SEW RELAXING, a sewing retreat with the ladies of Measure Twice.

    If she made it a monthly event, the added income would move the store from drowning to treading water, and right now, for Lydia, that was enough. She would have the local shoppers in Peridot, but she could also woo sewists from Atlanta, sewists who might want to start making day trips to a cute fabric shop in the mountains long after the weekend was over.

She had picked a weekend and started to plan, but now that it was actually happening, she felt overwhelmed. Three days. Three entire days away from the store. Three days with no in-store sales. Three days that had to run smoothly. Lydia looked around the shop. Since she had taken over ownership of Measure Twice six months ago, she had opened the store every day except Christmas and New Year's. Now she had to close it in order to save it.

Before she spiraled into all the things that could go wrong, and, honestly, she was really good at that, she needed to focus on the tasks at hand. She checked the display, made sure all the bolts of fabric were neatly tucked into the shelves. Then she double checked that the register was locked, since she'd already taken the money to the bank earlier in the day.

It was time to leave the store, to go up to her apartment, just above Measure Twice, and finish her preparations. She breathed in, deeply. The store smelled like a blend of laundry, old coffee from the breakroom, and dust, combining to make her favorite scent in the world.

The door's small bell jangled as she locked it, and she held on to the sound as she walked up to her apartment and faced the last of her to-do list.

Her fabric was already folded in bins and waiting by the front door. As always, Lydia did all fabric-related tasks before anything else. She glanced at the linen, the quilting cotton, and the soft, slinky rayon already washed and ironed and ready to be transformed. Still, a sewing retreat, her first-ever Sew Relaxing event, needed more than just fabric.

Lydia had also offered to bring food for the first full night. It was a no-brainer. She knew what she would bring: lasagna. If any good thing had come out of her laughably short marriage, it was her lasagna recipe. Never mind the failed attempts, the quiet dinners pushing gloppy pasta around on their wedding plates. All those burnt pans and mushy noodles had led to this: the best lasagna. So, she set to it.

The turkey sausage browned in her cast-iron skillet while she mixed the egg, Parmesan, mozzarella, and ricotta together in a mixing bowl. Then crushed tomatoes and spices went in with the sausage as the wide, ribbon-like noodles went into a pot of boiling, salted water. Lydia wasn't coordinated, but she could dance this one recipe with her eyes closed. The sauce finished as she tipped the noodles into the colander. She rubbed three small baking tins with olive oil and started the layering. Sauce, noodles, cheese, sauce, noodles again. Whenever she lost count or got distracted, Lydia added more cheese. More cheese, she believed, covered a multitude of sins.

Even if the retreat didn't go exactly as planned, how mad could anyone be eating delicious lasagna on a chilly February night in the mountains? Although, it felt like jinxing herself to say no one in that group would be mad, so she looked at the planning sheet one more time and walked herself through the attendees.

Fran. Of course, Fran was "going." It was her house, the Laurels, on Cherry Log Mountain that would host the event.

She had insisted. Fran had also already offered to provide three sewing machines *and* make dinner the second night. Since Lydia had bought the store from her, Fran had been determined to help Lydia make a success out of Measure Twice's new chapter. Sometimes Lydia thought of Fran as her fairy godmother. A fairy godmother in unflattering, high-waisted, pleated jeans, but a fairy godmother, nonetheless.

Just to balance out Fran, Clark was coming. He would be bringing no extra supplies to share and no food for the group. He would probably show up with his own stash of food for only him. Clark ran a small organic and upscale food store, the Pampered Pantry, on the Peridot town square, a few stores down from Measure Twice. No doubt he would be well stocked with seaweed chips and chia seeds. On top of that, he'd said he might be late. But the specific request part of the form? That Clark had filled out with gusto. Clark lived for specific requests. No gluten. No soy-based gluten substitute. Only alternative down pillows. The list went on.

Next on the list: The M's. Martha and Mary would be there, of course. One almost always guaranteed the other. They weren't sisters—Lydia had already asked them, and they had said "NO," in unison, appearing equally shocked by the brashness of her inquiry. But they might as well have been twins. The women, both in their late 70s at the youngest (even Lydia knew that question would definitely be too brash) dressed alike, talked alike, and were almost always in each other's company. Both were laughably polite, and completely exhausting. Sometimes, as a Northern transplant in her new small-town Southern home, Lydia thought of the M's as the living personification of the saying, "Bless your heart." They knew their way around a back-handed compliment better than anyone. Who else would run a church charity shop called Blessed Again and turn away so many donations with a sweetly said, "Honey, why don't you just keep that darling little knickknack for yourself?"

At least Lydia could count on Heather to be a steadying influence. She hadn't required Heather to come on the retreat, but if she were being honest with herself, she was relieved when the young woman had suggested it. Young woman. Was that how she thought of people now?

Candy-apple red hair cut right at her jawline, and a penchant for denim overalls cut pretty darn short, paired with combat boots, Heather always stood out of the crowd at Measure Twice. Lydia knew she needed Heather, needed her social media savvy, her creative approach to programming, and her more-than-honest opinion when Lydia showed her what fabrics and notions she wanted to order next. A twenty-five-year-old with a clear sense of what was cool, Heather was invaluable.

Toiletries packed, Lydia looked in her meager closet. Black leggings? Check. Sewing-related T-shirts? Check. Rainbow-colored hand-knit socks? Check. Add some underwear and Lydia was ready to be SEW RELAXED. She zipped up the duffel bag full of barely folded clothes and tried to breathe a sigh of relief. Who else was coming? Who was she forgetting?

Then she remembered Cynde, of course, with a hastily added *plus one* after her name. Cynde, a court stenographer with a penchant for long anecdotes, was apparently bringing a work friend. Cynde was a regular at the shop, since the courthouse sat in the middle of Peridot's town square, and she was always game to try a new class or buy a new kit. She promised Lydia that Amy, her friend, was the same and would be nothing but added value. Cynde might be well into her fifties, but she made friends and gossiped as well as any teenager Lydia had ever met. Since Amy was driving up from Atlanta, Lydia hoped the new addition could help spread the Measure Twice gospel among her friends, whoever they were.

The weekend, if she were being honest, was mostly about saving the store, but there were other goals, too, one of which was to teach the group how to make garments. Everyone coming knew how to sew, most knew how to knit, and some, like Cynde, could turn out a quilt with astonishing speed. She had already led them through making a simple shirt, and now she wanted to challenge them with a slightly more difficult project: a coat.

Lydia really loved to sew clothes. In the mood for a pink shirt with sushi on it? Boom. A blue linen pinafore-style dress covered in gold constellations? To be honest, Lydia had already made one of those, using her trusted York Pinafore Pattern from Helen's Closet and some Miss Matatabi fabric shipped all the way from Japan. Sewing clothes meant the only limit was your imagination. Well, that and your patience.

Like a lot of sewists, Lydia had fallen in love with the recent trend of "quilt coats." Some sewists used secondhand quilts, while some fast fashion shops just used fabric that looked like it had been quilted but wasn't. She knew the M's would consider it sacrilege to cut into old quilts for the sake of a jacket, but she hoped she could convince the group to love the garment by quilting fabric specifically for the project. All it would take was a lining fabric, cotton quilting batting, and an outer fabric. At the retreat, she would show them how to quilt the layers together for the sake of a garment rather than a blanket.

Lydia checked her final bin. Pattern weights. Rotary cutters. Dress shears, hefty and able to glide through any fabric. Batting to add warmth and bulk to the coats. Bias tape. Pins. Tailor's chalk. She was ready. She needed to breathe. Then she heard it, the off-key chime of her doorbell.

She looked out her front window. Cynde's old beat-up tan Honda minivan was parked outside the shop. Fran owned the apartment, but Lydia had been renting it for the last six months or so and had come to think of it as her home. Living right above Measure Twice had a lot of advantages, and Lydia was glad she almost never had to give people directions these days.

Lydia still needed to settle her cat in with her neighbor, Jeff, who lived in the next apartment over. Her cat, Baby Lobster, wasn't a great traveler, and Clark had some seriously negative opinions about cat dander, so it was easier to leave her behind. She just needed to get the supplies sorted with Cynde and her friend.

"Something smells *good*," Cynde declared as she walked into the small apartment the moment Lydia opened the door. Cynde was wearing one of her classic outfits, as Lydia thought of them, this time a matching set of linen top with autumnal leaves appliqued around the hem and linen pants with leaves around each pant leg. She always looked comfortable, but Cynde always looked a little what Lydia's mom would call snazzy, as well.

Interestingly, Amy looked far more buttoned up. A nondescript white button-down topped what could only be described as black slacks. Who wore slacks when they didn't have to?

Cynde didn't immediately introduce Amy, which surprised Lydia. And even more noticeable was the fact that, while both women looked at Lydia, they steadfastly refused to look at each other. Had there been a fight on the way over? Lydia needed this retreat to work, and it already felt like it was slipping toward disaster. Cynde's next comment brought Lydia back from her imagined troubles.

"Oh, Lydia, you can't be serious," Cynde chided, gesturing to the save-the-date card propped against the toaster in the kitchen. "Why on earth," she continued, "would they invite you? And why on earth would you keep the invitation?"

Amy looked back and forth between Cynde and Lydia, clearly hoping one of them would offer further explanation. Lydia just fussed with her supplies, blushing a deeper and deeper pink.

Lydia could still see it perfectly: her diet lemonade spilled and spreading across the floor. All that good ice ruined. Lydia could see her own shoes, fancy wedge espadrilles she had worn to try to fit in at the Junior League that Graham had encouraged her to attend. Her funny stories of snotty women and silly agenda points died on her lips. Her handsome husband, Graham, in their bed. Naked. Her former teaching assistant, Emma-Grace, in their bed. Naked.

Cynde held up the card. The invitation was Pinterest perfect and featured a photo of the smiling couple. Lydia looked again at the glamour shot of the happy couple, wearing matching plaid shirts in an apple orchard. "Graham and Emma-Grace are getting married!" read the card, with the loopy white calligraphy that seemed ubiquitous lately. What a name: Emma-Grace.

"This is Lydia's ex-husband," Cynde said, jabbing a finger at the smiling face of Graham in the orchard. "And this is the woman he had an affair with!" Cynde continued, jabbing Emma-Grace next. "For some reason I cannot figure out, they have invited Lydia, of all people, to their wedding! Lydia," Cynde turned her attention from Amy back to her, "why on earth have you kept this ridiculous invitation?"

The invitation was part of Emma-Grace's desperate attempt to rewrite history, convince herself that Graham's first marriage had ended in a conscious uncoupling rather than a blistering screaming match soaked in lemonade. But that didn't mean Lydia wasn't tempted to attend. Still, she was not about to admit she fantasized about attending the wedding as a successful shop owner, dressed in one of her own creations, with a gorgeous mystery man on her arm. The shop was failing, she hadn't done any of her own sewing in weeks, and her dog, Charlie, was the only man in her life these days. Instead, she offered, "It's just a save-the-date. And I don't think I'm actually going to go."

Amy looked unconvinced and Lydia didn't blame her. She hadn't even convinced herself.

Cynde dropped the card, moved toward the covered lasagna pans, and sighed, looking longingly at them, adding, "Do you need a taste tester for these?"

"Cynde, we already had dinner," Amy countered, more seriously than Lydia thought was warranted.

Lydia could guess what they had eaten, since Cynde was still holding the large Styrofoam cup of what was sure to be sweet tea. A drive-through, fried-chicken sandwich wasn't the worst way to start a road trip, in Lydia's opinion.

"That's the lasagna I made for the first dinner tomorrow." Lydia tucked the hot pans into a warm dish carrier. "Cynde, would you mind?" She struggled to zip the bag and then passed it to Cynde. "If you could take this down to the car? I just need to drop Baby Lobster off with my neighbor who is cat-sitting, and then I'll meet you down at the van. Sound good?"

"Baby what?" Amy asked, clearly concerned that the woman leading this sewing retreat was a few donuts short of a dozen.

"Baby Lobster is my cat," Lydia explained, realizing any chance of a good first impression was lost at this point. "I adopted her last summer. If I am being honest, the name got my attention first, but her awesome personality really won me over."

At this proclamation, all three women turned to see the calico cat grooming herself on the back of the couch with a clear air of superiority.

"She warms up once she gets to know you, I swear," Lydia added, sensing Amy's unspoken disbelief. "Besides, I don't know how much Cynde has told you, but it was Baby Lobster that saved my life when . . . when everything happened here."

Before Lydia explained the two murders that happened in Peridot this past summer, Cynde cut her off, grabbing the lasagnas and calling out, "We're on it!" as she headed to the door. Amy reluctantly picked up the sewing supplies, and the two women headed back down to the street. Lydia was grateful for the interruption. Now she just needed to drop off her cat, grab her own duffle bag, and Charlie's gear, and head down to the van. Easy.

Leaving Charlie behind for the moment, she picked up Baby Lobster and headed over to her neighbor, Jeff's, apartment.

Quilty as Charged

Jeff answered the door so quickly, Lydia wondered if he had been standing just behind it, waiting for her to arrive. As soon as Jeff opened the door, Baby Lobster leapt from Lydia's arms and darted over to Jeff's couch, making herself at home, while also studiously ignoring Jeff himself.

Lydia couldn't blame the cat. Jeff was perfectly nice. And Lydia hoped if she kept telling herself that, she would finally believe it.

Behind Jeff, she could see his trains. That is what Jeff did, buy and sell toy trains. He really, really loved trains. And Italian silk button-down shirts. And hugging Lydia for just a little too long.

Today the shirt was a garish purple vertical stripe, but it was only unbuttoned two buttons down. That was how Lydia gauged Jeff's moods, and two buttons down meant he was in a good mood but not too good. Lydia needed to get going, but Jeff clearly wanted to chat. She caved.

"How's business, Jeff? I can't tell you how much I appreciate you looking after Baby Lobster."

"Business is brisk, Lydia, thanks for asking. I just had an online auction for this beauty. I'm sending it off to its new home tomorrow," he added, gesturing to the train he lovingly cradled in his hands. Placing the train on a stand, he picked up something and held it out toward her.

"Here, why not take a business card with you on that retreat thing. Maybe someone on the retreat will have a train to sell." Jeff passed her the heavy card stock business card that read *Jeff's Trains*, his business buying and reselling model trains from his home. "And why don't you give me the address of where you're headed, Lydia?"

"Huh? The address? Why would you need the address? I mean," Lydia was torn between feeling confused as to why he would want to know and not wanting to offend him so much that he rescinded the offer to watch Baby Lobster.

Jeff smiled, seemingly unaware of her discomfort, and replied, "Just to be safe. You can't be too careful. And I know how much Baby Lobster means to you."

Was he planning on coming up to the retreat? Was he going to fake some cat emergency and show up at the Laurels? Jeff put down the train and opened his arms to give Lydia a hug. She scolded herself, yet again, for assuming the worst, and leaned in for the hug.

Jeff wrapped her tightly in his arms, enveloping her in the scent of what she guessed was Drakkar Noir with a faint whiff of mildew. Mid-hug, Jeff slid one arm down her side, resting his hand above her hip and squeezed what she could only think of as her love handle. Lydia bit back a squeak of surprise, and stepped back, breaking the hug.

"Thanks again for looking after Baby Lobster. I'll be back midday on Monday and come get her then," Lydia offered weakly. Jeff just smiled.

She turned to head to her apartment but could still hear Jeff say quietly, "Anything for you, Lydia."

As soon as she got back to her apartment, she took a minute to smooth her shirt over her hips and give a little shake to her whole body. Ugh. Lydia grabbed her duffle bag and tucked Charlie's supplies under her free arm. Leaving the apartment, she whistled for her dog to follow and then wrestled the door shut and locked it. Fran's apartment—well, her apartment now—was convenient, but it wasn't exactly modern, and the front door lock required elbow grease and a certain amount of optimism to get locked correctly.

It was slow going down the stairs, but soon, with the gear stored in the back, Charlie lounging and looking out the window, and all three ladies more than a little red and breathless, the minivan headed out of Peridot's town square and out to Cherry Log Mountain.

"Lydia, meet Amy. Amy, meet Lydia, officially," Cynde said as she guided the old van onto the road.

Poor Amy already knew about Lydia's failed marriage, the attempt on her life last year, and her weirdly named cat, but there was nowhere to go but up. Lydia waved as she settled into her seat in the middle row of the old minivan. "Hi, Amy! So glad you can join us this weekend."

Truth be told, Cynde hadn't told her much about Amy, just that she had a friend she wanted to bring on the retreat. Amy would apparently drive up to Peridot and then they would carpool over in Cynde's van, pick up Lydia, and make a fun trip of it up to the Laurels. Lydia, never one to look a gift horse in the mouth, had immediately agreed to the idea. Faced with an hour in the car together, however, Lydia realized she knew almost nothing about Amy, who now knew so much about her. Well, Lydia was too much of an anxious extrovert not to rectify the situation with needlessly personal questions.

"So, Amy, how long have you and Cynde been friends?" Lydia started with a softball.

Frustratingly, Cynde answered before Amy could. "Oh, we met back in college. First comp class she sat down right next to me."

Lydia briefly registered that this conflicted with Cynde's earlier claim that Amy was a work friend but then told herself, "It could be that both are true," and reminded herself to stop being so nosy. Amy still hadn't spoken.

Once they hit the highway, it was almost comforting to realize that Cynde's minivan was never going to be pulling to the left, flying down the fast lane. In fact, it stayed just one lane over, trucking along just above the speed limit. Lydia relaxed and put her head against the window and watched the Beamers stream past, listening for the occasional roar of a motorcycle weaving back and forth between lanes.

Lydia tried again to kick-start a conversation.

"Cynde, did you see that Shenanigans is having a comedy night next month? What do you say to a girls' night out? Drinks on me," Lydia offered, wanting to make Cynde smile and more than a little hoping it would actually happen. It would do Lydia good to get out of her sweatpants and off of her couch every now and then.

Cynde took the bait, responding, "First round is on you, then. *And* the second round if the comedy stinks!"

They were joking, but Lydia noticed again how quiet and silent Amy seemed in the dark front seat of the minivan while they planned. Was Lydia just imagining the tension in the air? Or had she hurt Amy's feelings? Should she invite Amy to her only-probably outing? She let it go but remained a little worried that she had already gotten off to a bad start with Cynde's friend. One bad attitude could really impact the retreat, since it was such a small group. Plus, it wasn't just the dynamics of the retreat that had Lydia worried.

Fran had also seemed off lately. Almost fragile. She had moved out to the Laurels full time and was coming into the shop less and less. Did she regret renting her Peridot apartment out to Lydia? Was Fran going to quit the little town completely? Lydia forced herself to concentrate on the drive.

"How about some music for the ride?" Cynde offered. Unsurprisingly, Cynde still had a CD player, and, since it was her car, she played DJ, quickly selecting an Indigo Girls CD.

Lydia loved their harmonies and was pleased with the choice, immediately feeling more optimistic.

If Lydia had expected that to be the background for a new conversation, she was sorely disappointed. Amy nodded and stared out the window into the dark, winter evening. Lydia struggled to not feel miffed, but the silence felt awkward, so she tried a different approach.

"Cynde, how is work going these days?" It wasn't the most creative question, but it was something.

"Court? It's okay, nothing too exciting to report. Amy has been up at the Peridot Courthouse part-time, so it's been fun to have a friend around."

So, Amy *was* a work friend.

Cynde continued, "That's actually how she met . . ."

Cynde was interrupted by a loud thwack of something hitting the front of the van. Whatever hit them wasn't large enough to knock the van off course, but it startled the women and Charlie. He began to whine anxiously, while Lydia scanned the dark, trying to see what they had hit.

"What *was* that?" Lydia asked Cynde from the backseat. "A deer?"

"Couldn't have been a deer, we would have seen it in the headlights. And it would have done way more damage. Maybe there was some sort of trash on the road? I'll check the grill as soon as we get to a gas station. I don't really want to just pull over on the side of the road."

Lydia liked that plan. The route to the Laurels mostly followed Highway 52, but it was getting emptier as the night went on and certainly wasn't well lit. Better to check the car somewhere that felt more like civilization. How bad could it be?